THE LUCKIEST

THE STUBBORN LOVE SERIES

WENDY OWENS

ORANGEWILLOW PUBLISHING

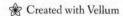

This book is dedicated to all the widows in my life.
You are strong and brave women. You are loved.

SERIES NOTE

The Stubborn Love Series consists of stories about the tough journey of the heart. They are companion novels and do not have to be read together to understand each story. All books focus on a different couple. Love isn't always easy and often can be painful, but if we open our hearts the rewards can be endless.

*Did you realize all the Stubborn Love Series book titles are inspired by songs?

STUBBORN LOVE

ONLY IN DREAMS

THE LUCKIEST

NEWSLETTER SIGNUP

Do you want to make sure you don't miss any upcoming releases or giveaways? Be sure to sign up for my newsletter at http://signup.wendyowensbooks.com/

PROLOGUE

I STRUGGLE to take a deep breath as the humidity over-takes my lungs; the pressure makes me feel as if I might drown. Squeezing my eyes shut, I try my best to block out all the sounds around me. The random coughs and whisper-ing, the shuffling of shoes, rustling of papers, and in the rear of the room, the cries of a restless baby as the mother tries to comfort him.

There's no movement to the air in the old stone build-ing, and I can't help wish to be anywhere else but here. There is a stench of sweat mixed with various perfumes hanging in the room, and I cover my mouth for fear I might be ill.

A hand settles on my arm. I know it's my friend Monica; she hasn't left my side all week. Her delicate skin on my flesh reminds me of a child—it reminds me of my Katie. I keep my eyes shut, steady my breath, and allow my thoughts to wander to Katie's smile, then her laugh. She's always had a joyous laugh, one that's fully committed. One that when someone hears it they can't help but smile.

I wonder if she is smiling now, wherever she is. Is she

laughing? Is she making the people around her laugh and smile as well? I miss smiling. I wish she were here with me so I could remember what that felt like. I haven't smiled in so long.

My breathing is so shallow, I wonder if I might slip into unconsciousness at any moment. Does anyone around me notice I'm about to completely disappear from existence? I don't look—I can't. If I look, I know I'll see all the pity staring back at me. The eyes that tell me I'm alone now. The eyes that tell me I must have done something wrong, something that made my husband and daughter leave me alone in this miserable world.

As my heart begins to sink even lower, I'm consumed by the image of Travis's grin. He's waving to me. We're on the beach, and it's the summer right after our junior year in high school. His smile is so perfect. Suddenly, we're on the soccer field, and it's the day he first spoke to me, the day he changed my life forever. The day he took me from a wallflower, hidden from the world, and transformed me into a girl who everyone wanted to know, the girl who captured Travis Phillips's heart.

Does he still love me like he once did? He married me as soon as we graduated high school; he'd told me he couldn't be away from me another night. What changed? What did I do to make him leave me now? He can't have loved me as much as he said he did and leave me alone like this. I know Katie loves me.

Swallowing hard, I swipe the tear away that manages to escape down my cheek. What if Katie is cold wherever she is? She needs her momma to tuck the blankets around her tiny body. My lips on her forehead each night are what push the good thoughts in, but who will do that? Who will read her a bedtime story?

I expel all the air from my lungs, and a calm settles over me as I remember she has Travis. He's such a good father. He will never leave her side. He will keep her warm. He'll read to her when I'm not there. He'll make sure the nightmares stay at bay when Momma can't kiss her goodnight.

"Mac? Are you ready?" I hear Monica's tiny voice whisper in my ear. I don't want to open my eyes. I know I need to, but when I do, time will begin to move again. I won't be able to stop it. This new world will become my reality. I will be alone. Once my eyes are open, everything that is wrong will sink in around me, pulling me into the darkness with its black tentacles, into the pits of tar that await to steal the last bit of life I have left inside me.

I feel Monica's forehead press against my cheek and her free hand cup the other side of my head, pressing me into her. The tender gesture sets off a reaction I can't seem to stop. I scream at myself within my own head to pull it together, but all composure is gone. My body starts to violently convulse, and I heave a breath of air in and out. A steady stream of tears follows the single tear that escaped only a moment ago, rushing from both of my eyes.

Monica grips me tighter and, turning into my crumpled frame, she begins to rock me. A whimper flees from my lips as she begins to pat my back. My father is a row behind me. I can feel his presence, but he doesn't reach out and touch me. He does nothing. He has done nothing to lessen my pain since I was twelve years old and my mother died. The cancer not only ate away at her body from the inside, but it didn't stop until it had consumed every last bit of the relationship between my father and me.

Somewhere in me, I know it hurts him to see me in such a state, but I don't have the energy to pretend everything is all right. If Monica were not here to hold me up, I know I would be in a ball on the floor—weeping and asking for mercy to end it. Daddy once told me it's better to feel pain than nothing at all, but I know now he was wrong. So wrong. A pain like this is worse than death.

When Mom died, it was like the wind was knocked out of me. What I feel today is so much worse. It's like the air has been stripped away, and I'm not even left with the desire to take in another breath. There's no fight for survival. There's no desire to see the sun set again. There's nothing but the pain and the hope it will end soon.

I hear the pastor's voice as a hush falls over the crowd. My back stiffens, and I manage to quiet myself for a moment. I need to hear every word. I know it will be like torture, but I have to. I'm here, and it's what I deserve for being here.

As if a switch shut off, the tears are gone, and I'm left with only damp cheeks and swollen eyes. Pushing myself upright, I inhale, the air shaking as it passes through my teeth. Monica's hand slides down and tightly grabs mine. I want her to release me. A desire to be completely isolated in this moment creeps in, but I don't pull away. I need to place my focus on what is about to happen, and I won't be able to do that without her supporting me.

"I want to thank everyone for coming out today. I'm sure I'm not the only one whose heart is breaking from this tragedy," the man standing at the front of the room begins.

I don't look at him. My nostrils flare in disgust; he doesn't know the first thing about a broken heart. I think he should be ashamed for even saying such a thing. His words string together into one meaningless token after another, until they fade into a dull murmur in my ears as my gaze falls onto the boxes only feet away from me.

Looking at them, it doesn't feel real. How can they be

inside of them? They seem so small. They can't be comfortable, and even though I made sure the lining was soft and plush, I don't see how anyone could be comfortable inside. The outside of the casket is a pearl color. I have to fight the urge to stand and open the lids. The funeral home staff told me it would be best to keep them closed for the service. I understood why; they didn't look like themselves due to the impact of the accident. I was scared to say it at the time, but now I'm quite sure there could have been a mistake. If they don't look like themselves, then maybe it's because it's not them.

Though I'm trying to fight it, my mind wanders to that night. I wasn't conscious afterward. Maybe they took Travis and Katie to another hospital. Maybe they woke up and they're searching for me. I don't know who is in the boxes in front of me, but I can't believe it's them. I know if it were my Katie, I would feel it. I'd have to, wouldn't I?

The preacher my father hired is still talking. I try to stand, but Monica's grip on me is too tight. I look at her, my brow narrowed. I want her to release me, why won't she...

She is looking directly at me. She shakes her head no, and her eyes are glistening. I clutch my chest. I can't breathe. The room is spinning. I want to pretend—why can't she just let me pretend? Maybe she sees it too. I don't deserve to pretend. I lived and they did not. I need to feel every second of life as I know it ending. The entire room sees it. They see that my innocent daughter was robbed of her life while I'm still here, still breathing, in and out. I want to tell them all that I wish I could take her place. Or even more, I wish I could take Travis's place. I'm jealous of him. Jealous that he gets to be the one to take care of her forever. He was always the strong one; he should be here, not me.

I'm smiling now, but I don't understand why. Perhaps

out of fear that if I don't I may slip into an eternal madness. Married at eighteen, mother at nineteen, widowed and alone at twenty-one, I've lived enough pain for ten lifetimes. The smile slips from my face, and I'm again reduced to tears. Roller coasters of random emotions render me into a trembling mess. And in this moment I know there was no mistake. I'm alone. Alone on the brink of madness, left with only my dreams of once again holding them in my arms.

———

ONE

THREE YEARS LATER...

The sound of the television stirs me from my restful state in the reclining chair. Buttons, my dachshund, is licking the last of the crumbs off the front of my shirt. I don't have the energy to stop her, or perhaps it's that I don't particularly care.

I can hear that the rain outside has stopped, but it doesn't seem to lessen the gloom that has settled over my living room. I glance at the drawn curtains and consider opening them, but with a sigh, I shift my attention to my rumbling stomach.

Even though I know I should eat something for sustenance, all I can think about is ice cream. Not just any ice cream, but my favorite from the local ice cream shop, Graeter's, called Buckeye Blitz. I push myself up, but Buttons doesn't budge. She stakes her territory on my face. Shoving her off to one side, I stand and cross the room to the kitchen.

Pulling open the freezer door, I peer inside but soon discover what I seek is not within. Then I remember I finished off the last of the blissful dessert the night before. Leaning against the counter, I decide sulking is the best course of action at this point. I glance down at the yoga pants that I've now been wearing for two days and my stained T-shirt. The idea of changing my clothes seems exhausting.

My breath catches in my throat as the cell phone on the counter begins to vibrate wildly. I grasp it firmly in my hands and look at the caller ID, seeing Monica's number. I swipe my finger across the face and take a deep breath. Exhaling, I gasp, "Hello?"

"Mac!" Monica exclaims. "I was about to send out the National Guard to search for you."

"Huh?" I groan, my mind still not able to fully process her words.

"Are you all right?" Monica presses when I don't answer. She raises her voice. "Are you even listening to me?"

"Damn it, Monica," I snap. "Can you please be a little quieter? I was napping."

"Of course you were." Her snarl puts me off.

"What's that supposed to mean?"

"Never mind." I hear her huff, and instinctively I want to press her, but decide I already know what answers lie at the end of that line of questioning. Answers that will only lead to a discussion I don't really feel like having. "I was worried about you, that's all. How are you doing?"

"Fine," I answer matter-of-factly. I already know she isn't going to accept this as my answer, but it's worth a try. I regret even picking up the call.

Her voice is now somber as she says, "He was still your father."

I feel an ache in my chest, and I want my ice cream. "I promise, I'm fine."

"Have you seen Priscilla since the funeral?"

"No, but I'm not really sure why I would though. I didn't see her much while my dad was alive."

"She is your stepmom," Monica says, as if it should mean something to me.

"Percy and I have never been close; you know that." A corner of my mouth lifts, attempting a smile at the nickname. Priscilla hates when I call her Percy, which means I've been calling her that since my dad married her when I was thirteen.

"When is the estate settlement meeting with the lawyers? I'll take off and go with you," she offers.

"No need, it was today."

"What?" she gasps.

I realize I'm rolling my eyes and immediately stop myself. Being away from people for the past few years has made me lack in basic manners, but this is a fact I've come to terms with. "Yeah, it's really not a big deal," I assure her.

"Not a big deal? Mac, I hate to be the one to burst the fairytale bubble you're living in, but your father's estate is very important. It's all you've got, sweetheart." I cringe at her fairytale comment. Everything in me wants to hang up at this point. My life is as far from a storybook as one could imagine.

The first few months after my Travis and Katie were taken from me, the apartment was filled with visitors who were always bringing gift baskets overflowing with tasty goodies. Then the visitors began to slow, and after the first year I was left to fend for myself with the occasional call from a friend or family member. I suppose those only checked in to satisfy their conscience.

The second year was when I discovered that all of the food my visitors had been bringing me had been filling the empty void in my life quite nicely, so I found my own ways to fill it with tasty treats. As long as I was snacking on some delectable treat and distracting myself with episodes of mindless television about the pointless lives of celebrities or bratty children wearing crowns, I wasn't thinking about the complete hollowness in my own life.

The third year was probably the worst though. It wasn't enough that my entire reason for living had been torn away from me. No, now I had everyone who claimed they were just looking out for me telling me that I had mourned, but I was still so young, so it was time to move on. In fact, one of the last conversations I had with my dad was about just that. It wasn't like him to meddle in the emotional side of our relationship, though, so I'm quite confident the talk was at the prompting of Percy.

"I'm sorry, I don't mean to snap at you. I know you're still dealing with losing your dad, too," Monica adds.

"People die; it's life."

"Wow..." I can tell she doesn't know what to say, a rare thing for my friend. I've known her since she started attending the same elementary school as me in second grade; Monica is rarely short on words or advice. However, she has always been the one person who is always there for me, even though I know I don't always return the favor.

"I'm not saying I'm glad he's gone," I attempt to clarify.

"I know you've lost a lot, sweetie."

A lot? I want to scream. A lot? I would say that is putting it mildly. My mother dies from cancer when I'm twelve years old. No little girl should have to watch her mother be robbed of her youth and beauty by such an unforgiving disease. Then I find my one true love, and I marry him, and we have a beautiful baby girl. But can I find happiness? No. God decides I get to be the only one to survive a car crash. Forgive me if I don't crumble into a blathering mess when my father has a sudden heart attack, but I'm a pro with death by this point.

"I'll be fine," I say instead.

"Do you need me to come over and go to the meeting with you?"

"I'm not going," I explain. "I told Percy to just let me know what happens, and she can give me anything I need to sign."

"What did she say?" I can hear the disappointment in Monica's voice.

I sigh. "You know, same old stuff. She started to launch into her lecture that I need to learn how to take care of myself, but I told her I had to go."

"She's just worried about you, hon."

"Please, she is the last woman in the world who needs to be giving me that lecture. She's only ten years older than me; I know exactly why she married my dad. Don't even get me started on what it was like to have a twenty-three year old stepmom as a kid. Back then she wanted to be my best friend, and now she wants to play the part of the wise older woman. I don't want any part of it."

"It's your inheritance, Mac," Monica stresses to me.

"And it's still mine, whether I'm there for the reading of the will or not," I snap. "Look, I gotta go."

"What? Where?" It doesn't surprise me Monica asks.

While I could tell her I've run out of Buckeye Blitz, and I have to run to the store for more, I don't, because I know it will lead to her worrying about how I'm not concerned about my health anymore. Instead, I tell a variation of the truth, "I've got to go to the grocery store."

"Really?" she gasps.

"Yes, you know I do that sometimes." This is nearly untrue.

"I know," she defends. "It just seems like you mostly eat out or get delivery lately."

She's half right. I definitely live on delivery food. Eating out would require too much interaction with people. Something I've decided just isn't for me. "Well I need to pick up some fruit and vegetables." Okay, now I'm just flat-out lying.

"That's amazing! Do you want me to come by after work, and we can walk around the neighborhood?" She nearly is leaping through the phone in excitement. I know for the past year she has bit her tongue about the thirty pounds I've put on, and for that I love her a little more. My appearance has dropped to a bottom priority in my life at this point.

"Oh—umm ... no..." I stumble through my words. "I'm sure Percy will have a lot to go over with me later."

"That's true. I didn't think about that. Well, promise you'll call me tomorrow? Let me know how it goes?"

"You know I will," I say before I hang up. We both know that is a lie.

TWO

THERE WAS a time in my life when I loved spring. The rain would come and wash away all of the darkness and death of the winter. It would signal the rebirth of the world around us, but that doesn't seem to happen anymore. I believe there is a quotient of death and tragedy that a single person can handle in one short period of time. I've far exceeded that, so now not even the rain can wash away the rotted corpses that linger in the air all around me. All I can do is close my eyes and hope that for a moment I can forget the nightmare that is my existence.

My heart leaps in my chest as I hear the loud car horn blaring behind me. I shake my head as if trying to shake away the cloak of blackness that blankets me wherever I go. Swallowing hard, I pull the wheel to the right, easing into the parking lot of the local Kroger grocery store. I see the finish line in sight. I tell myself this is it—just make your way in through those doors, avoid eye contact with all those people living in blissful ignorance, get your sweet treat, and then you're on your way home.

I park my Ford Focus and grab my iPhone wallet case,

shoving it into the pocket of my sweatshirt. Yanking up the hoodie, I secure myself behind the veil, and somehow this makes me certain nobody can see me in my disheveled appearance. I'm not sure, in the three years since Travis and Katie left me, I have been on a real trip to the store. If I'm not getting delivery food, I'm living on a bag full of junk food I occasionally pick up, but since I discovered the Prime Pantry online I barely see a reason to leave home. Percy once tried to tell me that a person could not live on a diet of Chinese take-out and Captain Crunch; I'm determined to prove her wrong.

Pulling open the door in the freezer section, I retrieve a gallon of the Buckeye Blitz ice cream, and then hesitate. My intake of the delectable treat has been increasing, and if I'm honest with myself, I know I will be right back here within the next four days. Perhaps I should save myself the bother of getting dressed and facing the scrutinizing gazes of the world and purchase a second gallon now.

Suddenly, my tongue catches in my throat, the door handle slips from my fingertips, and it swings shut. Directly in front of me, I find myself staring at the back of a little girl's head. Her hair is a mess of long golden ringlets with hints of strawberry tones. I can't swallow. I try to breathe, but my body is no longer responding to the commands from my brain. I reach out with my free hand, as a tear tickles the corner of my eye, threatening to spill out. I know I shouldn't let it, but a hopeful thought enters my head. It wasn't real, none of it. The last three years has all been a horrible dream. Right here in front of me, now only feet away, is my little Katie.

I open my mouth to speak her name, but nothing comes out. I can't reach her; she's too far away. When I take a step forward, the gallon of ice cream falls from my hand, tumbling to the floor, and my foot kicks it across the aisle. It comes to rest at the heels of my Katie. I wait, all sound now fading to a dull white noise.

Her head lowers, and she turns and looks at the dessert container. Bending down, she picks it up in her tiny hands, turns, and shifts her body upright, looking into my eyes. And in that moment, my Katie fades away, disappearing back into my nightmare. The divine conspiracy for me to be absolutely miserable in every moment of my short existence has returned. The little girl smiles at me, and while she's quite cute with her one-sided dimple, she isn't my Katie.

"Is this yours?" she asks in her small voice.

My bottom lip is shaking, and before I can stop it, a tear manages to slip out. I reach out and take the gallon of ice cream from her, croaking out a weak "Thank you."

"Maddy," the little girl's mother calls out. She lingers, staring at me. I wonder if she can see the lonely place I'm in. I'm frozen, and I know I must look insane, but I can't take my eyes off of the little girl.

"Mommy," the little girl says, rushing over and grabbing onto her mother's coat—her mother who has now continued to move down the aisle. "That lady looks sad."

My heart aches as I realize she can actually see me in the dark place I live now, a place where I'm always lost and waiting to understand my new life. Waiting on an understanding I know will never actually come. People tell me how lucky I am that I survived the crash, but here, a shell of a woman I once was, staring into the eyes of this little girl, I know she sees the truth as much as I do. The luckiest thing that could have happened to me that day three years ago would have been dying with Travis and Katie.

"Honey, you shouldn't talk to strangers," the mother begins, not looking at her daughter. I want to scream at her, to tell her to hug her little girl. I want to shake the woman wildly and tell her she has a priceless gift at her feet and she's ignoring it. A grocery trip doesn't matter—none of it matters except for your little girl. But I don't; I stand there silently and watch the little girl, glancing back at me, walk away with her mother.

I know the mother has done nothing wrong, and really, I want to scream at myself. I should have cherished the little moments more.

Then, as if the mother could hear the thoughts inside my head, she stops, kneels, and looks her little girl in the eyes. "What lady are you talking about?" she asks.

The bright blue-eyed little girl points in my direction and says, "That fat lady; she's crying."

The mother's face flushes red as she glances up at me, grasping her child's finger and pulling it down to her side. She's trying to whisper, but I can still hear. "It's not nice to point, and it's certainly not nice to call someone fat. Now come along." The woman is on her feet and making her way out of the section as quickly as she possibly can.

I look around me, half expecting to see someone else standing near me, but I'm not surprised when I see I am alone. Looking down at the ice cream in my hand, my eyes shift to the round, T-shirt clad belly that protrudes from the flaps of my sweatshirt. Without thinking, I rip open the freezer door and haphazardly shove the tub of ice cream back onto the shelf, tearing out of the store and into the parking lot as fast as I can.

And then, like a wave rolling over me, I release it, the flood of tears I'd been holding back. Peering into the rearview mirror, my eyes are not the only things that are puffy. My face is full and round—a face I'd begun to avoid looking at.

Nobody can ever understand how much I will always blame myself. I was driving; I'm the reason they're gone. I've tried to eat away the pain a little at a time. Every cupcake a way to try and forget, but no matter how much I eat, it's never enough to get them completely off my mind. Now I look at myself, and all I feel is shame. My baby girl would not even recognize her momma. Would Travis still think I'm beautiful? I can't help thinking my weakness would be an embarrassment to him.

I'm lost; there's no more road for me to travel down. I already know the only thing that awaits me at the end of each avenue is a dead end. Sometimes I don't think I will have the strength to get up off my knees and keep going. Everyone thinks I should put the pain behind me and move on with my life, but how can a woman put the death of her husband and precious little girl behind her? I don't want to think about it anymore. I wish I could put my pain in a box and place it on a shelf, but it's always there.

If only I had the courage to end it all, but growing up Catholic I think ending my own life might mean I won't get a chance to see my Katie in the next one. It's the only thought that keeps me breathing in and out.

I turn the ignition and whip out of the space, deciding everyone around me can watch out, because I'm getting home now, no matter who gets in my way. The rain pounds my windshield. At first I try to crank my wiper blades, my vision blurred, but I quickly realize they are already on high, and the reason I can't see is the tears that won't stop flowing out of my eyes.

My head is throbbing, and the image of the little girl in the store flashes through my mind. "Damn it!" I shout to nobody in particular.

I press my foot on the gas, racing through the parking lot

and whipping around the corner so I can drive behind the building. I squeal as the back end of my compact car swings out. Trying to take a deep breath, I wipe the tears away, pressing on my brakes because I can't see anything in front of me. I pull my hand away just in time to see the blur of red brake lights.

My arms lock, hands grip the wheel, and my foot slams the brake pedal to the floor. The wheels lock up, and I can feel the tires leave the road. In an instant, the night from three years ago flashes through my thoughts. I'm there. It's night; the wipers are clicking in their harmonious rhythm. Katie is asleep behind me. Travis is flipping through the email messages on his phone. The heat is on in an attempt to defrost the windows. My lids are heavy, and though I'm fighting them to stay open, one blink lasts too long. Just an instant too long, or were they closed for an eternity? The sound of Travis shouting, tires skidding, crashing metal, flashing lights, and then nothing. I remember nothing except waking up in the hospital.

The Ford Focus attempts to stop, but the tires are locked, and there is nothing to do except brace for the impact. Much to my surprise, the seven mile per hour collision packs quite a jolt of force, throwing me back against my seat. My heart feels like it might burst from my chest, the adrenaline pumping through me at full steam. I'm still pressing with all my might on the brake, even though both cars have come to a sudden stop.

I'm staring through the rain at the brake lights and blurry image of a crumpled New York license plate in front of me when there's a knock at my window. A dark figure stands on the other side, the rain obscuring a clear picture. A second later the door pulls open.

"Are you okay?" a voice calls to me.

The head of the voice is out of sight, but I see a pair of men's distressed jeans are next to me, a gray V-neck, now wet, is clinging to a set of well-defined abdominal muscles, and a black leather coat hides the man's skin from the rain. I don't say anything. The engine hums, the car jerking forward as my foot slips off the brake.

"Whoa there," the man says, bending down and leaning over me, sliding the car into park. He crouches now, looking at me with concern in his oversized brown eyes. His jawline is strong. The rain is gathering on his back and flowing directly into my lap, but I don't move. I feel the stiffness on my cheeks from the dried tears. I can tell he can see it—see that I've been crying.

"Can you hear me?" he asks.

I nod.

"Okay, sweetie, you seem pretty shaken up. Let's make sure you're okay." He reaches across me, unbuckles my seatbelt. He pauses, removes the keys from the ignition, and stands up, offering me a hand. I don't know why I take his hand, but I do. When I stand, I see the crumpled front end of my Focus pressed against his old Mustang, which only has a small dent, besides the license plate, from what I can see.

The stranger doesn't release my hand. He leads me to the passenger side of his car. Pulling open the door, he motions for me to get in. I hesitate, and he sees this.

"We need to exchange insurance, and I really don't want to do it out in the rain, do you?"

"Oh—" I relent, taking a seat. When he pulls his hand away, he's left my keys in my hand. If he's a psycho killer, he wouldn't give me back my keys, would he? I familiarize myself with where the door handle is while I wait for him to join me, just in case he is crazy.

When he sits down on the leather seat, he presses his hands back through his dark brown hair, causing the water to drip off the back of his head. He then wipes his hands on his soaked jeans.

"Now, let's try this again. How many fingers am I holding up?" he asks, waving two fingers in front of my face.

I surprise myself when I laugh in response. "I'm fine."

"Are you sure?" he asks, dropping his hand and leaning forward to look at my eyes. I wish he couldn't see me. I wish I had put on clean clothes. "You look like you've been crying."

Suddenly I'm angry. I don't know this guy, so how dare he say something like that to me. I stiffen and insist, "I said I'm fine."

"Okay, sorry, I just hate to see a woman cry."

"I'm not crying," I snap quickly, knowing it's a technicality that I'm not crying in that exact moment. "Didn't you say you wanted to exchange insurance info?"

"Yeah, of course," the man says, leaning over and opening the glove box to pull out a paper card. As he slams it shut, I begin flipping through my phone for my agent's contact info.

"Do you have something I can write on?" I ask, glancing around the car.

He reaches over the backseat and retrieves a fistful of blue flyers. "I guess the back of one of these will work." He hands me a sheet along with a pen that's resting in the cup holder. I jot down my name and the insurance info as fast as I possibly can.

When I'm done I hand him the pen, and he proceeds to do the same for me. Dropping the pen back into the cup holder, he hands me the sheet with his information. Before I can grasp the door handle, my breath catches in my throat as I realize his hand is gripping my arm.

"Are you sure you're okay to drive?" he asks. There is something in his eyes that makes me feel bad. A pureness that says he is genuinely concerned for my well-being. The well-being of a complete stranger.

I glance down at the paper in my lap and see his name written on it. "Christian?"

He smiles at me, glancing at the paper I'd handed him. "Yeah, MacKenzie, is that right?"

"Uh-huh," I begin, offering a slight smile, and he releases my arm. "I promise, I'm fine."

"Well, I promise I'm not going to ask you about why you were crying, but maybe you should stay here for a minute, just until the rain lightens up," he offers, and I wonder if he is just kind or if he might be flirting. Glancing down at my body, I think it must be that he's just a sweet guy.

"Really, I'm all right," I answer, but I don't move. I hesitate, and I can't tell him why. I can't tell him that in this moment I would rather be sitting next to a complete stranger than spend another single second alone. I flip over the flyer in my hand and read the other side. Immediately, a word jumps out and catches my attention.

"Personal chef?" I question.

He looks at what I'm reading. "Oh, do you know anyone?"

"I might," I answer, and my heartbeat begins to quicken. I'd been attending culinary school when the accident happened. I was close to finishing, but it never seemed important after—well ... after.

"It's for a band. We need a chef to travel with us on tour. Our last one got poached by an act we were opening for," he explains, but he seems amused by the story rather than annoyed.

"Are you in the band?" The question slips from my mouth before I realize what I'm asking.

"God no, my brother is the one with musical talent, not me," he begins.

"So it's your brother's band?"

"No," he continues. "Actually, I'm just a roadie. It's kind of a long story, but my brother and I own a building in New York that a bar rents from us, and the band is one of the acts that plays there sometimes. They got a nationwide tour, needed a hand, and I had nothing better going on."

"Seriously? You just had nothing better to do, so you decided to pick up and travel across the country."

He hesitates, and I wonder if I've offended him. "Let's just say running away is sometimes a good way to forget about your problems."

I swallow hard; maybe this stranger gets me more than I think.

"So do you know someone?"

"Excuse me?"

"For the chef job?"

"I doubt it," I answer.

"Well, think about it, and if you do, the information is all on there. Starting tomorrow, applicants can bring their résumé to the address at the bottom. It's the place we're practicing while we're in Cincinnati."

I look at the address and instantly recognize it. "I know it. It's the old brewery district, right?"

"Yup, that's it. Well, if you think of someone, we need to fill the spot before we hit the road again this weekend."

I pull on the door handle and step out, lean down, and add, "Like I said, I doubt it. Sorry about hitting you." He opens his mouth as if he is going to say something else, but before he can, I push the door shut, smile, and wave at him through the glass before crossing over to my car.

As I get in, put the car in reverse and pull away, I don't dare look over at Christian, but I can feel his eyes on me. The rain is now just a light sprinkling and, without the tears, my vision is unobstructed. Carefully I make my way out of the parking lot, heading in the direction of my apartment, trying my best to ignore the crunched front end of my car and the opportunity that's staring me in the face. An opportunity to be a chef—one I would have jumped at years ago.

THREE

I SIT IN MY CAR, in a parking spot in front of my home, but I don't get out. I'm not sure how long I've been sitting here. The rain has stopped completely, and the sun has found its way back into the world. The car has heated up under its rays, wrapping me in a cocoon of warmth. It's paralyzing. My head is resting against the back of my seat, and I watch the small particles of dust dance in the sunlight. A ballet of the things so small, they often go unnoticed. A car horn blares to the left of me. A man angry at a woman who took too long to cross the street in front of him. I shake my head, wondering the question again that has haunted me for years. Why would Travis leave me alone in this world?

Pushing open the door, I climb out; suddenly I regret not purchasing the ice cream I had originally set out to buy. I ventured out into the world for a treat to drown my sorrows in and come home with a bashed up car. This was not how I envisioned my morning going. The trauma of the little girl's comments has faded, and now all I want is to find comfort within the walls of my home and a gallon of ice cream, with Buttons on my lap. I don't have it in me to try again, though. I'm already tired. I'm often tired these days.

I climb the stairs slowly, focusing on each one, using the iron railing to pull my weary body up to the next one. My chest feels tight and my eyes are burning. I tell myself I'll be home soon, in my favorite chair, Katie's blanket wrapped around me. Just a few more steps. Taking the last forward movement up to the landing, I spy a small yellow envelope peeking out from the corner of my welcome mat. Walking over, I retrieve it, and immediately recognize the hand-writing on the front. It's from Percy. Relief washes over me as I realize my trip was not a complete waste; I'd managed to avoid a visit from my stepmother. Of course, now that my father is dead, is she still my stepmother. If they parted at death, doesn't that mean I get to part with her as well? She isn't a horrible woman; in my heart I know that. I just choose to hate her, but I always have. I don't really see the need for an explanation.

I slide my key into the door and make my way inside. Hanging the cluster on a hook near the entrance, all I can think about is the bliss of my chair. Rushing over, I collapse into the overstuffed goodness of the recliner that years ago I'd hated. The recliner was a purchase of Travis's. I nagged him for the entire first year we were married to burn the damn thing. It was hideous. I hated it, and I was certain there was no possible way I could make it work with my furnishings. It wasn't until my Travis was gone that I learned to appreciate that the beauty of the chair was in the comfort it held. I curled up the night after the funeral and didn't leave its embrace for nearly the entire next day. Since that time, it has become my favorite spot.

The yellow envelope is still in my hand. I assume it has something to do with the meeting with the lawyer I chose not to attend. I can't imagine the contents of the envelope affecting me in any direct way. My father always took care of me, at least financially. I know that wouldn't change in his death. Sliding a finger along the lip of the envelope, I tear into it, revealing multiple pieces of paper hidden inside. One piece falls into my lap. Lifting up the rectangular shape, I see it's a check made out to me for eight thousand dollars. Uncertain what I'm looking at, I proceed to unfold the letter that's included as well. It's Percy's handwriting again.

MacKenzie,
I hope this letter finds you well.

That's just like Percy. My father just died, and she is hoping a letter finds me well. Of course I'm not well!

We missed you at the meeting today. I hope you are feeling better, and since you're not home, I assume you are.

What she really means is, if you were sick, you would be home so I know you're a little liar.

Your father's attorney has reviewed the estate, and unfortunately it appears your father made some choices that left the finances in a less-than-desirable state.

Again, I can see what this actually means. She was never happy with the fact that after Travis died, my father stepped up and paid all of my bills. I knew this had particularly bothered her that he had taken on the expense for so long. I quit coming for Christmas a couple years ago when she suggested a year had been long enough for me to grieve, and perhaps I should think about what I wanted to do with my life. Something she would never understand was that I had already done what I wanted to do. I married Travis and had Katie, and now that they were gone, there was really nothing else I desired out of life.

The remainder of his liquid assets has been divided among his children, and this check reflects that amount.

As I read these words my stomach drops, my chest aches. My father had always made wise investments. We never wanted for anything. How can it be possible that it is all gone? But I know the answer to this. He paid for everything. Travis and I had been so young. We didn't plan for what happened to us. After the accident, Daddy took care of the funeral and burial expenses. But it didn't stop there; he knew I couldn't bear the idea of living with them again. He bought me anything and everything I needed. He made sure my rent and bills were paid, that I always had money in my account. I am the reason there is nothing left. I feel like I'm going to be sick.

He paid cash for your car, and he wanted you to have it so I will have the title transferred to your name.

I think of the crumpled disaster in front of the apartment, heaving a heavy sigh.

I know this is probably a shock for you. Your father didn't want to worry you, but his business had been off the past couple years. I love you as one of my own, dear, and I want to offer our home to you. You are always welcome, and

I know your sisters would love to have you. Take some time to think about it and let me know what you want to do.

Much Love,

Priscilla

At least she knew better than to sign it 'Mom.' I drop the letter, and before I can even think about it, I am dialing Monica. She is always the one I can unload on. When I come unraveled, she has this amazing way of helping me hold it together.

"Hello," Monica answers.

"It's me."

"Are you all right?"

"No."

"What's wrong? Do you need me to come over?"

"I don't know. I can't deal with this, Mon." I'm shaking as I speak.

"Slow down," she instructs me. "Deal with what?"

"I get back from the store and there's a letter on my porch from Percy."

"Okay? And?"

"And it says my dad was nearly broke when he died."

"What?"

"Yeah? There's a check for eight grand, and she says I can keep the car."

"Wait, I don't understand. How is that possible?"

"She said business was bad for a couple years, but Dad didn't want to worry me," I explain. "Why would he not tell me? He didn't have to take care of me like he did. He should have kept that money."

"Mac, you know him, and there was no way he wasn't going to take care of you. He loved you so much."

"I guess."

"No guessing about it," she corrects me. "He may not have known how to talk to you, but him taking care of you was a way he felt like he could show you how he felt about you."

A silence hangs in the air between us before Monica asks, "So what are you going to do now?"

"I don't know. Percy offered to let me move in with her."

"Oh God," she quickly says, "that would not end well."

"Ya think?" I chime sarcastically.

"I guess you could move in here, but my roommates will insist you pay. Maybe you could go back to culinary school."

The idea of living with Monica's uptight roomies makes me almost as sick as the idea of living with Percy. Then I remember... "Wait!"

"What?"

I dig through my pockets for the flyer from the parking lot guy earlier. "I was in an accident, and the guy had a flyer, if I can just find—"

"You were in an accident! Are you okay?" I can tell Monica would jump through the phone if she could.

"Yes, I promise it was nothing. It was raining, and I could barely see. I accidentally rear-ended someone in a parking lot."

"Are you sure you're all right?"

"Yes, but he wrote his..." I start to explain before finding the sheet in my inside pocket and pulling it out. "Here it is. He wrote his information for insurance down on this sheet, and I saw on the back it was an advertisement for a personal chef."

"Really? What kind of personal chef?" she asks, her voice skeptical.

I peer at the flyer once again. "A band is in need of a cook to travel with them on tour."

"Are you kidding me? You've barely left your home for three years, and now you're going to go on tour with a band?"

"I doubt it," I reply dismissively. "I'm sure I wouldn't even get the job. But I have to do something. I can't live with Percy."

Monica is quiet; I know she is thinking about the idea. "All right, call about it, but if you get the creepy vibe at all, just hang up, promise?"

I laugh.

"Promise me!" she exclaims.

"Okay, I promise."

"Call me later."

"I will," I reply before hanging up.

I try not to think too much about what I'm going to say. I know if I over think it, I will chicken out. I'm not even sure I want the job, but I figure it doesn't hurt to call. The phone rings. Once, twice, and then I hear the familiar voice from earlier. I decide not to let him know it's me.

"Hello, this is Christian."

"Umm, yeah, I'm calling about the ad for a chef," I answer, nervous.

"Great, if you're interested, we're having an open call tomorrow at one of the warehouses on Liberty. Do you know the area?"

"Yeah, I do. Should I bring anything?"

"Bring your résumé, along with any references, and come to the side door. From there someone can direct you.

Interviews start at noon and go until they're done with everyone."

"Got it, thanks," I reply.

"You're welcome," I hear, and then the phone clicks. My heart is racing. What am I doing? References? I dropped out of culinary school. How in the hell can I even compete? Reaching to my side, I grab Katie's blanket. I pull it all around me and close my eyes. I can't panic about this anymore. I need the silence of sleep to consume me. The comfort of a state where worry and sadness leave you alone. Closing my eyes, I welcome the darkness.

FOUR

THE NEW MORNING light hasn't brought me a new perspective on my situation. If anything, the panic has taken a firm grip on me, wrapping its fingers tight around my throat. I can't live with my stepmother; that much I know from our past. Monica seems like the next best option; however, I think our friendship will suffer if we are roommates. Her constant mothering and worrying would drive me absolutely mad. This means I have no other choice but to rely solely on myself.

I need work. There's no way around that. My inheritance is meager at best, and might keep me going for a couple months, but then what? I need a plan. First, I think about my skills. Then I remember food is the only skill I ever had. I know I can cook, and I can even find a job at a local restaurant starting out, but in all honestly, I doubt I could hold the job. A kitchen is hectic. There's a team there that relies on you, and I'm not exactly what one might call reliable right now. Even though it's been three years since the accident, there are some days when my reality becomes too much, and I simply check out. A kitchen job won't give me that.

The flyer from Christian keeps popping back into my head. How hard can it be to cook for a band? I would think the schedule isn't insane, and without family and friends around me, prying into all the details of my life, maybe I can find a moment of peace. A moment to myself, without someone asking if I'm going to be okay. Without the people around me telling me to count my blessings, or worse, giving me those looks of pity. Growing up, I worked in the kitchen of my father's restaurant, but he sold that some years after my mother passed away. Cooking is in my blood.

I've never applied for a job like this. I'm not sure where one would even begin or what qualifications they are looking for. I make a decision; I'm going to let my cooking speak for me. After all, it is a job as a chef, so what better way to win over an employer than with food. After an early morning trip to the grocery store, I'm now staring at all the ingredients to make Katie's favorite dish: chicken and dumplings. I've decided to go with comfort food—men love comfort food.

I don't recall the last time I truly cooked. That is, not opening up a can of soup and dumping the contents into a microwave-safe bowl. I used to love cooking. Now it seems I will put anything in my body; fatty fast food, fried take-out, antibiotic laced meat. Anything seems to go if it's quick, easy, and gives me an immediate high.

Part of me misses it: choosing the right ingredients, the perfect spices, the aromas that would fill the air. I quickly learned that cooking isn't as enjoyable for me when I don't have people to share it with. Now, when I plan a meal, and I'm forced to reduce the calculations so the servings are for one, which is just a reminder that I'm alone. With a deep breath, the preparation begins.

Generously, I sprinkle salt and pepper on the cut-up pieces of a whole chicken. Next, I dredge each piece in flour on a nearby paper plate. I spent the extra money for local, stone-milled flour, as I'm a strong believer in the finest and least processed ingredients in order to make the most delicious food. In a pan, a melted tablespoon of ghee and another of coconut oil is waiting for me.

Grabbing the set of tongs, the chicken goes into the oil with a crackle and pop. There is something comforting in the smell of the browning meat. Something that reminds me of a life before it was wrecked by grief. Browning all the sides, I pull out the pieces of crisped chicken and set them on a paper towel. A worry enters my mind. Is this too simplistic of a dish to win over my potential employers? Will they see right through it and realize I'm nothing more than a culinary school dropout, who is terrified of life or taking risks? I push down the crowding thoughts of doubt and try to focus on making the best damn chicken and dumplings I have ever made.

I dice the celery and carrots, and just as Katie liked, I choose to leave out the onions. With a dollop of ghee, I sauté the vegetables, adding in a bit more salt and pepper. I giggle when I sprinkle in the thyme, remembering Travis's frequent joke in the kitchen. He would always throw me the bottle and say, 'Look, thyme's flying.' Every single time he said it I would laugh, even when I didn't think it was very funny.

In goes the chicken broth to the pan of veggies. I used to make my own broth, and when I would, Katie would complain that the house stunk like feet. But I haven't done that since before everything changed. Carefully, I drop in the chicken and turn the heat to a simmer. Pulling out the biscuit dough I made earlier, I glance at the clock. I have one hour to finish the food, get ready, and drive to the interview. Panic washes over me as the looming deadline approaches.

Dropping in the balls of dough, I run to my closet. I don't want to look like I'm trying too hard, but I also want to appear clean and professional. I don't think my yoga pants are going to cut it. I pull out a pair of black slacks I haven't set eyes on in years. Dropping my pajama pants to the floor I slide one leg on and then the other. When I go to pull them up the thirty pounds I've gained is suddenly much more apparent. Stepping out of the pants, I quickly slide through the garments one after another. Nothing is going to fit me. This realization sets my mind spinning. Do I just forget it? If I do, that would mean living with Percy is almost a certainty. No. I need to do this.

The funeral! I remember. I had worn a knee-length black dress to my father's funeral. The stretchy material was forgiving on my newly formed curves. I slide the dress over my head, fluff my hair, add a little powder to my face, and finish off with lip gloss. Pressing my lips together, I declare to myself ready.

In a few frantic moments of rushing around, I manage to package up my delicious meal, update and print my resume, which makes me feel like a complete fraud, and blow out the door with a couple seconds to spare. I'm doing my best to not let the anxiety creep in. I tell myself over and over, You're fine, no big deal. You've got this. Now if only I can make myself believe it.

FIVE

I SIT IN MY CAR, staring at the other people walking by. As I see each one, I wonder if they are my competition—are they who will take away my opportunity for escape, take my chance to run from my ghosts. My heart is beating so hard I can feel my chest pounding in and out. I know I need this, a distraction, a way to distance myself from the reality that has tormented me for years. Yet I find myself unable to move.

"Travis," I whisper. "If you're looking down on me right now, I need you. I need you to help me be strong ... God, I miss you so much." I know I must force the thoughts from my mind before the tears come. The tears always come when the loneliness sets in.

Glancing in the rearview mirror, I confirm my chestnut hair is still in place, half pulled back to reveal my cheek-bones, one of the few places on my body that has not been affected by my weight gain. There's a knock on my window. Startled, I gasp as I peer up. The gorgeous man I had rear-ended in the parking lot is staring down at me. I smile at him, and he motions for me to roll down the window. Realizing what an idiot I must look like, I quickly press the button, the sound of the motor buzzing as the glass lowers.

"Hi stranger." He's smiling, and I notice a dimple I hadn't before.

"Oh—hi."

"Yikes, I couldn't see the damage too well in the rain, but you really did a number on your car, didn't you?"

I don't answer; instead, I get a goofy wide mouth grin and nod at him. Jesus, I must look like a complete idiot.

"Umm, yeah, so did I not put my number on there correctly?" he inquires. I furrow my brow in confusion, then realize I hadn't told him it was me when I called about the chef position.

I laugh nervously. "No, sorry. Actually, I'm here about the job."

He staggers back slightly. "You're a cook?"

I hesitate. How do I answer such a question? I've never worked as a personal chef. Saying I dropped out of culinary school after the death of my husband and daughter seems like a heavy way to start a conversation. I decide to keep it simple. "Yes."

"Why didn't you say something yesterday?" He looks at me suspiciously.

"I don't know. I guess I wasn't thinking straight after the accident," I say, trying to think quickly. He lingers a moment, still glaring at me, until suddenly his entire demeanor shifts.

"Well great, come on in, and I'll introduce you to everyone," he says, pulling on the door handle, waiting for me to exit. This is it. There is no more stalling to be done. I step out, making sure my dress is lying properly in the back. He presses the door shut, and I begin to follow him when I suddenly remember my dish.

"Oh wait!" I exclaim, turning and running back to the car. "I forgot the food."

"What food?" Christian asks, and in a second, he is at my side, curiously looking over my shoulder as I pull the pot from the backseat. "You cooked?"

"Well, I am interviewing to be a personal chef. It seems like the least I could do is let them see if they enjoy my food." I suddenly feel much more confident. "Do you mind carrying this so I can grab my resume?"

"Only if I can try it, too." He grins, taking the dish off my hands.

"Of course," I reply in a voice that even I think sounds flirtatious and wonder what in the hell I am doing.

"What is it?"

"Chicken and dumplings," I explain, and without thinking about it, the next words slip out of my mouth before I can stop them. "They're my daughter's favorite."

"Oh, you have a kid?" he asks, turning and walking back toward the building.

I mentally chastise myself. How could I have brought up Katie? I wanted this job so I could get a break from my life, from all the people who know the constant hell I'm in. I say I want to get away from the looks everyone gives me, and what is one of the first things I bring up? My dead daughter. "She passed away a few years ago."

"Oh, wow, I'm so sorry," he adds, looking over his shoulder at me and slowing his pace.

I'm shaking my head, and I lie. "It's okay."

"You seem so young," he begins, then quickly stops himself. "You know what, I'm sorry, it's really none of my business."

"No, really, it's fine, I brought her up." I even hate the

term 'passed away,' but whenever I use the 'died,' people get extra weird on me.

"I really am sorry for your loss," he offers again softly, stepping through the open door.

"Let's just not talk about it, okay?" I try to say in a light voice, but I know the trembling is obvious.

"Of course." I imagine he's relieved. My eyes adjust to the dim light in a matter of a few seconds. My gaze narrows on the crowd of other young twenty-somethings sitting around in folding chairs. "Don't worry, I won't make you wait with the other applicants. After all, I think there is some kind of code between people once you've rear-ended them— in your car, that is."

I laugh at his correction of his unintentional innuendo. "I got it. Thanks. So, all these people are applying for the job as well?" There are at least a dozen individuals strewn about the seating area. Ripped jeans and concert T-shirts seem to be a standard wardrobe choice, and I suddenly feel very out of sorts. I have a flower tattoo on my upper arm that Travis took me to get on our honeymoon, and suddenly I'm wishing I had worn something that made it more visible. Perhaps I could have fooled everyone into thinking I was cool enough to be here.

"Yeah, but none of them brought food. That bumps you automatically to the front of the list."

"Really? They didn't?" I'm wondering if I've made a mistake.

"Nah, not exactly a crowd of over-achievers out there. They figure they're cooking for a rock band and need to play it cool."

"And did they pick right?"

"I'd pick the food I can taste over the food I can't," Christian begins, "unless yours completely sucks.

My nerves kick into high gear, and I wish I were any place but here. I force myself to laugh at Christian's attempt at humor, even though I am far too nervous to think much of anything is funny. "Well, I don't think it sucks, but I'm not really sure that counts."

"It would be really bad if you thought your food sucked, wouldn't it?"

"Yeah..." Now I laugh for real. "I guess it would. Now really, you don't have to get me in ahead of everyone; I'm fine waiting with everyone else."

"Nonsense—" Christian starts.

"What do we have here?" a man questions, peeking into the pot in Christian's arms. His dark hair is mussed as if he doesn't care how it looks; yet somehow it still appears incredibly sexy. His eyes are blue, which I hadn't expected when I first saw his hair. He has short stubble on his face, and perfectly shaped lips that can be best described as extremely kissable. My breath catches in my throat, and I don't know what to say. I'm speechless, sandwiched between two insanely hot guys. I'm so out of my element, I wonder if everyone else can see it as well.

"Oh, hey Dean, this is MacKenzie. I met her at the grocery store yesterday when I was putting up flyers."

"Wait a second." He looks me up and down. "Is this the girl who can't drive?"

"Excuse me?" My voice is no longer missing. In fact, I've found it along with a few choice words. "I can drive! Quite well, thank you. And for your information, it was storming out when I barely tapped into him."

"Well, I don't know if I would call it barely," Christian interjects, wincing at the memory.

"Oh, shut up," I command, glaring at him. Did I really just say that?

"Whoa there," Dean protests, raising his hands and waving them in the air. "I'm just kidding. Strung a little tight, isn't she?"

I'm not sure if it's the fact that he just criticized my driving, or the fact that he looks so damn cocky with that crooked grin, but I'm revved up. I'm not going to take his condescending bullshit. I don't even know this guy. Who in the hell is he to say these things? "Strung a little tight? I'll show you strung a little tight," I snarl and act as though I'm going to lunge forward in his direction. Anyone who actually knows me understands just how absurd this is, since I don't have a violent bone in my body.

"Mackenzie," Christian snaps at me. "This is Dean."

"Yeah, I heard you the first time," I grumble, not taking my eyes off my target.

"The lead singer of Head Case. You know, the band you're here to cook for."

I feel my face go instantly hot. I look away from Dean. I'm certain he must be thrilled by my embarrassment. I can't believe I have such a short fuse. Obviously, during the past few years of isolation, there have been some other changes, including the complete loss of the ability to communicate with the rest of society. Taking a long blink, I swallow deep, and turn back to face my victim. I'm right; he has a smug smile on his face, and he's so cute I can't figure out if I want to punch him or kiss him.

"I'm so sorry. I don't know what got into me," I offer, then grit my teeth to stop any other rude remarks from flying out.

"It's fine, but do you mind if me and the guys try the food you brought?" he asks, acting as though he is trying to be overly cautious.

I laugh, even though I don't think it's very funny.

"Of course not, and I also brought my resume," I add as he turns and walks away without a word. I look at Christian. This whole interaction puzzles me.

"Follow me," Christian directs, taking off in the direction Dean headed. We make our way around the end of a bar into a side room. There is a jukebox along the far wall and pool tables just in front of it. Sitting all around the pool table are three other guys.

Dean approaches them, and in a loud voice announces, "Lunch is served."

I stand back and watch as Christian places the pot on the bar and the men swarm around it. As they scoop helpings into beer mugs, I realize it never crossed my mind to bring plates or utensils, but they don't seem to mind. A shorter guy with a full and lush beard lifts his mug up to his mouth first, intensely eyeing the contents. I hold my breath, waiting for him to taste, but nothing. He pulls it away.

"What's wrong?" I hear Dean ask him.

"Can't eat it—well, I can, but then the rest of you get to deal with the consequences," the man answers. I crinkle my nose. There must be some sort of sensitivity with what I've prepared. I want to slip away and disappear in this moment.

"Alex, you try it," Dean instructs one of the others.

A tall and slender ginger tilts the mug up, taking a taste.

"Well?" Dean prods him as I watch in silence.

"Damn, that's good," the slender man moans.

"Oh, sure, rub it in," the first man grimaces.

Christian walks over to stand next to me and whispers, "Pete's the drummer, and we just found out he has a gluten sensitivity. He's kinda pissed, but mostly about beer. Alex, the red head, is the bass player, and you already met the lead singer, Dean. He also plays the guitar."

"And the other guy?" I ask, nodding in the direction of

the sandy blond fellow with the larger nose and strong jaw line.

"Andrew, he pretty much does it all," Christian explains. "They seem to like it."

"Well, all of them except Dean," I say. "He's not eating."

No sooner than the words leave my mouth do I see Dean lifting up his mug to his nose, cautiously sniffing it. I'm not sure if I should be offended, so I decide to silently watch him instead. He presses the mug to his lips and sips the creamy broth. I can't see his expression. He doesn't pull the mug away, but instead he lifts it higher, opening his mouth wide, taking in a dumpling. Setting the mug down, I study him as he shifts the food from side to side in his mouth before swallowing.

He looks to the other guys who are all peering back at him. He stands quiet, and finally says, "Agreed?"

I wonder what he means. The other guys are nodding and chiming their answers in the affirmative. Without hesitation, Dean turns and walks over to stand directly in front of me. "We leave in five days, can you be ready?"

"What?" I gasp.

"Christian can give you all the details you need."

"What about my resume, and don't you have questions you want to ask me? Or ... but ... one of you couldn't even try it," I stammer.

"He agreed on you, but it might be nice if you make something that won't having him stinking up the tour bus all night." Dean laughs at his joke. I crinkle my nose again.

"You don't have any other questions?" I ask in disbelief.

"Is there anything I should know about you? Have you ever poisoned a client?" Dean smiles.

I laugh, and my heart is racing. "No." I think about

adding that I've never had a client, but decide it's best to leave that out. "What about all the other applicants?"

"Would you rather I hire one of them?" Dean asks me pointedly.

"No, I didn't mean—" I begin.

"Great! We like your food, we have stuff to do, so see you soon," he speaks quickly before turning to face Christian. "Can you send everyone else home and give MacKenzie all the information she'll need?"

Dean doesn't say another word. He turns around and walks over to his band mates. In an instant they are all engaged in a boisterous conversation. Christian takes my arm, leading me back to my car. "Welcome aboard, I guess."

"Okay, can I just say that's the weirdest interview I've ever had," I state, though I haven't had any other interviews to compare it to.

"That's Dean, but you'll get used to him."

"I suppose." My head is still spinning.

"Is the number on your resume correct?" Christian asks, holding open my door.

Nodding in response, I take a seat behind the steering wheel.

"Great, I need to send all of these other people home, then I'll call you after practice to go over the details. Does that work for you?"

"Yeah, I mean—" I'm not sure now if I want this job for sure, but it seems too late to stop the train; it's already out of control. This is going to take what I know as my normal and turn it on its head. "Thank you, Christian."

"For what?"

"You got me in front of them. I know I have you to thank a lot for this job."

"Don't be silly, it was your food. We'll talk later."

"Okay." I smile. Christian closes the door, standing and watching me as I pull away. I can feel myself blushing.

My mind is racing with ideas. I'm going to be leaving my home, the only home I've known as an adult. The home I created with my husband. Am I ready for this?

He's still looking at me, waving. My thoughts wonder to Christian ... why is so nice to me? Is he waving because he wants to be my friend? Is it because he's kind, or because he sees the opportunity for more? Can I even think about more? Am I capable of more after Travis? All I know is I have five days to pack up everything I've known. I swallow hard, my face hot and red, and all I want to do now is get home and call Monica. She's always prepared to tell me if I'm making a rash, or just plain stupid, decision.

SIX

MONICA PIVOTS, and I watch as she searches for something. Monica is quite beautiful; she always keeps her long auburn hair pulled back from her face, even though I tell her how great it looks when she wears it down. Her tall and slender frame moves with grace. I remember envying her shape while we were growing up, but once I met Travis those feelings faded. He had told me once how pleased he was that he had fallen in love with a woman with curves.

"What are you looking at?" she asks, pausing and glancing in my direction.

"Just thinking about how much I'm going to miss you," I answer truthfully.

"It's not like you're leaving forever," she returns to her searching. "At least you better come back."

"Don't be silly, of course I'm coming back. I have to get my dog."

We laugh. "You better watch it, or I might just kill that damn dog of yours while you're gone."

"Don't say that, she'll hear you."

"She's a damn doxie who is so fat she can't see her own feet."

"That's not fair; she has a thyroid issue."

"You do know that is something you've made up in your head to make yourself feel better about having a fat-ass dog."

"Shut up," I snarl playfully.

"Where is the damn packing tape?" Monica grumbles.

Glancing behind me, I pull out the green tape dispenser that is wedged under a nearby box and lift it high into the air as if victorious. With a huff, she walks over and swipes it from my hand.

"You know what I want to hear more about?" Monica asks before dragging the tape across the box in front of her and flipping it over so the open end is right side up.

"What's that?"

"More about these dreamy sexpots you're going to be in close quarters with."

I laugh; I should have guessed she would have taken the conversation in that direction. "There's nothing to tell."

"Nothing to tell!" she exclaims. "Based on your description, there is tons more to tell."

"First off, I doubt we'll be sharing a hotel room or anything like that, and second, there's no way either of them would be interested in me."

"Either of them? So there are definitely two who rose to the top?"

"No, I just happened to only speak to two of them."

"Ah, I see, so when you get a chance to speak to the others, there will be even more options."

Shaking my head, unable to stop myself from grinning, I grumble, "You're too much."

"Tell me more about this Christian. You said he was sexy and sweet?"

"I guess."

"You guess he's sexy, or you guess he's sweet?"

"Oh no, he's definitely sexy," I quickly confirm with giggle. "But he appears to be one of those types of guys who spends way more time in the gym than I ever would."

"Well, that just means he has a great body, right?"

"Yeah, I suppose. A little lumpy for my taste."

"Have you ever had lumpy?"

"Well—no."

She shoves me in the arm and teases, "Then how do you know you don't like it. One never knows they like ice cream until they've had their first bite."

"And I do love ice cream," I add with a devilish grin.

"Mac! You bad girl, what's gotten into you?"

"You've always been a bad influence."

"I try," she says. "What about the other guy? Is he ... lumpy?"

"No..." I pause and think about Dean. "He's more lean. From what I could see, his arms were covered in tattoos."

"Is that a good thing or bad?"

"It looks good on him."

"Did you show him your ink?" Monica inquires.

"No, it didn't exactly come up. Besides, I'm sure he has a different girl in his bed every night."

"What makes you say that?"

"I don't know ... isn't that what musicians do?"

"Oh Mac, I love you." Monica is nearly giddy at my comment. "But you are such a prude sometimes."

"Shut up," I huff.

A silence settles between us. I stand and walk over to the bookcase Monica has been working on packing up.

There's a row of Jim Butcher books, which belonged to Travis. I pull one out and run my hand across the cover. He would always pre-order his copy so that he could get the book the day before it was officially released.

"Are you okay?"

"Huh? Oh, yeah, just a little overwhelmed by all there is to do."

"You like him?" she questions.

I furrow my brow; her question puzzles me. "Jim Butcher?"

"No goof, the tattooed one. Did you say his name was Dean?"

"Seriously?" I snap, shoving the book into the box before grabbing another handful of novels, placing them in the box as well. "I said like ten words to the guy."

"When you first described him to me you told me he was gorgeous. You've never used that word to describe someone before."

"That's not true," I argue, avoiding eye contact and keeping busy packing.

"Yes, you did."

"Well, I may have used that word, but just because I think a guy is attractive doesn't mean I have any interest in dating them," I inform her.

"And why not?"

"I'm married." The instant the words leave my mouth the cold reality settles in over me once again. I revise my statement, "I was married."

She takes my arm and gestures toward the couch. My knees are buckling, but I follow her lead, taking a seat. She sits next to me, her hand resting on my leg. My eyes are growing wet, but I refuse to let the tears fall.

"Are you okay?" she asks, leaning forward, forcing me to look into her eyes.

"When does it go away?"

"When does what go away?"

"The pain?"

"Honey, I don't think it ever completely goes away."

"Well, you're no help." I try to laugh when I speak and lighten the mood.

"I don't want to lie to you. You were dealt a bad hand in life, but it's been three years, sweetheart, so it's more than all right for you to think someone's hot."

"I know that!" I exclaim, hopping to my feet and crossing the room. I'm about to leave all of this here—my old life, the sadness, the loneliness—at least for a few months. To think about the pain like this, right before I leave, is too much.

"Please don't yell at me. You know I'm just trying to help."

I shake my head, grabbing more books and placing them in the now half-full box. "I'm sorry. It's just—" I stop myself, unsure how to say what I'm feeling.

"It's just what?"

"I thought after a while people were able to remember and talk about who they've lost. Laugh about the craziness that happened when they were here. It's been three years, and I still want to cry every time I talk about them."

"You've been a living monument to them. There is nothing about your life that doesn't reflect Travis and Katie."

"What else am I supposed to do?"

"I'm not saying you're wrong. Everyone begins to let go in their own time."

"But what if I don't want to let go?"

The phone rings, and I nearly jump out of my skin. I freeze, looking around the room, trying to remember where I last set the device. It rings again. Monica hops to her feet and crosses the room; she retrieves my cell from the windowsill, rushing it over to my hand, just as the third ring sounds. I swipe my finger across the front and answer, "Hello?"

"MacKenzie? This is Christian, I— uh, I work for Head Case."

I laugh. "Yeah, I remember."

"Oh yeah, of course," he quickly replies. "I was calling to let you know I'll be picking you up for a supply run. Is two days enough time for you to get a list together of what you'll need?"

I really have no idea if it's enough, but I also want to seem like I know what I'm talking about. "Yeah, sounds great."

"Perfect! I'll call before I come to get you. Oh yeah, and just a heads up: all staff only gets two suitcases, so be sure to pack carefully."

"Okay, thanks," I say, then hear the phone click. I hate when people don't say goodbye; it always has come across as rude to me. I stare at the darkened phone face.

"What was that?" Monica asks.

I shake my head in disbelief, unsure what I just agreed to. "That was my new job. Apparently I only get to take two bags. What am I going to do with all of my stuff? With Travis and Katie's—I can't do this job, there's no way I can sort it all out." I'm having a panic attack, but there seems to be nothing I can do to stop it now. I'm too far gone down the rabbit hole. My heart is racing; I can hear it pounding in my ears.

"Stop it! You're not backing out now!" Monica exclaims.

"I can't," I insist. "What am I going to do?"

"Yes, you can," she reaffirms. "We'll get it all packed up and call Percy to see if we can store everything in her garage."

"I don't know," I reply apprehensively.

"She loves you, Mac, and she'll take care of it. No matter what you think of her, you know she will."

"It's all my pictures, everything I have of them."

"It'll be okay. We'll put a picture in your bag, so you can look at it whenever you need to. I'm a phone call away if you freak out."

"I don't—"

"You're just upset right now because it's new, and new is scary. You can do this, I know you." She now has a grip on my shoulders and is staring me directly in the eyes.

"I can do this," I repeat, though I'm not sure I believe myself, so I repeat the words again and again. "I can do this. I can do this."

"Yes, you can, now let's finish packing. You're starting to creep me out." She laughs. I'm going to miss her laugh.

SEVEN

I CLOSE my eyes and pop in the sample size of the German chocolate, releasing an orgasmic moan of delight as it melts on my tongue and spreads the sugary sensation throughout my mouth. Realizing once again I'm in public, I open my eyes and peer at the woman behind the sample table, and I wonder how long she's been staring at me.

"There you are," Christian's voice sounds off behind me. "Sorry I didn't pick you up ... busier day than I thought."

"Oh, no worries, it's really—" I begin, but a girl runs up and interrupts me.

"Really, Christian?" The girl shouts, rushing toward us. Her hair is bleached blond—well, all of it but her dark, one-inch roots. She has dangling star earrings and her cut off T-shirt and jean shorts makes me feel suddenly self-conscious about my own body. I check the corners of my mouth to ensure there is no trace of the chocolate bliss I just sampled. "You couldn't even wait for me to get my shoes on?"

"I told you not to take them off in my car." I watch as he rolls his eyes as he responds.

"You know my feet get sweaty if I leave my shoes on too long," the girl reminds him, her hands planted firmly on her hips.

"Enough already!" Christian snaps. This surprises me, as I never imagined him losing his temper, but I suppose I don't really know him. "Kristen, this is MacKenzie. MacKenzie, Kristen."

"I told you, call me Storm," she corrects him. He rolls his eyes again.

"Whatever. MacKenzie, she'll be helping you get everything you need," he explains. "The crew is fed separately, understand?"

"No, not really," I answer.

Storm looks me up and down. "Yeah, only the band gets the fancy food."

"Kristen, be quiet," Christian waves her off.

"Storm, damn it!"

"We tend to get carry out. The band needs to have their nutrition looked after, so that's what you're here for. Got it? Here," he continues without me answering, handing me a binder. "Inside you'll find any info about allergies, likes, dislikes."

I flip through the pages, reading the contents. "Really? Dean's favorite food is mac-and-cheese? You've got to be kidding me."

"Yup, and you need to find a way to make it gluten free for Pete," Storm states, popping her gum obnoxiously.

"Yeah, I know," I say with a half-smile.

She pushes her hands in my direction. "Well, excuse me."

"I'm sorry, I didn't mean anything by—" I start.

"Just ignore her. She's annoyed Pete can't sit around and drink after shows with her."

"Why don't you just shut up, Christian?" the girl taunts, and I wonder how young she actually is.

"Anyway, read over everything and call my cell when you girls are done and ready to check out."

"Alex has a peanut allergy?" I exclaim, reading through the list. I huff, now extremely frustrated. "I could have used this information days ago."

"Sorry, take a few minutes and try to rework your plan. Storm will help you," he emphasizes her self-proclaimed nickname, not shielding his annoyance. "I've got a bunch of calls to make. We had some cancellations, and I need to get ahold of the right people to get the spots filled. Any questions, just ask her."

Christian turns to walk away before I can say a word. "Oh..." He pauses, turning around. "And don't worry, MacKenzie, you're going to do great."

"Actually, my friends call me Mac," I correct him, a huge smile now on my face.

He grins in response, revealing those dimples I could go swimming in. "I like it. Does that mean we're friends?"

My cheeks go hot. Why am I blushing? Before I answer he winks and then turns, rushing out the entrance of the bulk grocery warehouse.

"I think I'm going to vomit." Storm sighs. "He can be such an asshole."

I choose to ignore her comment. "Well, it's nice to meet you, Storm."

"Yeah, you too." She nods, no enthusiasm in her voice.

"How about we head over to the furniture department so I can sit down and go through my notes?"

She shrugs her shoulders in response. "I'm yours, whatever you need."

We make our way across the store, and I search out the

most comfortable looking sofa before taking a seat. A sales associate catches sight of us in a matter of seconds. I frown when I see him rushing over to greet us. "Hello ladies, is there something I can help you with?"

"Just looking," I respond.

"Okay, well you just let me know if you have any questions." He smiles and skulks back over to the column he had been waiting at.

Storm doesn't sit; she's standing over my shoulder, legs slightly open, swaying as she plays with her hair with one hand and twisting her gum around a finger with her other.

Doubts assault my mind. What am I doing here? Am I really a chef? They're going to figure me out. I'm a fraud. Allergies? I'm going to kill someone. I know I must push these thoughts aside. My home is packed away into boxes. I actually went through the misery of asking Percy if I could store them at her place. Even though I hated to admit it, she was really sweet about the entire thing. I'd asked about using the garage, and she'd insisted I use Dad's office to store all of the boxes, so there was no risk of damaging anything. I'm still not willing to say I like her, but I definitely appreciate her.

I squeeze my eyes shut, trying to blur out the thoughts that are racing through my head.

"Are you all right?" Storm's voice sounds behind me.

"Yeah, sorry, just a little overwhelmed," I say, as I look up at her. "Do you want to sit down?"

"I guess, but it's kind of gross how many asses have been on this thing, ya know?" I laugh; I wouldn't have gotten the germaphobe vibe from looking at her.

"Sorry," I offer.

"Not your fault," she adds before taking a seat next to me on the sofa. I can feel myself forcing my smile. Monica told me I sometimes scare people with my serious, sad eyes, and that my eyes can't be sad if I'm smiling. The problem is, I only genuinely smile for a few seconds before it becomes forced, and then it has an altogether creepy look to it.

I look back at the binder, reading through the allergies and dislikes first. Pulling out a pen, I begin to cross things off my list.

"So you're a cook?" Storm inquires.

I don't look away from my papers. "Yup, what do you do for the band?"

"Whatever needs to be done." Her reply is quick, and my mind begins to ponder if she means absolutely anything the band needs. "You know, like a female roadie."

"Oh!" I exclaim, chuckling.

"Gross! Did you think I was some kind of slut or something?"

"What? No!" I gasp, trying to act shocked, hoping she won't see through my act.

"Good, because I'm only involved with Pete, plus Andrew is my brother." It makes much more sense why she is here.

"Oh, I didn't realize you were related to one of the guys. That must be nice for him to have family on tour with him."

"Nah, we hate each other," she adds as if it were a completely normal statement.

"I see, so you are dating Pete?" I ask, wanting desperately to change the subject.

"I guess you could call it that. He's not really into labeling things." I want to shake her and tell her that is what men say to women who are simply a booty call, but I refrain. "So do you have a boyfriend?"

The question is innocent, but one that packs a punch. "I was married actually."

"Was, huh?" she asks as if she has just discovered my life's big secret. "Ended up being an asshole, right?"

I swallow hard, staring down at the binder, studying the notes. "Actually, I'm a widow."

"Damn, seriously? That sucks."

"Sure does," I agree with a tight-lipped smile. I want the subject to change. To anything but what we are currently talking about. "So what happened to the last cook?"

"What?"

"I assume I'm replacing someone?"

"Oh, that guy? Jesus, he sucked. He quit to cook for some other act. I wouldn't mention him to any of the guys, though; he just left with the other band after a gig, no notice, nothing. He was just gone."

"I see, thanks for the warning."

The more I look at things, I actually only need to make a few modifications and we should be good. Perhaps I might actually be equipped to handle this position after all. Dean's favorite dish of mac-and-cheese can be made with quinoa pasta to keep it gluten free. Pete's rice noodle pad thai request is going to be a toughie with Alex's peanut allergy, but with a little research I know I can figure it out.

I glance over my revised list one more time, then nod my head. "Ready for some shopping?"

"Whatever," she replies, standing. I wish Monica could meet the girl. She would think it a hoot that the girl is the very definition of angst.

I take in a deep breath, nerves and excitement consuming me. My very first shopping trip of my first job as a personal chef.

EIGHT

THE CAR RIDE to my stepmother's house from Monica's is uneventful. When we dropped the last of the storage off to her house the night before, she had wanted me to spend the night. One last good bonding experience before my big adventure. That, of course, wasn't something that sounded at all interesting, so I was thrilled when Monica chimed in, explaining I'd already committed to a night out with her. Though our night out consisted of pajamas in her living room with a gallon of ice cream and our favorite bad nineties movies, it felt like absolute perfection to me. Even though I hate to admit it, staying at Monica's place gave me a little more time with Buttons.

I pull down the long blacktopped drive that is covered in whirly copters. It makes me think of my father and how he hated those things. He had always wanted to chop down the two massive maple trees in his front yard, but Percy would never let him.

The oversized ranch home sits on three acres of well-manicured lawn. It had been a nice place to grow up—that had never been my problem. It just wasn't my mother's home, and therefore, I somehow felt like I'd be betraying her if I ever allowed it to be my home. At the end of the drive I see Percy waiting for me in front of the detached two-car garage. One of the doors is open, and she is waving me inside.

I roll down my window, confused. "You want me to park in the garage?"

"Yeah, the one on the right."

"Are you sure?"

"Yeah, I'm positive," she says, smiling. My father's car is in the other stall, so I know Percy is choosing to let me use the vacant spot, resulting in her parking in the driveway while I'm away. She makes it so damn hard to hate her.

I pull in, directly next to my dad's Corvette convertible. Stepping out, I shove the door closed behind me and make my way to the rear to retrieve my suitcases. I can feel Percy close behind me. "Where are the girls?" I ask, referring to my two half-sisters.

"They're still at school. They wanted to stay home and see you off today, but they've already missed so much with the funeral," she explains.

I nod; sometimes I forget I'm not the only one who lost Daddy. "What are you going to do with that?" I inquire, motioning over to the classic car, hidden under the tarp. I can't believe it hasn't crossed my mind until this moment.

"I don't know. He loved that thing," Percy answers sadly.

I remember when he bought it. It needed restoration. He'd gotten it soon after we found out Mom was sick. He used to take her out for rides, and even though it was in pretty rough shape, it always made her smile. He told me once that when he worked on it, he felt close to her. He made me promise it was our little secret; he never wanted to upset Percy. I know he loved both of them, but there's something about that first true love.

"I can't imagine it not being here anymore," I remark, wanting to make sure I make it clear how I feel. I know it's not fair to put that kind of pressure on her, especially with her looking at the debt she must be facing, but that was a piece of our history. A piece of my original family history.

"Don't worry about it, all right?" She attempts to comfort me by wrapping an arm around my shoulder. "I'm sure I'll figure something out; I always do."

I look at her hand and then back to her face. She takes the hint. As she lowers her chin, her voice grows softer. "You know your dad loved you very much, and—"

"It's okay, we don't have to do this," I suggest, slamming the trunk shut and taking hold of my two bags, moving them to the center of the driveway.

"I know you're not into the emotional stuff, but I want you to know you mean a lot to me, and your sisters love you as well."

"Thanks," I say, my eyes shifting around wildly, searching for my ride.

"So..." Percy shifts the conversation, "don't worry about any of your stuff. It'll be here safe and sound until you return."

"I know." My clipped response makes her squirm. I sigh. Damn it, it's so hard to be cold to this woman. "I really appreciate you doing this for me."

She beams a smile like it's Christmas morning. "I'm so proud of you for getting out there and doing something adventurous."

"I'm riding around on a bus and cooking for a group of smelly musicians," I dismiss.

"Well, I'm a little jealous. Sometimes I think I missed out on a lot getting married so young."

This perspective from her surprises me. Percy isn't one to talk about regret. She has also never acted like she ever wanted anything in life other than to be the wife of my father. It's one of the things that annoyed me about her. My mother was a dreamer, so I never understood how my dad could turn around and marry Percy after her.

"I'm sure it's going to be much less thrilling than what you think."

A silence hangs in the air, weaving its way all around us. Until suddenly, out of nowhere, Percy adds in a solemn voice, "I miss your dad."

It knocks the wind out of me. Percy had been married to my dad for eleven years. If anyone knows what it was like to lose a spouse, it's her. She understands me in a way she never could before dad died. I feel compelled to comfort her, but how? I know comfort is something nobody has ever been able to give me.

"Me too," I say at last, offering my true feelings instead of some empty promise that everything is going to be okay. We both know nothing will ever be okay again.

I grip Percy's wrist and read the time: 9:25 AM. A cool breeze grazes my arm, and I shiver.

"Are you nervous?" she asks.

"A little. I think I'm more afraid that they'll realize I have no clue what I'm doing and fire me when we're three states away." A laugh mingles with my words.

"Oh, please, you're the best cook I know. Your dad never stopped talking about how as soon as you were tall enough to reach the stove you were always cooking right alongside him in the restaurant."

I sigh. "Yeah, those were fun times."

A crunching sound of large tires on asphalt fills the air around us, and we both catch sight of the first tour bus turning down the driveway. And then another. Finally, a couple cargo vans follow up the rear. My heart is pounding in my chest. I expected a van, but not the entire tour. This is it; there's no turning back.

"You know, I looked up Head Case—"

I'm laughing. "Oh God, please tell me you didn't."

"Wait a minute ... they're actually pretty popular. Oh, and that lead singer, wow is he—"

"A complete ass? Yeah, pretty much," I interject.

"Well, he's a hot ass," she quickly adds.

I laugh. I can't believe those words just came out of Miss Proper Percy's mouth.

The oversized vehicle hisses as it comes to a stop. My hands are sweating—why on earth are my hands sweating? The door opens, and the first face I see come off the bus is Christian's. He's wearing a smile from ear to ear, emphasizing those delicious dimples.

"Oh dear God," Percy whispers under her breath.

There's a smirk on my face as I turn and give her a look of shock.

"What?" she whispers, a blush filling her cheeks. "All I'm saying is he's attractive." Her tone shifts as she adds, "Not like your dad was, of course."

"Way to bring it full circle to depressing."

"I do what I can," she says with a shrug. "Who's that?"

I glance back to the bus and watch as Dean steps off, running a hand through his messed hair. "You don't recognize him from all your Googling?" I tease her.

"He seems taller in person," Percy notes.

Christian lifts the side panel on the second bus before making his way over to me. "Morning MacKenzie—"

"Mac, call me Mac," I remind him.

He nods, then asks, "Are these your bags?"

Nodding, I hand them to him and offer a thank you. "I appreciate you all picking me up on the way out of town. I'm storing my car at my stepmom's, so this saves her from driving me."

"No problem," Dean interjects, walking past me and straight over to Percy. "Besides, it will give the nosey neighborhood ladies lots to gossip about."

Percy giggles, and I roll my eyes.

"And you are?" Dean is standing next to Percy, peering at her with his big, ocean-colored eyes.

"A recent widow." I slap my hand across my mouth, overcome by my statement. Why would I say that? I look at Percy's face, and she's horrified. I took all of her pain, and I put it out there for the world to see. Why would I do that? Jesus, I really am a horrible person. I may not like her, but she doesn't deserve that.

Dean is only quiet for a moment; he scoops Percy's hand into his and pulls it to his chest. Peering into her widened eyes, he says, "I'm so sorry for your loss."

His sincerity rocks me to my core. It's as if he has known her his entire life and the idea of her lost love breaks his heart in the deepest of ways. Speechless, motionless, I say nothing as he briefly embraces Percy. He expresses how wonderful it is meeting her and that he looks forward to their next encounter. He then turns and walks back to the bus without a word to me, not even so much as a glance.

I take a few steps toward Percy and gasp pathetically. "I'm sorry—I don't know why I said that."

She smiles at me, reaches out, and squeezes me tightly. "Be safe. I love you."

I pull away and smile. The words float through my

mind, and I consider saying them. I think those three words might be the perfect ones to tell her just how sorry I am about my remark. But instead I nod and tell her, "I'll call."

Turning toward the long line of vehicles, I make my way to the second bus—the one Christian is loading my bags under. He stands, closes the hatch, and smiles at me. I'm relieved he walked away before my rude comment moments ago. "This is the ladies' bus," he explains. "Kristen, I mean Storm, is on board."

I lean in and hug him. "Thank you," I whisper in his ear. In the one week it's been since I met Christian, my life has completely changed. I appreciate his kindness and I know this opportunity is in large part due to him.

Pulling back, he looks at me with confusion in his eyes. "You're welcome, I guess." Then he walks away.

I look back one last time at Percy, standing next to the open door of the bus. I wave and smile at her. I see a familiar sadness on her face, one that I want to get away from. It's a look that, when I see it, reminds me of the similar pain I feel. Though she doesn't know the loss of a child, she is still there, in the garden of the darkness—the place I have lived for three years. I'm relieved to be distancing myself from the suffocating grief that plagues our family.

Climbing up the stairs, I smile at the middle-aged bus driver, who I notice is missing a large corner of one of his front teeth. I walk past him, exchanging some kind words with Storm, or as kind as Storm can be. She shows me where I'll be bunking, and at that, I collapse onto the tiniest bed I have ever slept on.

Panic washes over me. The idea that I have no clue with whom or where I am is stuck, playing repeatedly in my head. I'm broken into a million pieces, the shards spreading out from my center, floating away from me to all corners of the earth. Helpless and hopeless to be whole again. A tear escapes from the corner of one eye, but I don't bother to wipe it away. Instead, I keep my eyes closed. Storm is jabbering on from the bunk above me, but I'm not listening to what she has to say. I'm trying to fight my way through the fear that is consuming me. The bus vibrates beneath me, and I pray I'm making the right decision.

NINE

THUMBING THROUGH THE recipes in my notebook, I try to pick the perfect selection. This is the first official meal I'm cooking for the guys. My guess is most of them don't even remember my name, not that I mind it that way. I simply would like to keep this job longer than a few days.

"Hello?" I hear Storm huff behind me. I turn to reply, and see her bottom lip is sticking out, pouting at my lack of immediate response. I have no clue why she is looking at me like this. "Haven't you been listening to me?"

"Huh?"

"Seriously? I've been talking to you for like five minutes."

"I'm sorry." I quickly refocus my attention on her. "I was trying to figure out which dish to make tonight."

"Christian wants to know which grocery boxes to pull from the truck," she repeats herself again, though I'm not sure how many times this has been.

"Oh, let me see," I stammer, flipping to my pages again. I have a system—a system that has to work. A system that I pretended I'd used before. I shop for the food I need for each meal within three to five days, depending on the schedule; the ingredients for each meal are then boxed and numbered. Now all I have to do is pick a meal so Christian can pull the box with the corresponding number. "One, tell him to pull the box labeled one."

I can't decide, so the first meal I will make them will be the first one in my binder. Seems like the easiest way to make the decision.

"All right," she snarls. "I'll tell him."

Staring at the recipe noted box one, I try to focus long enough to read the words. I sigh with happiness; this recipe has always made me think of home. A clothesline in the back yard, lavender being carried on a breeze, golden light filtering through green trees, friends gathered around a patio fire pit roasting marshmallows. A recipe that makes me think of what home should feel like. Not empty hallways or quiet bedrooms, not dark rooms, and certainly not loneliness.

Today, I will treat these men to a symphony of tastes. There would be a summer vegetable hash, with onions, garlic, fresh rosemary, red potatoes, carrots, portobello mushrooms, and snap peas sautéed in coconut oil. But the truest treat will be the pork medallions with a cherry sauce. There is simply no way this dish won't wow my new employers.

"Box one, m'lady," Christian says, presenting me with the brown cardboard box.

"Did you get the meat package from—"

"The refrigerator? Yes, I put the one with a number one on it inside the box, so you're ready to go. Do you need help prepping?"

"No, just curious, when will they eat? I want to time

everything correctly," I ask, taking stock of the items in front of me.

"They prefer not to eat something heavy before the show so you'll be prepping for just after they come off stage."

"Which is?" I press, wanting a more exact time to plan when the pork medallions should hit the pan.

Christian pulls out his phone from his pocket and glances at the time on the face of it. "They take stage at 7:30 so you can expect them about an hour or so after that. It won't always be that early, so sometimes you might have to make them a late lunch or evening snacks. I can go over their schedule in more detail with you later and what they need."

I nod, taking in all of his instructions. "Sounds good. I better get started on prep."

"Okay, if you need Storm, she'll be helping with equipment and sound check."

"I think I've got it."

A large wind gusts, blowing through the tent and knocking over some spices on the nearby makeshift table.

"I'll get some of the crew over here to get some walls zipped in, which should help cut down this wind," Christian adds. I can feel him looking at me. I avoid looking back for fear I might drift off into his dark eyes or brilliant smile. "Have you ever cooked in conditions like this?"

I think about lying, but I've had enough of pretending I'm something I'm not. That, and Christian has this way about him that makes me want to tell him everything. "Honestly? No, this is going to be new for me. But it doesn't seem too bad."

It doesn't take long for me to learn I am completely mistaken. Cooking like this is a complete nightmare. The crew came and put up the vinyl walls just as Christian had asked, but the wind was the least of my worries. In order to find water, I had to go in and retrieve it from one of the bathroom sinks at the facility. This in itself just seems wrong, but since I'm boiling it I decide I can overlook it. Then, when I heat the pan in order to get a nice sear on the pork medallions I can't get it hot enough. The little burners simply don't pack enough of a punch.

But I press on, all day, determined to make my first meal for the group perfect. And here we are, it's now 8:30, and everything is in their warming containers, ready to be consumed. The vegetable hash turned out to be absolute perfection, I'm confident they'll all love it. The pork medallions, on the other hand, proved to be quite difficult. I lost an entire batch that turned out rubbery because they were cooked on too low of a temperature. Tossing them, I figured out if I cooked one at a time I was able to get enough heat to properly sear it, and this is exactly what I did to each and every one.

My heart jumps when I hear footsteps approaching; this is it. They're about to be treated to a delight they probably never expected. Dean is about to see just what a genius I can be with food.

"How's it going in here?" Christian's voice fills the tent.

"Oh." I sigh.

"Gee, sorry to disappoint you."

"No, sorry, my fault, I thought you were the band."

"Nope, they're still on stage."

"What? I thought the show was supposed to be over," I blurt out, watching as Christian inspects my food.

"Is this bread?" he asks, and I can hear the worry in his voice.

"It's flax seed bread, so it's gluten free," I inform him

firmly. "How long are they going to be? The food is warm now."

"I don't know. The first act ran over, and I'm sure they'll get an encore."

"Wait! What?" I feel my heart sink. "They need to eat this stuff while it's fresh."

"Just keep it on the warmers. I'm sure it'll be fine," Christian suggests before exiting the tent. I don't even have a chance to argue. Put it on a warmer. What does he think this is? I've slaved over this food all day; the last thing I want is for them to sample my skills when it's not at its peak. But here I am, with nothing to do but wait.

The minutes tick by, one after another. The anxiety in the pit of my stomach is growing. I take the lid off of the vegetable hash to stir it, and see a pool of liquid has gathered from the condensation of the lid. I stir it as quickly as I can, the potatoes losing their firmness and starting to mash into one big gooey mess with the other veggies. I place the lid back on and decide it's best I not disturb them again, for fear of making matters worse.

Nine o'clock has come and gone. The food has been sitting on the warmers for thirty minutes. I begin to pace. My worry shifts to frustration. Is this what it will be like to work for them? Will they always be inconsiderate like this? Is this how it works? Am I being unreasonable? If food sat like this in the restaurant, it would be tossed.

I hear a commotion down the path and the roar of a crowd. I look at my phone: 9:17. I exhale, preparing myself. I want them to love it, but there's a voice in the back of my head that tells me it's going to be a disaster. The band mates file into the tent, one after the other. None of them seem to notice me aside from a quick sideways glance from Dean.

That is the most he has given me since the embarrassing moment in Percy's driveway.

I hear them discussing the show, clawing over each other to reach the plates and utensils I set out. Ripping the lid off the vegetable hash, I cringe, waiting for grumbles, but they scoop heaping mounds of it onto their plates, barely looking at it. And then, one by one, they move to the pork medallions, loading their plates up, and I'm suddenly glad I made extra.

It's Dean's turn. The others are already shoving the food into their mouths, little bits spraying out left and right. I'm not sure what I expected, perhaps more fawning over all the work I put into the food. I tell myself their enjoyment should be enough. They continue to fill their mouths, laughing and enjoying the moment. They must like it or they wouldn't keep eating, I tell myself.

Then Dean catches my attention again. He is fishing around inside the container of pork medallions, his nose pulled up as he snarls as if something is disgusting. Panic floods my body as I worry something has fallen in with the pork medallions. I rush over to assist.

"Is something wrong?" I ask.

"What is this?" His words come out as venom, and the other guys fall silent.

I peer inside the container and realize there is nothing in there except the food I'd prepared. Proudly, I announce, "Pork medallions in a cherry sauce."

He moves the tongs around in the sauce. "Look at it," he groans, "it's all congealed."

"I—I—" are the only words I can manage.

"Oh, shut up and eat it," Pete shouts, shoving another bite into his only partially empty cheeks. Then, with a full mouth, he adds a muffled, "It's delicious."

"Thank you," I say with a nod and return to the corner.

I hear the tongs hit the pan, and when I turn around I see Dean has decided to pass on the medallions. He takes a bite of the vegetable hash and begins talking to his friends. I can't take it. I want to shout at him. I want to tell him how rude he is, how I worked on that food all day and he—I try and stop the thoughts from racing through my head. He's my boss, and it's his choice not to like something I make.

The heat inside me is building, and I think I might snap if I don't say something. I can't though. Without a word, I leave the tent, darting off in the direction of the parking lot and the safety of my bus.

"Hey, wait up," Christian shouts behind me, but I don't stop. It doesn't take much effort on his part, and he has caught up with me.

"Hi." I don't stop.

"You all right?" I wonder what tipped him off, my red face or my flared nostrils.

"Your boss has some nerve." The words start tumbling out of my mouth, and now there seems to be nothing I can do to put them back in.

"Who? Dean? Last I checked, he's your boss too."

"Fine," I huff, coming to a stop in front of the women's bus. "Our boss has some nerve. Although, I doubt after tonight he's my boss much longer."

"What?" Christian stops my pacing with a well-placed hand on my shoulder. In that instant I want to crumple into him and let his strong arms rock me. What the hell, Mac, get it together. "What happened?"

"He hated my food." I'm nearly gasping for breath.

Christian shakes his head. "He said that? That's not like him."

"Well, no—not exactly," I begin, trying to remember

how it happened. "But he didn't even taste the pork medallions, and he complained about the sauce being congealed. I mean seriously?" I cross my arms, getting angry all over again.

Christian is laughing.

"Excuse me, is there something funny I'm missing?"

"That's just Dean. He's a picky eater. He knows that, and he's not going to fire you over it," he explains.

I raise a finger into the air, wildly waving it around. "No, well, he shouldn't. I should fire him."

"Oh yeah?" Christian is still laughing at me. This is infuriating.

"I'm serious. There is no way a chef can cook like this. A hot plate can only do so much you know. And I need an accurate timeline on when they'll be eating," I rattle off my grievances.

"Already making demands, huh?"

With those words it hits me. I am being a complete nut job. This isn't a fine dining establishment. They aren't expecting me to put out food that would be prepared in a massive and well-equipped kitchen. I'm placing my own expectations on them. I start laughing.

"I'm so sorry. I must seem like a psychotic witch."

"No, you seem like someone who takes pride in what she does, and I don't think there's anything wrong with that. Why do you think Dean picked you?"

"Please, he didn't want to bother with interviewing people. He picked me because I was the first person he spoke to."

"That's not true. He did interviews in two other cities before he met you." Christian's revelation leaves me speechless. "He saw someone who loves what she does and wants to share her talent with others. Why else would you have made chicken and dumplings for your interview?"

"Are you being for real?"

"Yes." Christian narrows his brow.

"He really interviewed a bunch of people before me?"

He takes in a deep breath, looking around him for a moment, ensuring we are alone. "There is a lot more to Dean than meets the eye."

"What's that supposed to mean?"

"I mean he puts a lot of thought into everything in his life. He's a pretty deep guy."

"Deep?" Now I'm laughing harder. "That's not a word I would use to describe him."

"You don't really know him."

"Oh, and you do?"

"I do actually," Christian confirms. "He's been through a lot, it changes the way he looks at things."

"Yeah, I bet Boy Wonder's life has been just terrible," I grumble, the image of him rejecting my food flashing through my mind.

"Mac, I'm serious. You shouldn't be too hard on him," Christian is looking directly into my eyes now. I shift uncomfortably. "He's had a pretty shitty life."

"Like how?" I question in disbelief.

He looks out at the parking lot full of people filing to their cars. "I'm in the mood for ice cream. How about you?"

"What?"

"Do you want to go out for some ice cream with me?"

"Are you serious?" My question mixes with my laugh.

"I'm always serious about ice cream," he replies. There it is—those eyes and that smile I'm afraid I will get lost in. Christian is too much sometimes. I can't stop smiling. It's an expression I'm not used to, and I notice my face is hurting.

"Okay, Mr. Bennett, you're on."

"Great, but I'm driving. It's safer that way," he jokes, extending me an arm. I gladly take hold, eager to stop thinking about Dean and the rejection of my food.

"Don't start on my driving," I instruct him playfully.

A gorgeous guy who likes to get ice cream. This really is shaping up to be a pretty perfect job ... well, besides Dean.

TEN

IT TAKES me nearly an hour to get ready. Preparing food outdoors does a number on me, as well. My face feels as if it's caked in grease, and my hair is a frizzy mess. I shower, dry my hair, add just the right amount of makeup to conceal the circles under my eyes, then slip into my favorite jeans. Okay, the only jeans that still fit me.

Bounding down the stairs of the bus, I freeze when I hear Christian's voice. He's leaning against the side, one foot bent, perched behind his perfectly round bottom. "I forgot how long it takes women to get ready."

"Don't blame me," I say defensively. "Blame the deplorable conditions I'm forced to work in."

"You're pretty spoiled, aren't you?"

"Excuse me?" I gasp. We're walking toward the street at this point, Christian leading the way.

"I'm just saying, you seem to complain a lot. I assume that must mean you usually get your way." His words mix with laughter.

I take a strand of my hair and begin to wrap it around a finger. "I've just never had a job like this."

"That's obvious," he states matter-of-factly. I shove him playfully.

"All right, that's enough beating up on Mac for one night." I giggle, wanting to smack my forehead for actually referring to myself in the third person.

"I wasn't trying to be mean. I think a woman should be spoiled; it shows they're cared for."

"Seriously? Or it makes them a royal pain in the ass," I suggest.

He grins, glancing over at me. "Well, yeah, that too."

"I grew up in a kitchen—a real kitchen—not some back-yard barbecue. That doesn't make me spoiled. It means I have standards."

"Ah, I see, so you're a restaurant brat?"

"From the time I could walk," I boast proudly. Thinking about my mom and those years doesn't hurt like it used to. It actually feels good to talk about. Once Daddy married Percy, there wasn't much discussion of her. After he sold the restaurant it was like that entire chapter of our life was closed. "My mom always dreamed of having a restaurant. My dad was head over heels in love with her and wanted to make all her dreams happen. So, he found a little place in an area of town that was undergoing gentrification and spent all of his life savings opening Poppy Hill."

"So why are you working here and not there?"

"My mom passed away when I was twelve. A few years later he sold the restaurant."

"I'm sorry," Christian offers. "I didn't think. I totally forgot about meeting your stepmom, and I should have put it together."

"It's okay, it's been a long time," I answer with a tight-lipped smile.

When we round the corner and continue up the sidewalk, I realize we're not heading to his car. "We're walking?"

"If that's all right with you, someone told me about this little place up the street."

"Works for me," I say, wishing I had worn more comfortable shoes.

"So your dad recently passed away?" His question surprises me.

I nod. "Yeah, he was the glue, ya know?"

"I do," he answers softly. "That was always my brother for me."

"Oh yeah? I'm surprised you'd want to leave him."

"Eh, he's with someone now, and I just figured they needed some space."

"That's awfully nice of you."

"I guess." I can see the topic is starting to make him uncomfortable. "Is your dad's death why you wanted this job?"

I laugh. "Wow, you just say whatever pops into your mind, don't you?"

"Sorry, habit."

"He took care of me after my husband and daughter passed away."

"What?" he exclaims. "I remember during your interview you said your daughter had passed away. I didn't realize you'd lost a husband too."

I nod. "Yeah, what can I say, death seems to follow me." My attempt at a joke doesn't seem to be finding a welcoming audience.

"Jesus," he huffs. "That has to be hard. Do you mind me asking how?"

"Car crash," I reply, staring blankly into the distance.

"Wow, that's terrible. I'm so sorry."

I try my best to smile. People always tell you they're sorry when they find out you've lost someone. This seems so odd to me. Did they kill them? Did they cause the illness or accident? I'd much rather people just tell me, 'That sucks.' It seems the only thing that's appropriate.

"What were we talking about?" I think hard, wanting to get off the topic of my dead husband and daughter. "Oh, my dad! After he died, I found out there wasn't much left financially for the family, and well, that was it. I needed to find work so I could take care of myself."

He smiles at me again, but it's a different kind of smile. He looks devious. A thought pops into my mind, and I wonder if he's thinking about kissing me. I never had a ton of experience in the dating world before I met Travis. It's been three years since a man has touched me, and I'm not sure if I would know the difference between a friendly hug or something more.

"The directions said the ice cream place should be up ahead on our right," he informs me, lowering his gaze to the ground in front of us.

I glance up, the neon outline of a cone catching my eye. "There it is."

"So what made you look for a job like this instead of another restaurant job?" he inquires.

"Boy, you sure do ask a lot of questions."

"You don't have to tell me if you don't want." He shakes his hands in the air. "But I will assume you're probably some criminal running from the law if you don't tell me."

"Nice," I huff, coming to a stop, standing and waiting as Christian opens the door for me. An entrance bell dings, and I step through. A confectionary smell hits me in the face as soon as I walk in, my mouth immediately watering.

We order our flavors. Christian tries to guess what I want. "Cookies and cream?"

I shake my head.

"Orange sherbet."

This makes me laugh. "Nope."

"Okay, I give up."

"If we were back home, I would be getting a buckeye blitz, but since we're here, the closest they have would be—" I scan the case. "Peanut butter chocolate chunk."

"That sounds good." He smiles and motions to the worker that we'll take two. I can't shake the idea he's flirting with me, and I'm not sure if it excites me or terrifies me.

He pays and we take our scoops to a nearby cafe table. He's the first to take a taste, and when he does, he grabs his chest and moans, "Oh my God, this is good." I blush as the idea of how lucky that ice cream is flashes through my mind.

I give him a half laugh. "Yeah, based on your body, I'd say ice cream isn't something you have very often."

"What's that supposed to mean?" By the way he's grinning, I know he knows exactly what it means.

"I'm serious. This is the last thing I should be having right now."

"Why?"

"I've picked up a little weight over the past few years, and I'm just trying to take it off."

"I think you look great. Besides, curves on a woman aren't a bad thing." Okay, I can't be crazy. He has to be flirting with me, I think to myself.

I'm not about to tell him, but I'm actually enjoying myself, enjoying the company of someone else for a change. For a split second, a glimpse of Travis and Katie enters my thoughts, and I lower my head in an effort to shield the grief I must be wearing on my face. Every time I have a happy moment, I'm reminded that they're not here to share it with me. I wonder if this will ever stop, or if this is simply my existence now.

"Are you okay?" Christian asks me. My face must make it obvious.

I feign a smile and nod, then lie, "Ice cream headache." I'm not sure if he buys it, but I hope so.

"Mac, can I ask you a question?"

"As long as it's not something creepy like the color of my underwear."

"Well, it wasn't, though now I'm curious." As soon as he says those words I feel the area between my legs go hot. "It was actually about something kind of personal."

He looks apprehensive ... this makes me nervous. "You said you had a daughter who passed away?"

A shot of ice bolts through my veins, and I stiffen in my seat. "Yeah, that's right."

"How old are you? I mean—you don't have to tell me if you don't want to. You just seem so young."

When I decided to go on this journey, I told myself I wouldn't tell anyone about my past, but there is something about Christian that makes me want to open up to him. Something about him that tells me if I talk to him, it will make me feel better.

"I understand. It's fine. I know it seems weird to a lot of people."

"No," he quickly interjects. "Not weird, just trying to put it together."

I take a deep breath, then tell him my story. "I got married right out of high school, and within a year we had a baby."

"Wow, really? That's so fast. I dated my high school sweetheart up until last year."

"Didn't work out?"

"Bad timing." His voice is solemn. "So what happened?"

"Three years ago, there was a car accident, and both my husband and daughter were killed."

"You weren't with them?"

"I was, and miraculously I wasn't hurt." There's a sarcastic tone to my voice that appears to confuse him.

"Jesus, you were so lucky."

"Yeah," I quip. I'm not lucky. I was the unluckiest one in that car because I get to keep going through this long and drawn out life all by myself. No Travis and no Katie, all the promises of forever broken.

"Hey, would you mind if we keep this between us?"

"No, of course not."

"Thanks. It's just sometimes people tend to feel sorry for me, and I'd rather not deal with that."

"I get it. I promise I won't say a word," he confirms.

"So what was wrong with your timing?"

"What?"

"This girl you broke up with ... what happened?"

"I guess she wants something I can't give her."

"Ah." I smile. "Commitment phobic."

He stands up and laughs, and, leaning in close to my ear, he whispers, "You should stick to cooking. You're pretty bad at the shrink stuff."

Taking his arm, I ask coyly, "Or is it that I'm really good at it?"

"Let's get you back," he says, avoiding my question. "I go running in the mornings, would you like to go with me?"

With a wide smile, I bait him with a question he can't get right. "Do I look like a runner?"

"What's a runner look like?" Oh, he is good. "You

mentioned you wanted to drop a little weight, and while I think you're fine just the way you are, I thought you may want to join me."

"I was just teasing, and I'd love to."

"Great," he announces. "I'll be at your bus at seven."

I bite the side of my jaw; I'm not a morning person. The idea of waking up that early seems like torture. Based on Christian's fitness level, though, he might just be the one to help me kick my Jell-O ass back into shape. Now I just need to figure out if these were dates or if Christian is just looking for a friend until he can reunite with his lost love.

ELEVEN

MORNING IS HERE before I know it, and all I can do is wonder why I agreed to this. Did I think if I committed to a routine, it would become easy for me? Magically I would suddenly be a fitness nut. Here I am, on morning number one, and all I want is to pull the blankets back over my head and fall fast asleep. Instead, I'm lacing up my running shoes, which have obviously been rarely worn.

I stand up and think to tell Storm where I'm headed, but her bunk is empty. This doesn't worry me. The way I've seen her on top of Pete, I assume most of their after dark hours are spent together.

There's a knock on the window. Placing one knee onto the couch, I peek out of the heavy curtains to see Christian standing below. My heartbeat quickens, and the dread I'd been feeling suddenly shifts into excitement. I like talking to him; I never get that he feels sorry for me.

Racing down the narrow walkway of the bus, I press on the lever to open the doors. A breath sticks in my throat as I inhale sharply in surprise. A smile looks up at me, but it's not Christian.

"Good morning," Dean offers in a smooth voice.

"Wha—I— I..." My face grows warm in an instant as I stumble across my words. The scene the night before is racing through my mind. The insult of him not even tasting the food I'd spent all day preparing for him.

"Dean heard me getting ready and wanted to join us." Christian comes into view. "I told him you wouldn't mind. You don't, do you?"

I'm frozen, still speechless. My eyes dart to Dean who is now leaning on one of the door flaps. His arms are crossed, and he's staring up at me from under his lashes with a half-cocked grin. Paranoid thoughts begin to move through my head, as I wonder if he's here to torment me, if he knows how much he upset me the night before, and if this is just some sick way to rub it in my face.

"I think she does mind," Dean laughs.

Hopping down the stairs, I barely give him a glance as I announce over my shoulder, "I couldn't care less."

"Ouch," Dean hisses. "That seems passive aggressive to me ... what do you think, Christian?"

As if in protest, Christian waves his hands in the air before saying, "Leave me out of this."

I stop and turn to face Dean. "I have no idea what you're talking about. I'm here to run, so what are you here for?"

"Why, for the stimulating company, of course." He smiles, then takes off running in the direction Christian and I had walked the night before. Christian follows him, and in a panic, I take off, as well. Dean turns around, and running backward, he adds, "Oh yeah, and there's nothing like a little sexual tension in the morning to get your heart pumping, so I'm here for that, too."

Spinning back around, he picks up his pace. I'm already

starting to feel winded, but I yell after Dean anyways, "I didn't know you were that into Christian."

He doesn't turn around, and the distance between us is growing. I hear Christian laughing, and jerking my head in his direction, I snap, "What's so funny?"

"Was that your attempt at a comeback?" He's still laughing, slowing his pace so that he's next to me. I barely have the breath to keep running, even though we've only made it out of the parking lot. Christian's laughter makes me wheeze, and I snort softly with a snicker of my own.

"Yeah, I guess that was pretty bad," I admit.

"You think?"

I can't respond anymore, as I'm focusing on keeping my body moving forward. Before I know it, we are rounding the corner, heading past the ice cream shop and into a new area of town. I look up and see Dean at least twenty paces ahead of us.

"Come on, slow pokes!" When I hear him shout this I grit my teeth instinctively.

"Is he always such an ass?" I grumble.

"He can surprise you. He's been a huge help with all the shit I've been going through," Christian isn't even breathing heavily. I want to give up and sulk back to my bunk, but that would be far too humiliating.

"If you say so." I choose the fewest number of words possible in order to conserve my energy.

My legs are burning, and I wonder if Christian can see how much I've been struggling up until this point. "How far are we going?"

"I figure once we warm up, we can get three or four miles—nothing too strenuous." His answer twists my stomach.

Warm up? This is a freaking warm up. I have to stop. I

can't do this. Just as every fiber of my being is telling me to give up, an amazing thing happens. A surge of adrenaline floods my body, and my pace quickens. The sidewalk is a blur under my feet. The steady pounding of my feet echoes in my ears and sends a vibration through my body. My hair is clinging to my forehead. I force the air up my throat and out of my mouth, taking another deep draw as soon as the exhale is complete. The delicious rush of oxygen floods throughout my body, my muscles contracting and stretching outward. I don't know what has gotten into me, but I feel amazing.

Christian is matching my pace, and we are closing the gap on Dean. At the bottom of the hill I see Dean make a sharp right into a park. We follow closely behind, and he turns his head at the sound of our feet. The wind blowing through my hair, the air pumping in and out of my lungs, I wonder why on earth I ever stopped running. And then I remember: my husband and daughter died, and it all seemed so pointless.

Like a freight train hit me in the stomach, I'm knocked back. There's a cramp in one of my legs, which causes me to stumble to a clumsy stop, crouching on the ground and rubbing as fast as I can, trying to get the sharp pain to cease. My thighs are still burning, and a bead of sweat that has been gathering at my hairline sets off a chain reaction of droplets running down my face.

Dean and Christian stop immediately, and Dean appears next to me in almost an instant. "Are you okay?"

I nod, and through gritted teeth, I grunt, "Cramp."

"Where?" Dean follows up. I don't reply, but he looks at where I'm rubbing, and before I know what's happening his warm hands are massaging my hamstring. I stop breathing for a second, but then quickly I'm wheezing again from my recent speedy pace. He's rubbing me, I think. Why am I letting this guy rub me? Why do I like that he's rubbing me?

"Are you sure you're okay?" Christian asks, and I look over to see him extending a hand. I take the offering, which causes Dean to release me from his grasp and take my other hand. They get me to my feet.

"I'm fine," I insist. Placing weight on the leg causes me to wince in pain.

"You're not fine," Dean insists.

"I am; I just need to walk it off," I argue, favoring the injury, a little relieved I have an excuse not to run any more. The amazing and invigorating feeling running had given me quickly fades.

"Christian, why don't you go ahead and get your run in, and I'll walk back with Mac," Dean offers.

"What?" The word slips out of my mouth.

"Yeah, it's really no problem. I'm not a huge runner anyway."

Christian studies Dean and then me. I'm trying to plead with my eyes. Plead for him not to leave my side. He wouldn't invite me to go running, and then at the first sign of trouble pass me off to this guy he knows I can't stand.

"Are you sure?" he asks Dean. Damn it! He is going to ditch me.

"Positive. Besides, it will give me a chance to get to know our new resident chef," Dean replies. I look at Christian with wide eyes and then back over at Dean, and feign a smile. "Well, that is, if you don't mind having to walk with me?"

What in the hell am I supposed to say? Well, actually, you offended me by not tasting my food last night. Or maybe I should just really put it all out there and tell him what a cocky bastard I think he is.

"No, of course not," I lie with the stupidest looking grin on my face.

"Great," Christian continues. "I was really looking forward to getting a long run in anyway. If you've got her, I think I'll go ahead and go for my ten-miler."

"Eat your heart out, bro," Dean laughs. With a quick wave from Christian, he's gone. "Oh, thank God, I thought he would never leave."

"What?" Shock from his statement overwhelms me. "I thought you and Christian were like best friends."

"Oh, I love the guy, don't get me wrong," Dean protests, then begins to laugh as he leads me over to a nearby park bench. "Like a brother, but damn, it's hard to act like running that fast isn't killing me. Sometimes I think the guy can't be human. At least with him gone I can take a rest."

He helps me take a seat before sitting down next to me.

Smiling, I offer a little honesty myself, "Okay, confession time, I'm not really much of an exerciser myself."

"Yeah, not many people hit it as hard as Christian does," Dean says, scanning the park.

Furrowing my brow, I ask the first question that pops into my mind, "Then why did you come?"

"Honestly?" He looks directly at me.

"Of course."

"To get to know you better." His response makes my heart rate quicken. What kind of answer is that? Is he trying to tell me something? What in the hell is happening? Is he playing a game?

"Well, that doesn't make any sense," I argue.

He laughs quietly. "And why is that?"

"Why would you want to get to know someone you are getting ready to fire?" Damn it! Brain, stop telling my mouth to say these crazy things. Just because you think it, doesn't mean you should say it, Mac!

"Why on earth would you think I'm firing you?" He leans forward to look me in the eyes, which of course makes me look around uncomfortably. He leans a little closer, and in avoiding his eyes, I look to his lips, which makes me think about kissing him. You can't stand this guy! What are you doing? Are you really this horny after three years? My gaze shifts down to my leg, and though the pain is now dull, I focus my eyes on it as I rub the muscle.

"Last night you wouldn't eat my food," I answer at last.

He laughs. "I didn't eat it because I don't like pork ... well, I take that back. I don't like pork except for bacon. Everyone likes bacon."

"What? No! That wasn't on the list of dislikes."

He smiles. "Because Pete would eat pork for every single meal of the day if he could. I knew if I put that I disliked it, then you would probably choose never to make it. I can't be that cruel to him."

"You said the sauce was congealed," I argue, not believing his excuse.

"Well, it was."

"Because you guys were a half hour late getting off stage —" As soon as the snarl comes out I regret it. "I'm sorry, I shouldn't have said that. You're my boss and—"

Dean is shaking his head. "No, you're exactly right to say something. We were late, and that wasn't fair to you. I'll try and make sure we get you a more accurate schedule in the future."

"You really don't have to."

"Nonsense, I want to enjoy my food. It would be silly of me not to. I'm excited to see what you can do, as I'm a bit of a foodie myself," he explains.

This completely surprises me. "Really? I would have never imagined that."

"Why is that?"

I look him up and down, a huge grin on my face.

"What?" he presses again.

"Just the rocker, and all the tattoos—it doesn't seem to fit."

"Wow..." He's laughing. "Don't we judge a book by its cover? For your information, my mom loved to bake when I was a kid."

"Oh really? She doesn't bake for you anymore?"

"No, not possible." I can tell this makes him uncomfortable.

"Oh my God, I'm so sorry. I just keep putting my foot in my mouth. It's really none of my business if your mom still bakes for you." I hate when people ask me probing questions that always seem to lead to the conversation of my dead family. I worry I might have done the same thing to Dean.

"No, it's fine, just complicated." His answer piques my curiosity, but I resist the urge to inquire further. "What about you? What made you become a chef?"

I look out into the distance, a smile on my face as I think fondly on the memory I enjoy sharing. "My mom, too. She was the head chef at our family restaurant. We were a farm-to-plate place before it was hip. When she cooked, it was like a dance was unfolding with intricate choreography all across your taste buds."

"Wow, sounds amazing."

I look at Dean and softly add, "She passed away when I was twelve."

He nods. "Hence the stepmom?"

"Yeah."

"Oh wow, and your dad just died, too. That's gotta be tough..." He stops speaking, but it feels as if something unsaid is hanging in the air. He shifts on the bench, and I wonder if the discussion of death is something he shies away from. Is it his mother? Did she die? Is that why she doesn't bake for him anymore?

"We don't have to talk about this stuff," I offer.

He doesn't say anything. He looks at me, then straight ahead, then back at me. "I lost my dad, too."

"Oh really? I'm so sorry. Was it recent?"

"No, when I was a kid."

"It's never easy on a kid." I think about all the lines people have fed me over the past few years, trying to think of any that were comforting, but I can't, because they never are.

"I guess," he replies, barely audible. I can see it on his face, that pain. It's more than his father, and while I'm not sure what it is, it's obvious Dean is hurting in a way that is much deeper than losing a parent. I lean in, allowing my shoulder to rest against his. That simple touch of another human being is sometimes the only thing that can bring me any comfort, and I hope it will do the same for him. I wonder if Christian was right and I misjudged this man.

"I'm really glad you're here," he says at last, his words making me panic. I don't know what they mean. Maybe there's no significance in them at all or maybe they matter more than anything in the world. All I know is right now, I don't want to explore what it means; I only want to enjoy it for the moment.

"Me too," I offer, then hop to my feet and slap my leg. "Well, seems better. Ready to walk back?"

"Sure, and you can tell me all about the dinner you have planned for tonight. Oh, and maybe we can stop in at that little pastry shop I saw on the way back, but just don't tell Christian."

Laughing, I happily agree.

———

TWELVE

WE PULL INTO A TOWN, unpack, I make the food, I go to the store, then we pack up, and the next day I do it all over again. Sometimes we're on the road the very same night after a concert, but other times we stay put for multiple days. After a few weeks I'm already used to the hectic pace of life on the road. Downtime is spent hanging out in parking lots or green rooms, listening to music, laughing, and enjoying each other's company. This is what people do in the real world. They converse with one another. They live. It felt foreign to me at first, but over time, it's started to feel normal.

At home I had a cocoon. It was home—a place I could shield out the world and be alone in my misery. Alone. That's the perfect word to describe my life in Cincinnati. There was no way for my friends or family to find their way into my life, as I had too expertly crafted the walls around me. In a few short weeks, being surrounded by life had done something to me I never expected. The world that had been standing still has begun to turn again.

There isn't a day that goes by that I don't miss Travis or

Katie, but rather than lying in bed, numbing myself with food and television, I'm feeling the slightest tingles of living again. Dean and Christian have made it a habit of visiting the local farmers' markets with me when the schedule lines up. This strange thing has happened where I've started to laugh again. I thought perhaps I was only capable of tears anymore, but they've proven there is a small piece of joy inside me, if only just a sliver. There are still friends to be made.

Christian still confuses me. He talks all the time about this girl he was once in love with, Paige, but then in the next breath he'll tell me how beautiful I look. I wonder if this is his personality—does he thrive on making women feel good about themselves? Travis was that way with me; he never shied away from giving compliments, eager to see me smile or blush. Dean is a different creature. It's not shocking that he's the lead singer of a band. He always likes to be the center of attention, and if there's an opportunity for a cheap laugh, he will always go for it. I like laughing, though—I've missed it—so I enjoy having him close. I'm surprised now that I didn't like him at first.

Storm has softened since I met her; I've learned that the rough exterior she shows everyone is just an act. She's young, and she has been hurt; I think maybe if I hadn't found Travis so young, I would have ended up a lot like her. There's a hurt behind her eyes, a loss that is not so easily disguised. Most nights, when she actually sleeps on our bus, she tosses and she turns. While awake, we often joke about how the entire tour is like the roving island of misfits, each of us running from our own demons. Maybe that's why we're all here. We're drawn to this because it gives us a chance to try and forget what waits for us back in the real world.

"Hey Macaroon," I hear Dean's voice outside the bus. I smile at the nickname he gave me, which annoyed me initially, but has since grown on me.

I exit the bus, shifting the shorts on my waist, which in only three weeks' time have gone from being skin tight to actually offering breathing room. "What's up?" I ask.

He looks at me from head to toe, and I suddenly feel self-conscious, tucking a strand of my dark hair behind my ear. "I was wondering if you were hungry?"

"Isn't that something I should be asking you? After all, feeding you is my job," I tease.

He looks away from me, dragging his Converse-clad toe through the dirt in front of him. "I noticed a place up the street called The London Underground, and I just thought you might want to grab some lunch."

"Sure, where's Christian?"

"Uh— he's busy," Dean answers quickly.

"Okay," I say, my tone suspicious.

"No, really, he is," Dean insists. "He had to run and get a part for one of the vans. But hey, if you don't trust yourself alone with me, I completely understand."

And now I'm laughing. Why is it with him I am always laughing? Raising a finger, I tell him to wait, as I run up and grab a wad of cash from under my pillow before leaping down the stairs.

"Ready?" he asks, a huge smile spreading across his face.

"Yup."

The bus is parked in the parking lot of an old condemned school. This evening's venue did not have anywhere for us to set up, so we found the closest space available. I shove my hands in my pockets, and we start off in the direction of the main sidewalk.

"So how far is this place?"

"Not far on my bike," Dean says, and I realize he is no longer next to me. He has taken a sharp turn, standing near the back of the bus, where his motorcycle is waiting for him —for us. He grabs the spare helmet from the back of the bike and hands it to me. I feel my fingers tingle with a rush of adrenaline.

"You can't be serious," I scoff.

He says nothing, putting his own black helmet on and fastening the strap. He straddles the seat, grabbing the handles firmly, causing the tattoos on his arm muscles to flex. "No helmet, no ride."

"I'm all right with that." I smile.

"Oh, come on, I'm a great driver."

"Yeah, you're not the one I'm worried about."

"What?" He looks at me.

"I'm more worried about the other big cars or trucks running over us."

He reaches out a single hand, waiting for me to grasp it. I hesitate, looking at it cautiously. In a soft voice, he says, "Trust me."

Shaking my head, I stumble forward. Apprehensively, I moan, "I don't know."

"I promise, it's amazing," he insists, not taking his eyes off me.

I swallow hard, hold my breath, and take his hand. He pulls me close, and I climb on behind him. As I place the helmet on my head, securing it, he starts the bike.

"Ready?" he asks.

I joke, "Not really."

"Hold on tight," he instructs, and with a stiff jerk we're moving.

I reach forward, wrapping my arms around his firm

body, burying my head into his back. He slows at the edge of the parking lot. In an instant, my perspective on everything changes. I feel the earth vibrate underneath me with the hum of the engine. First, the wind is tickling my arms, but that's not enough. I want to feel more. I lean back, allowing the wind to whip against my face, and with a surge of adrenaline I feel like my heart might pop. I'm not in control, and it's the best feelings in the world—scared, excited, thrilled—all at the same time.

I feel like I'm a little girl, lost and alone, rocketing through the world. I'm flying, soaring toward a destiny I don't even know. Life feels amazing for the first time since I can remember, and lost in the moment, I want to scream at the top of my lungs in joy.

I dig my fingers into Dean's chest. I feel him lean to the right, and instinctively I lean with him as we round a corner. The road beneath us is a blur, and I must fight the urge to release my grip and spread my wings. I remind myself that I can't actually fly. And just as quickly as the ride began, it comes to an end. We pull into a parking spot, and my heart sinks when Dean presses down the kickstand and turns off the engine.

He waits for me to step off first, then stands, straddling the bike, and taking off his helmet, he turns and takes mine from me, securing them onto the back.

"Well?" he asks with a half-cocked smile.

I want to hug him, tell him that it was one of the most incredible feelings I've ever had. I want him to understand that few things numb the pain that I'm constantly in, but those few moments on the back of that bike made me forget for an instant. "It was fine." Fine? God, you're such a bitch.

He's smiling. I'm sure he can see I'm lying.

"Okay, it was pretty freaking awesome!" I squeal.

"See, being afraid of life never gets you anywhere."

"Whatever," I laugh, waving him off and approaching the door to the restaurant. I've had enough of that smug look on his face.

The restaurant is quaint, with a number of small café-style tables in front of the window. When we approach the counter, we discover a tall and extremely slender man with a rather large nose and a bowl haircut awaiting us. Dean begins a conversation with him, something I would have never done, and we find out he and his wife are the owners of the establishment.

He tells us the story of how they met while on a trip to London. They fell in love with the city and returned there years later when the time came to exchange their vows. And when they decided to open a restaurant, the only choice was to open one with the theme of how he met the greatest woman he had ever known. Dean kept glancing at me as the man spoke, and though I tried to stop my cheeks from flushing a bright red, it seemed to be out of my control.

As we wait for our order, Nathan, the owner, makes our coffees while his wife prepares the food in the kitchen.

"Sweet, aren't they?" Dean whispers.

I smile, glancing over at Nathan, his gangly movement making me grin even wider. "I guess you could call them that."

"Don't tell me you're a cynic when it comes to love."

"No, I don't think so. I mean ... really, I just don't think a lot about love these days."

Dean is quiet as Nathan brings me my latte, before heading into the kitchen. He leans over and whispers close to my cheek, "That's a damn shame."

"What is?"

"That you don't think about love these days." His breath is warm and lingers all around my face.

The door swings open again, and Nathan sets my plate in front of me. I'm shaking … why in God's name am I shaking? Picking up the drink and sandwich, I move over to one of the small tables and sit down quietly. In a matter of seconds Dean is sitting across from me with his order.

Lifting the latte to my lips, I close my eyes and breathe in the sweetness of the mocha. A toasted bagel topped with bacon and avocado slices waits for me, and I decide not to linger too long on the crisp smell of the caffeine heaven at my lips. I open my eyes to see Dean staring at me, one nostril lifted in disgust.

"What?" I huff.

"Okay, I get a latte, and I get the bagel, but together? Avocado and mocha, that's just disgusting."

"Sorry, we can't all be twelve year olds and order dessert for lunch," I tease.

"A scone isn't dessert," he argues.

"One with chocolate chips is."

He picks the pastry up off his plate and takes a huge bite. Chewing for a moment, he smiles and laughs, "Oh yeah, it's dessert." As he moans, crumbs spray out, and he quickly covers his mouth.

"Gross!" I exclaim, but it's obvious by my tone I'm more entertained than upset.

He finishes his bite, and then takes a sip of his black coffee. There's something sexy about him drinking a cup of black coffee. I always load mine with cream and sugar. To see him take the bitterness head on makes him seem so strong and raw.

"It's good," he comments at last.

"Thanks for inviting me."

He nods, peering at me as though he's inspecting me. "I have to ask. Was that your first motorcycle ride?"

"Was it that obvious?"

He bites his lip, then shrugs. "Yeah, pretty much."

I take in a deep breath, sighing into my coffee mug. "My dad was never into them, and neither was Travis." I look down at my drink, my dead husband's name still stinging my lips.

"So you guys started dating in high school?" Dean asks. I'd shared little bits and pieces of my past over the last few weeks, careful never to reveal too much. Dean kept his past much closer, never willing to share any of his secrets.

I nod, taking another sip, then set my mug down and take a bite of my sandwich.

"Was he your first boyfriend?"

"Why so interested?" I taunt.

"I just find it amazing that you married your high school boyfriend. You don't really hear about that happening anymore."

"Sometimes you just know. Haven't you been in love?" I ask, trying to probe and knock loose one of those demons I know is tailing him.

"Nope, never."

So the pain he's carrying isn't from a woman, I think to myself.

"Well, trust me, when you find it, you know."

"Yeah, but some people are so scared of being hurt that even when they find it, they're too afraid to leap." His words make me wonder if he is trying to say something.

"Are you saying you're too scared to love?" I ask directly.

"No, but I know people who are."

My cheeks are hot; I think he must be talking about me. "Like who?"

He presses his lips together, hesitating to reveal a name.

"You can't just put that out there and let it hang in the air."

Lifting a shoulder, he easily relents to my protests, "Fine, Christian."

I'm still lost in a cloud of confusion. Is he saying I'm afraid of Christian or that Christian is afraid of finding love? "What about him?"

"He's so stuck in his past he's missing his chance at happiness." Does he mean Paige? I wonder. Does he think Paige is Christian's past? If that's the case, is he trying to say I'm his chance at happiness? Am I reading into everything completely wrong? God, this makes my head hurt.

"Have you said something to him?"

"I try, but he'll only listen when he's ready."

I stare at Dean. What is he thinking? There is so much more to him than I ever realized. Does he have insight on me he isn't sharing? I'm not sure I'm ready to hear it anyway. I take another bite of my sandwich, content with the company and no more major revelations for the day.

———

THIRTEEN

AFTER MY LUNCH WITH DEAN, all I've been able to think about are his insightful words. I've been analyzing them repeatedly, trying to figure out what exactly he was trying to tell me about Christian. I like Christian, at least as a friend. Does Dean see something there I don't? While Christian isn't exactly what I would call my type, he is very sexy, and the idea of kissing him doesn't exactly turn me off.

I stepped outside of my comfort zone, confronted my fears to take this job, and as a result it's been the most alive I've felt in three years. I never thought I'd feel excited to wake up again. What if there are other things I'm afraid to experience? I convinced myself you only get one shot at love, but what if that isn't true? I'll never have my first love back, and I know that. Maybe Dean was trying to tell me I could find a new chance to love in a different way. Jesus, I need to stop obsessing. I'm probably reading into things, and it's making my head spin.

Across the parking lot I catch a glimpse of Christian—he's covered in grease, elbows deep under the hood of the cargo van. With a hard swallow I decide to go talk to him.

I've never even tried to imagine anything romantic with him. There are times I may have thought he might have been flirting with me a little, but maybe it was more.

He sees me approaching and smiles. He leans in lower with one arm, then pulls his body out of the engine compartment. "Hey beautiful, give me a hand?"

"Huh?" I grunt.

He beckons me with his head, and I move in closer. I'm only inches from him now, and he moves behind me, pressing me up against the van with his body. My breath catches in my throat. "See this?" he holds up a black rubber tube.

I nod, trying to ignore his mouth as he speaks, which I soon realize is impossible.

"I can't seem to fit my hands down in there to slide this onto the spot it needs to go. There's a half-inch piece of metal that juts out, and this piece needs to slide over it, got it?"

"I don't know how to do this," I protest in a high-pitched voice.

Taking hold of my hand, he guides it deep into the engine. "There, feel what my fingertips are on, go slow, ease it on. You don't have to rush it."

My god, I'm sweating, my heart is racing, and if I didn't know better, I would think he was talking about something quite different than an engine. Grasping his long fingers, I follow them down to the piece of metal he described. The tube slips with a slight shove. I linger, keeping Christian close to me a few more seconds before I lean back and free my hand.

"Thank you!" he exclaims, and I notice his eyes catch the grease on my hand. He grabs a nearby rag and begins cleaning off my fingers. I tremble at the tender move. Maybe this is right; maybe Christian is exactly what I need.

I look up to see he's staring into my eyes. Why would he do that if he didn't want me? There are only inches between us, so if he didn't like me in that way he'd move away, right? I ask myself.

I lick my lips; this is it, now or never. I lean in. Our lips are going to touch, and I'm going to kiss a man who's not Travis. My chest is aching. Our lips are less than an inch apart now, there's no stopping th—without warning, Christian grabs hold of my upper arms and steps back.

"Whoa, Mac, what are you doing?"

"I—I thought—I…" The words are tumbling out of my mouth, but I can't seem to put them together in a way that makes sense.

I want to run, run as far away as I possibly can, and hide my head. My face is hot and red; there is nothing I can do to erase this mistake. Leaning away from him, I prepare to dart back to the bus, but when my feet begin to move I realize Christian has a tight grip on one of my arms.

"Let go," I plead, my voice cracking.

He pulls me back and wedges me against the van. I'm helpless in his strong arms.

"Don't run away, talk to me. Why did you do that?"

"I don't know, I thought—I guess I misread the signs."

He breathes out a heavy breath. "Damn it, Christian," he mumbles to himself.

"I'm sorry," the words squeak from my lips.

"No, Mac, don't do that. You're very beautiful," he continues, and I look anywhere but in his eyes. "And you're exactly the type of girl I would be with."

I stop struggling when I hear those words. A stitch knits

itself across my brow, and I can't stop the questions from spilling out, "Then why didn't you want me to kiss you?"

"Because it's not fair to you. I like you a lot. I might be single, but I'm not really available."

"Paige?" I whisper.

He nods. "I like you too much to hurt you, and I know that's what would happen."

My head collapses into his chest. I want to cry, but I manage to hold in the flood of emotions. He wraps his arms around me, and in that moment I feel safe. I'm embarrassed, but at the same time, I just discovered what an incredible friend I have in Christian. I'm sure once I get back to my bunk, though, I will shrivel up into a ball of misery.

I pull back and smile up at him. "Christian, I can't ever get my Travis back. I've lost him forever, but Paige is still here. Why don't you go after her?"

He lets go of me, turns his back to the van, leans against the grill, and crosses his arms. "It's not that simple. She needs me to be someone I can't be for her. So much of me would have to change for that to ever work."

"I guess you should probably get started on that."

Christian looks down at me. "I wish it were that easy."

"Really? My family is dead, and you're going to complain."

He forces a grin. "Gee, I feel like a real ass."

"Well, you are, but that's okay. We all have to start somewhere."

He laughs, nudging me with one arm. "Still friends?"

"Always," I answer, and the amazing thing is, as embarrassed as I am, I mean it.

FOURTEEN

WAKING UP, I fight to open my eyes against the thin layer of salty crust that has settled on the edges. They are tender and swollen, reminding me of all the tears I'd shed the night before. My tears weren't from embarrassment about Christian anymore. He'd handled my misstep so beautifully; I couldn't be upset about him. There would be no more confusion about his comments or lingering looks. He is a friend, and he made that abundantly clear. Nor did my tears stem from disappointment. A huge part of me didn't even know how I really felt about Christian. Had Dean not placed the thoughts in my mind, I doubt I would have ever pursued the idea.

The bus is dim, the morning light just starting to work its way through the curtains. I hear a snort above me and remember Storm. She and Pete had a very loud argument outside the bus last night, and though this wasn't anything one would consider strange for the two of them, it did result in her sleeping in her own bed. I push the blanket to the other side of my bunk, sitting up and rubbing the crust away from my eyes.

Last night's tears had been brought on by the reality that I'd almost kissed another man. A man who was not Travis. A man who was not the father of my daughter. Our vows had said until death do us part, but what if what that truly meant was both of our deaths?

When you divorce someone it's because you can't stand being with him or her anymore. I don't get that closure. I get a lifetime of still being in love with the man I married, but knowing I can never be with him. Or what about Katie? Am I a terrible mother if I choose to move on with my life? Maybe she would want me to be happy, and perhaps my grief is the way I'm dishonoring her. But then doubt creeps in, and I worry instead she would she think I forgot about her. These were the thoughts that made me cry myself to sleep last night.

I must be going mad. It's been three years, and everyone tells me I should move on, try to be happy again. What if I'm just broken? Maybe happy isn't something I'm capable of anymore. I wish I were home in my comfy recliner.

Stretching, I give a hardy yawn and, in my crop sweat-pants and tank top, I move to the back of the bus, maneuvering a bra on under my shirt. The stuffiness in the bus is making it hard to breathe. I peer out the curtains; a heavy fog has settled on the caravan. Yanking on a skullcap to cover up my bed head, I wrap myself in an oversized sweater, slip on a pair of shoes, and step out into the brisk morning air. Most mornings on the trip have been warm, but soon after reaching the West Coast we began experiencing brisk temperatures in the mornings and evenings.

Taking in a deep breath, the coolness washes over my lungs. I look around and realize it must still be early as nobody else in the camp is stirring. Glancing off to the right, I squint and see a playground in the distance. The haunting emptiness of it somehow seems to beckon me. As I walk in the direction of the swing set, kicking the earth up in front of me, the salty smell of the ocean fills my nostrils. I wonder how close we are to the water.

I take a seat on one of the swings, and see that directly next to me is an old wooden infant swing that is shaped like some sort of animal. It's so weathered I'm unsure what it is, perhaps a horse. In the early morning light and layers of fog I think how it feels like a graveyard.

"Hey, Macaroon." Dean's voice causes me to jump, like a ghost reaching out to touch me. I choke on my air, shifting anxiously on the swing. "Sorry, did I scare you?"

He rounds the corner to stand directly in front of me. I pull the layers of my sweater tight around my body and am suddenly thankful I chose to take the few extra seconds to put on my bra. He's wearing jeans, sandals, and a white T-shirt. He could be straight out of a '50s movie if it weren't for his modern tattoos.

"You did," I snarl. "But that's not why I'm mad at you."

He shifts from side to side, then moves over to the wooden infant swing, playing with the ropes for a moment. "Uh oh, what did I do to make you mad now?"

"You said something that caused me to make a fool of myself."

"So you're mad at me for something you did?" he asks, laughing softly.

I don't look away. Instead, I twist the swing and stare directly into his eyes. "You were the one who put the thought into my head."

"What thought?" He leans in, waiting for my answer, still holding the wooden swing.

"Never mind," I snap, looking away. I want to unload on him. Tell him that because of him I spiraled down into a complete free fall of emotions I had only recently managed to get a handle on, but instead I clam up. I'm not angry because I'm embarrassed. I'm angry because for a short moment he had me believing I might be able to find happiness again.

He lets go of the swing and moves to stand in front of me. I'm staring at his toes sticking out from his sandals. His toes distract me. I've never noticed that he has the most amazing feet. The muscles in them are lean; the hierarchy of the size of toes is perfection. No freakishly long random toe. I hate him a little for this flawlessness.

"Oh, come on, you can't be serious," he grumbles, moving a couple steps in my direction. I dig my feet into the ground and lock my legs, moving myself away from him.

"Just forget I said anything."

Lunging forward, he grabs the weathered ropes of the swing I'm sitting on and pulls until my face is planted only inches from his. "Tell me."

I duck under his arm, narrowly escaping his grasp. "I don't want to now."

"Well, too bad. You should have thought of that before you said anything in the first place."

A breeze whips my hair out to the side. I shiver and wrap my sweater even tighter around my body. "I can't believe this afternoon is supposed to be in the eighties."

He shakes his head wildly, moving into the dead space behind me. "No changing the subject. What did I do?"

"Fine! You put the thought in my head that I should go after Christian," I blurt out at last.

"I ... what—" Dean begins before quickly trailing off. He takes a step back from me, his sudden change of behavior causing me to take notice.

"What's wrong with you?" I bark, paranoid.

"I never said that to you." His voice is soft, and he's not looking at me. This isn't an act. Something is wrong with him.

"Well, no, not directly," I begin. "But you said he's so stuck in his past that he's missing his chance at happiness."

"And where in there did I say you're his chance at happiness?" Dean is nearly yelling now. The change in his mood sours mine.

"Well, I just assumed."

"Jesus, I didn't mean you and him. Don't you see, Christian is so hung up on his past it's ruining his life?"

"Yeah, his past with Paige."

"No!" Dean huffs, annoyed I'm not getting it. "His parents died when he was a kid. He can't get past their death long enough to see what his grief is doing to the people around him. If he could get his head out of his ass long enough to realize he and Paige were the real deal maybe he could fix everything he has screwed up."

"Well, I— I didn't know that part," I snap back, a quick swipe of my backhand to Dean's arm.

"What in the hell am I doing? You don't see it, do you?"

"See what?"

"It's right in front of you."

I bite my lip for a moment, fighting the screams of frustration inside my head.

"What is?"

Dean licks his lips, looks me in the eyes, and just when he is about to say something, he turns and takes off into a circular pacing pattern. He's lost in thought, and in this moment I would give anything to get a glimpse into his mind.

"Say it," I press. "What's right in front of me?"

He continues to pace, shaking his head. He looks at me,

and in the morning light, his eyes look like pools of gray water at the bottom of a well—sad and deep. "What do I have to do to make you see?"

"Jesus Christ, Dean! See what?"

"Why in the hell would I try to get you to go after Christian when I'm the one who's hung up on you?"

"What? No, you—"

"Yeah, you really don't see it, Macaroon?" His tone is softer.

I'm staring at him. His messed dark hair, the slight stubble on his face, his angular jaw line. He is handsome—exactly my type physically—but it never crossed my mind I could be his type. He's a rock star, who has women throwing themselves at him every night, and I'm—I don't even know who I am.

My heart begins to pump faster, and a tingling sensation surges throughout my body, all the way to my fingertips. He doesn't look away from me, and I can't seem to pry my eyes from him. I breathe out, the air shaking as it exits my mouth. My jaw clenches, and I know I should say something, but what? What do you say to something like that?

There's an intensity in his stare, and I feel the heat growing between my thighs. My lips part, and I'm hoping the perfect words will somehow magically fall out of my mouth, but there's nothing, only silence.

"Say something," he whispers desperately.

"I ... I don't know what to say," I reply honestly.

"How do you feel about me?" He closes the gap between us. His eyes widen, and he steps closer, taking one of the ropes of the swing I'm sitting on back into his hand again. He pushes on it, causing me to twist in his direction. My gaze shifts wildly, unsure where to look. Nervously, I stand, taking the other rope into my hand, facing him, only the small piece of wood between us.

"I've never thought about it," I answer, our eyes drifting back to meet one another again.

"Really? Because it's all I've thought about since I met you," he continues. "When you asked me the other day if I'd ever been in love, I didn't lie. I haven't been, but what I didn't say was when I met you I thought maybe I could be."

"What are you saying? You can have anyone you want."

"Unless I can have you, that's not true."

I'm shaking my head. I'm not sure if I'm trying to caution myself by the action or tell him I can't believe his words. "I can't."

"You can't what? All I'm asking is you spend some time with me."

"I know I'm twenty-four, but I'm not like most girls my age. I'm not interested in playing games and hooking up. I've had the real thing, and I don't have any interest in—I don't know ... whatever it is people do."

He laughs a little and smiles at me. "Who said I was into games? Why do you think I like you so much? It's because you are different."

"Please," I huff. "You hated me when we met."

"No, I didn't." He laughs again. "Wow, I've really made a mess of this."

"You haven't," I protest. "I just don't know what to say."

He extends a hand in my direction, and I take it. He pulls it to his chest, and I stumble nervously to him. I can feel the electricity building between us; my eyes roam to his mouth in anticipation of his next words.

"So don't say anything," he whispers, and I nearly fall down where I'm standing. He releases the swing and wraps that hand around my hips, pulling me into him. He looks at me with lust, and I know I'm mirroring the same expression. In that second, the rest of the world falls away. It's just him and me, our pasts nowhere to be found.

My chin is trembling, and I'm waiting. I know what's coming. I want to etch every second of this into my memory. I want to be able to recall the smells, and how fast my heart is beating, and the texture of his lips. I swallow hard, wondering how much longer he is going to keep me waiting. And as if it were the most perfect timing in all of the universe, right when I thought I might burst from the anticipation, his lips press against mine.

I close my eyes, and his hand that held mine to his chest releases, and I feel it sweep up, cradling the back of my head. I feel weightless, and a passing thought has me wondering how I'm still standing, but I quickly realize it's his strong arms that keep me upright. When I feel his tongue graze against my closed lips I freely part my mouth for him, drinking in the blissfulness.

A man hasn't tasted me in such a way for so long, but I'm not thinking about anything except Dean pressed against me. His hands tighten, one grasping a fistful of hair and the other digging into the flesh on my hip. I wrap my arms around him, clinging to his back. Our bodies tangle together—it's easy to lose track of where he begins and I end. My tongue meets his, and I feel him exhale in delight. I quiver, knowing I can make him feel such pleasure. I feel beautiful in a way I haven't since before the accident.

We cling to one another in an erotic ballet, but disbelief threatens to tear it all away. This can't be real, I tell myself. You don't get to be happy like this—you get pain. A tear escapes from the corner of my eye and rolls down to where Dean's hand meets my cheek.

He pulls away, breathless. Tenderly, he shifts his thumb and wipes away the wet and salty trail.

"Are you okay?" he asks me.

I nod, unable to verbalize the thoughts racing through my head.

He delivers a half smile before saying, "Every morning when I wake up, all I can think about is finding you. I want to make you laugh and smile. When I make you happy it's the most amazing feeling in the world."

I draw in a ragged breath, then ask, "What's a girl supposed to say to that?"

"Thank you." He smirks, and I have to fight the urge to kiss him again. "Now that you know how I feel about you, all I can think about is making you feel wanted."

"I don't know if I'm ready for this," I say at last. But he doesn't act disappointed; instead he smiles wider.

"Macaroon, you make me feel incredible, and all I want to do is make you feel even better. You're all I've ever wanted."

My instincts tell me to pull away from him, create some distance so I can resist his charms, but I fear if I do, my legs may not be able to stand on their own. "I come with a lot of baggage."

"I'm pretty sure I'm strong enough to carry it. Besides, everyone has baggage. If you don't, that just means you're boring."

My mind is telling me to turn and run, but my heart is screaming its desire to be loved again. It reminds me I didn't die in that crash three years ago. I collapse my head into his chest and let him hold me. I feel him shudder and know he is just as terrified as I am.

"I won't hurt you," he groans into my hair.

I want to believe him; with everything in me, I want to believe him.

FIFTEEN

DEAN HAS BEEN STRUMMING on his guitar for at least an hour. I could watch him work out new sounds, pulling them from his mind and getting them onto paper, all night. All evening he has been toying with the same song. I offer to write down the lyrics, but he informs me it doesn't work that way for him. He will work on it for weeks, come up with various versions in his head, and then the right one will rise to the top. I can't imagine keeping all of that straight in your mind; I can't even go to the grocery store without a list.

He pauses, and the bus goes quiet. I look up at him and smile; he's watching me. I feel my heart pounding faster with each passing second the beat quickens. He doesn't say anything. He doesn't even smile. He's just watching me.

Why are you looking at me? What do you want? Am I still smiling? Why in the hell are you smiling when all he's doing is looking at you? Maybe he's thinking about the song and he isn't actually looking at you.

Dean moves forward on the mini bench and leans his guitar against the back of the driver's chair. He swivels in his seat and turns to face me again. Okay, now I know he's looking at me. I'm sitting on the narrow piece of floor, my face is turning red, and I want to look away, but don't want to make it obvious that he's making me uncomfortable.

A brilliant idea enters my head. Do something that lets you look away while appearing to keep busy. I shift up onto my knees and turn toward the back of the bus. I look around and all I see is the bathroom and my bed. What in the hell am I going to do now? I can appear to be busy by taking either a shit or a nap.

"Everything okay?" he asks. I don't turn around, but I can feel him still staring at me.

Think quickly, I tell myself. Lunging forward, I swipe an oversized pillow off my bed and return back to the seated position on the floor. I try my best to spread out and lean back. I'm totally uncomfortable, but I'm determined to make it look like this was exactly what I had planned.

"Great—just getting comfortable," I lie.

Dean stands up and starts walking toward me. Oh, sweet baby Jesus, he is getting closer. My heart has now moved up to racing, and I wonder if he can hear the beating that is thundering in my ears. What in the hell is he doing? Is he going to—

The thoughts race through my head wildly as Dean steps over me and walks back into the small bathroom and closes the door. I take in a deep breath and expel. I feel like such an idiot. I think he's about to make a move on me, but all he was doing was taking a bathroom break.

My face turns red as I suddenly hear, through the door, the sound of him urinating. The door might as well be a thin piece of paper. Curiosity begins to play through my mind as I think about the fact that he's fully exposed, only feet away from me. My nose lifts as my mind shifts to the fact that he isn't only exposed, but now I know what it sounds like when he pees. Gross! Mental note, never pee in the bus while Dean is in it, or he will hear it and your life will come to an end. I hear the faucet kick on, and I'm relieved at the notion he actually washes his hands.

The door opens and Dean emerges, but I don't turn around to look at him, as it seems like an invasion of privacy to do so; although, on a tour bus, I've learned privacy is not something that actually exists. He's doing something behind me, but I still don't turn to see.

He steps back over me, a pillow dropping down on the floor next to me. "Think Storm will mind if I borrow her pillow?" he inquires, sitting down and leaning on it with one elbow before I even have a chance to answer.

"I won't tell her if you don't," I answer. He's grinning at me, and I can't help but think about how much I want to kiss those lips. "Done playing?"

"Yeah, I'd much rather be talking to you."

"Oh yeah?" I ask in my most flirtatious tone. "About what?"

"I don't know ... everything."

"That's an awfully large topic," I note.

"I want to know everything about you," he says, but I know that would be a mistake on his part. The last thing he wants is to know everything. The more you get to know me, the more jacked up you realize I am.

"My favorite color is teal." I grin, knowing this is not exactly what he meant.

He laughs. "All right, I'll take it. Mine is green."

"Of course it is," I scoff.

"What's wrong with green?" he asks defensively.

"I think every guy I've ever known has said green is their favorite color."

"Really?" he asks, looking in the distance, thinking about my statement. "I never realized it was so popular. I like that it's the color of life."

"I would think red is the color of life?"

"What?" he snarls. "Red is war and strife."

"No way," I argue. "Red is the color of blood, and blood is life."

"Okay, I can see that. But green is all over in nature. The grass, the trees, all of the life going on around us has green in it."

I shrug. "I guess. I still say red is the color of life."

He scoots closer. "I think red is the color of passion."

He is totally trying to make a move on me. I am so okay with this.

"All right, what's your favorite movie?" I ask, suddenly feeling a flood of panic rush over me.

Dean leans back, placing his hands behind his head and extending his legs, crossing his feet. I have to fight the urge to climb on top of him. "Hmm ... favorite movie? That's tough. I'm not sure. I'd have to think about it. What about you?"

"That's easy. 'We elves try to stick to the four main food groups: candy, candy cane, candy corn, and syrup.'"

I'm grinning wide, waiting eagerly for his response. He furrows his brow. "I don't get it."

"What?" I gasp. "You really don't know what that's from?"

"Should I?"

"It's only the best Christmas movie of all time."

"Seriously? A Christmas movie is your favorite movie of all time?"

"It's not just any Christmas movie! It's Elf with Will Ferrell," I explain.

"If you say so." He laughs.

"Okay," I begin, shaking my head wildly. "I'm not sure if I can have a boyfriend who doesn't know the movie Elf."

"Boyfriend, huh?" he interjects, his eyes locked onto mine so I can't look away.

"I mean—"

"No, I like it," he continues. "It's been a couple weeks, and I wasn't really sure what you were thinking about us."

I shift, allowing one of my legs to brush up against his legs. I feel him stiffen and then relax. My stomach is fluttering. "Your turn ... favorite movie."

"Oh geez," he huffs. "I guess if I had to pick one it would be..."

He's quiet for a second, staring at the ceiling. I can't quit thinking about what just went on between us. It was one thing for Dean to say how he felt about me, but now we've somehow actually defined what we are. I have a boyfriend. I am someone's girlfriend. I feel like I might puke.

"'Hello, my name is Inigo Montoya. You killed my father. Prepare to die,'" he quotes.

"'Inconceivable!'" I exclaim, knowing he would appreciate the reference.

"Oh Jesus, you know how to turn a guy on, don't you?" He laughs, rolling over on his side and wrapping an arm around me.

I shimmy so that I'm now completely lying down on the floor next to him, peering into his eyes. I love the way they shine when he looks at me, even in the dim light of the bus.

"I do what I can," I boast. "Though I've never had a Princess Bride quote get a guy's motor going before."

"I'm special," he whispers, our faces moving closer with each breath. His hand travels up my side, cupping my cheek.

"Yeah, that seems about right," I whisper back. Oh my God! He's going to kiss me. This is it. His lips are going to touch me. Will my lips be confused? Will they enjoy the touch of someone new?

He doesn't kiss me, but instead, he hovers inches away from me. "Favorite band?"

"What?" I gasp, shock clear in my voice. Dear God, please just kiss me already.

"I like some of the older bands; let's see, there's the Beatles, of course, The Rolling Stones, R.E.M., Nirvana." As he rattles off the bands I consider cutting off his words with my own lips, but I can't. I won't. If he wants a kiss from me, he will have to make the first move.

I shake my head slightly, my mind still reeling in disbelief that we are talking about our favorite bands instead of making out. "I guess, for me, my go-to band would be U2 ... oh yeah, and I love me some Dylan."

He leans back and tilts his head. "Jakob."

I laugh. "Bob."

"Oh yeah," he moans, extending and arm, so I could lie on his chest. "You're a keeper."

I smile, my head moving in to rest on his firm chest, his arm folding around me perfectly. His heart is beating under my cheek, and I sigh, soaking in the rhythm.

I feel his head shift, and I know he's looking down at me. I lift my chin so our eyes meet. His eyes drop to my mouth and, though the idea is fluttering around in the back of my thoughts, I won't be fooled again. I won't let myself hope that he wants to kiss me.

"Can I ask you a personal question?" he asks.

"Why do people start questions like that? I mean, really, does anyone ever actually say, 'Why no, you can't ask me a personal question, but thanks.'"

He laughs. "Okay, point taken." Then falls silent.

I prop myself up on an elbow and look in his eyes. "Oh no, it's too late. You can't put that out there and then drop it."

"I didn't think you wanted me to ask," he chimes defensively.

"No, I was just saying you shouldn't ever set up a question like that again because it's total bullshit," I explain, then return to my position with my head on his chest, his arm around me. My hand is on his stomach; he starts using his other hand to tickle the flesh of my arm, rubbing it up and down with his fingertips.

"How did you keep going after you lost them?"

I'm quiet. I'm not sure if my ears are playing tricks on me, or if Dean has actually just asked me that question. The silence continues to grow, as I have no answer. I'm not really sure I did keep going.

"I'm sorry, I shouldn't have asked," he ends the silence at last.

I shake my head. "No, it's fine..." I begin, still unsure what I'm supposed to say. I want to move on—that's what I'm doing right now—but I have no idea how I finally took that step, except out of necessity.

"What?" he asks.

"I didn't keep going. I shut down. I only started functioning again because I had no other choice. My dad died. There wasn't anyone else left to take care of me except for myself."

"How long has it been?"

Surprisingly, I'm not uncomfortable telling him these details. I'm able to speak without bursting into tears. "A few years."

"I wish you didn't have to go through that," Dean offers, and I can tell he means it.

"It's funny ... at first there are enough distractions that it really doesn't hit you completely. You're consumed with your feelings, don't get me wrong, and you're still processing the pain, but you don't realize just how much the loneliness hurts until a few months pass and the visitors with their casseroles disappear. Then it's just you and your pain."

"I'm sure it's hard on friends too," he suggests.

I tilt my head up and look at him. "Why would it be hard on them?"

"Death is hard on everyone. I'm sure there are people who loved you and felt helpless and frustrated that there was nothing they could do to take the pain away." I wonder how Dean knows so much about grieving.

"I guess," I say in a near whisper.

"Thank you," he whispers, pressing his lips against my forehead.

I shift, moving my head from his chest to his arm. "For what?"

He licks his lips, his eyes shift once again down to my lips. Oh hell. "For sharing that with me. I know it can't be easy."

I give a slight nod. He rocks up onto his hip, hovering over top of me. His body locks mine in place. His chest is pressed firmly on my shoulder against the floor. I close my eyes; I have to before I literally beg him to kiss me. His hand returns to my jaw line, tracing it gently.

I try and wiggle a hand loose. I want to lace it though the back of his dark hair, but as much as I try, I can't seem to break my limb free. I try my best not to move too much, as I don't want him to think I'm struggling. He might move away, and that's the last thing I want.

I can feel his breathing growing shallower the closer he

moves toward me. Then suddenly, our eyes locked on one another, his lips now only inches from mine, and I think his breathing has stopped entirely. He's looking at me. Why are you staring at me? Do you get off on torturing me? Why won't you just kiss me already?

And that's exactly what he does. Dean closes the last of the gap between us; my eyes close as our lips meet at last. My lips part, allowing his tongue to enter and find my own. His mouth is soft on the inside, a sensation I'd forgotten.

I've forgotten to breathe, and when I finally force the air in and out through the small breaks between our mouths, it causes a vibrating moan between us. Dean tightens his grip around me when I do this.

Dear God, don't let this end.

His hand shifts from my jaw to the back of my head, taking a hold of my hair and lifting me up into him. My back arches as I try to meld my body into his, fusing us. The kiss builds in intensity, then calms, then once again builds. It's a roller coaster of lust, and I can't keep the thoughts in my head from drifting to places that makes me burn from the inside out.

He tears his mouth away from mine, and both of us are gasping for the precious oxygen we've been deprived of. Desire swimming through my body, I wait for our lips to reconnect. Opening my eyes, I see his face is now hovering several inches above me.

"I've gotta go," he moans.

"What?" I cry.

"I'm already going to be late for sound check," he explains, still not moving.

I groan in frustration. This makes him smile.

"Don't worry, I don't mind picking up where we left off," he offers with a mischievous grin.

"Promise?" I whisper, lifting my head to free his arm.

He sits up and rolls off me, and, standing, he turns and offers to help me to my feet. "Oh, without a doubt."

"I guess I should probably go cook you guys some food, huh?"

He lifts his shoulders. "I know the guys might appreciate it." He laughs softly, before pulling me close and pressing his lips to my forehead. He looks into my eyes again, and I think I might see my reflection dancing in them. It's like joy might burst from my core and level everything within a mile radius.

"Tonight," he says, turning and leaving me. My skin is still tingling as I watch him walk away through the windows.

You kissed him. You're a damn sex kitten. You kissed him. Him. You kissed a man who isn't your husband. Your lips touched someone other than Travis. Stop! You have to stop. He kissed you, and it was good. Be happy, for once.

That kiss ... it was amazing. I could have continued to kiss him all night. But ... he was the one to stop. Was it just because of sound check? I know he's missed it before. Did he want to get away? Stop it! He likes you. Don't be paranoid. Be happy, damn it!

SIXTEEN

LETTING someone love me isn't something I ever thought I would do again. Dean makes it easy. If he's anywhere near me, there's a shared smile, a sweeping touch of his fingertips. We kiss every chance we get, despite the groans from the rest of the crew, but Dean never presses me for more. I'm not sure yet if this is something I'm happy about or not. I know he thinks I'm fragile, and I love that he's sweet and sensitive, but sometimes I think the only way it will ever progress between us is if he takes the lead.

I think the first few days were the hardest—mostly because they were awkward. It's in the first few days that people comment when they notice a budding romance. But on top of dealing with everyone else finding out, we get to deal with the extra baggage: this is my first relationship since Travis passed away.

Dean asks a lot of questions. If he sees that I'm sad, he always encourages me to talk through it. With each week that passes, this new thing in my life seems a little more natural. I worry it's more of a challenge than Dean thought it would be, but I think I'm the one who's been surprised.

When everything in your life you care about goes away, it's easy to accept you'll never care about anything ever again. So suddenly, when you do, it's like a plant you thought was dead begins to bloom again; a river you were certain was dried up years ago begins to flow. I'm that flower. I'm the water flowing over those rocks. I can breathe and move again, rather than only wither and decay.

The schedule has been intense over the past few weeks —we made it down the coast, over to Texas, and this morning we arrived in Atlanta. It's been the roughest portion of the trip, travel-wise, but Dean and I always manage to find a chance to spend time together every day.

Last night he asked me to make a batch of my mac-and-cheese for him today. I got up early and headed to a grocery where I found some incredible local farm cheeses and fresh smoked bacon. I'm determined to make it the best batch I've made for him yet. A romantic lunch with his favorite dish— maybe this will be the moment he will seize the opportunity and take our relationship to the next level.

"What smells so good?" Dean's voice makes my heart flutter.

"Hey you," I smile, pausing as he walks over and leans in for a kiss, those silky lips brushing against mine. "The mac and cheese is browning in the toaster oven."

In an instant, he shifts direction, peeking in the door, the heat waves beating him in the face. "Oh my God, it smells amazing."

"Thanks." My cheeks flush.

He closes the door again, peering in through the small glass window. "I just know she's going to love it."

"She?" I gasp. A hundred scenarios of what he meant by she fly through my head.

"Yeah, when do you think it will be done? I'm not sure

how long I'll have to deliver it and still get back on time," Dean explains as if I should just know what he's talking about.

He never had any intentions of this being a romantic lunch for us. I've misunderstood. There will be no next step. No, instead he had me make his favorite meal for ... well, for God only knows who. "Of course."

He turns to face me, cocking his head and curiously lifting an eyebrow. "Of course what?"

"I can't believe you had me make this for one of your— Jesus, I don't even know what."

"Wow, where the hell is this coming from?" he asks, his mouth hanging open in shock.

Honestly, I don't know where it is coming from. I've never been a jealous girl, but I've also never been with a man like Dean. I see the way all of the girls who come to the shows look at him. He never makes me feel insecure—in fact, quite the opposite. I always know I'm the center of his world ... at least I thought I was.

"I'm here to cook for the band, not to help you get a hook up."

He laughs, moving toward me. "Did you really just say that?"

He reaches out to take my hand, but I pull away, worried I'm going crazy. Why do I keep saying these horrible things? "I thought you wanted to have a special lunch with me."

Dean pauses, and I can tell he's frustrated, but then, much to my surprise, his expression shifts as he asks me, "I'm sorry I wasn't clear. What are you doing today?"

"I don't see where that's any of your business." Dear God, I'm still doing it!

"I'm trying here ... can you relax for one minute?"

I look behind me, but there is nowhere to run except to the bathroom. I face him, crossing my arms, and with as much contempt as I can muster, I say, "I have the band's meals to prep for tonight."

"What if I can have you back a few hours before the show? Is that enough time?" He's smirking. I'm pissed off, and he's smirking.

"Back?" I huff.

"Yes, I want you to come with me."

"Where?" I ask, softening my posture, realizing perhaps I may have overreacted. All right, I totally know I over-reacted.

"You'll see."

"Just tell me," I insist.

"You'll see," he repeats.

"I don't know."

"Please." He moves closer, and this time I don't pull away when he reaches out to take my hand. "I want you to meet her."

"Who?"

"Will you just trust me?"

I tilt my head, glaring at him suspiciously. "Okay. Do I need to change?"

"No—well, you don't have a lot of metal on you, do you?"

"What?"

"Never mind, I'm sure you'll be fine," he reassures me.

"Now you're weirding me out ... where are we going?"

Dean presses his lips to my forehead. Way to almost screw this up, idiot. Must be some sort of record, I silently curse myself.

"It's hard to explain, but, once we're there, I'll answer any of your questions. Can you pack up the food, and I'll meet you at the van in ten?" I nod and watch him leave the bus. He looks different. He's now a man shrouded in mystery. Why is that so damn sexy?

———————

SEVENTEEN

FRANTICALLY, I scoop up the dirty laundry that's strewn all around the bus. I've never been the tidiest of individuals, but Storm puts me to shame. In moments I know he'll be here. I've never cared if my bus was messy while he was around, but suddenly every detail seems to matter. I quickly give the small living quarters one last scan, when a cardboard box at the foot of my bed catches my eye.

I'd been so excited when Monica told me she was shipping a care package last week I literally squealed. It's not an easy feat to receive mail while on the road. Things have to be carefully planned. We chose a city we would be hitting a week out, and she sent it to the venue. I picked it up yesterday, but I've been so distracted I never got around to opening it.

I place the box on the small counter area in the kitchenette at the front of the bus. Pulling out a knife, I carefully run it down the packaging tape. Monica knows everything I love so I'm positive I'm going to like what's inside.

I open one flap and then the other; a small pink envelope sits on top of tissue paper. Tearing into it I find several pictures of Buttons and Monica all over our hometown. I flip the note over to read:

Hi Beautiful,

I'm missing you like crazy. I included some pictures of Chubbs and me around town. As you can see, she is getting some much-needed exercise. She's been eyeing a bull terrier at the park. I think we could have a love connection on our hands.

I hope you're finding a little love connection of your own, but no worries, in case you're not, I packed something for that too. Love you. Can't wait until you're home.

-Monica

My cheeks ache from smiling so hard. I've missed her too. I can't wait to call her and tell her what's happened lately. I can imagine how hilarious she'll think it is that I came on to Christian, but somehow ended up with Dean.

"Knock, knock," I hear Dean's voice directly behind me.

I gasp and turn around, holding the letter and photos tightly in my hand. "Hi! I— umm ..." I stammer, caught off guard.

"We had plans, right?" Dean asks, sensing my hesitation.

I shake my head, pausing for a moment to drink him in. He's wearing the distressed jeans that I love on him and, for a change, a button-down, dark gray shirt, untucked, and some charcoal loafer-style shoes that I would have never imagined him owning. His hair still looks wet and is slicked back, and, much to my surprise, he has shaved. I like a little stubble on a man, but it's nice to see Dean looks gorgeous either way.

"Yeah, we are. Sorry, just got distracted," I explain, tilting my head to tuck a sliver of hair behind my ear.

"Oh yeah?" He moves closer, trying to get a look at what might have pulled my attention away from our date.

"Oh." I shake my head and hand him the pictures from the envelope, careful to hold on to the letter. "That's my dog, Buttons, and my best friend."

"Monica, right?" he asks, flipping through the images. I'd only mentioned her a few times; I'm impressed he was listening.

"Yeah, she sent me a care package," I continue, turning and pulling apart the taped layers of tissue paper.

"Anything good?" he inquires, moving even closer and setting the images down next to the box.

I glance in, but the box is dark inside all of the tissue paper. My hands retrieve the first item. "Buckeyes!" I exclaim.

"I can see why she's your best friend." Dean leans on one elbow, watching me explore the contents one by one.

I reach in, continuing to pull out items—a black hair scarf with cherries, a pair of earrings from one of my favorite local jewelry designers in Cincinnati, Abbi Glines's newest steamy romance. My cheeks go hot as Dean sees the cover, lifting his eyebrows.

"Well, I think that's it," I say, lifting the box, the sound of something shifting inside catching my attention. "Oh, there's something else."

I reach in, and as I do, I can feel Dean's eyes locked on me. I feel something long and cool slip into my hand. Locking my fingers around it, I let the box fall away. Instantly, I see Dean straighten up, a half-cocked grin on his face.

Much to my horror, I look down to see a pink rubber

penis-shaped device in my hand. I freeze, but my cheeks are on fire. All I can think about is the different ways I am going to torture Monica before I kill her.

"I can explain," I begin. I'll tell him she's crazy—like actually certifiable.

He's still grinning at me as he gives me a slight nod. He closes the gap between us even more.

"You know, I can help with that," he offers, and I can't help but wonder if he's serious, or perhaps maybe I'm wishing.

"You think I'm that easy?" I hit the ball squarely back to him. I consider licking my lips, but worry that may be over the top. I'm looking directly at him, and damn, he's incredible.

"A guy can hope." He pauses, playfully lifting an eyebrow. "Can't he?"

I grin. In fact, I can't do anything but grin. He moves closer, and I glance down, realizing I'm still holding the device. My breath hitches, but he still moves closer. He's facing me, never moving those gorgeous blue eyes away from me. He slides his arm around my waist, and as he presses himself against me, I'm sure I can feel an erection. This surprises me, and my hand releases the dildo, which falls to the floor with a thud.

"What's wrong? Can't contain your excitement around me?" he whispers, his breath warm on my neck, just below my ear.

My mouth is watering, my heartbeat quickens, and my head is now spinning. I pull back, the distance giving me a slight bit of clarity. The idea of this kind of pleasure is tempting. The bulge in his jeans tells me he is interested.

In an attempt to casually conceal the pink rubber shaft, I use the toe of my platform sandals to kick it under a nearby chair. Dean cocks a brow, his face shifts, and he laughs softly.

"What?" I shrug innocently.

"Did you just kick a dick under a chair?" He's still laughing.

"Watch it, or I might make a habit of it."

"Ouch," he hisses, then winces, grabbing himself as if he were imagining the attack.

My eyes dart past his shoulder, where Storm is coming up the stairs. She has on her headphones, staring at the face of her phone. I nod my head at Dean, indicating we're no longer alone. I shift, moving to walk past him. He grabs my hip, pulling me into his grasp.

"We'll continue this later," he promises. He takes my hand and leads me past Storm and out of the bus without a word. I wonder if she can tell what had been transpiring from the look on my face.

As we move around the side of the bus, I feel his hand shift to the small of my back. It's like he knows all the places to touch me to drive me absolutely insane. Seemingly out of nowhere, my chest begins to ache, my head feels hot, and I double over, trying to catch my breath.

"Are you okay?" he gasps, taking my arm, pulling my hair back from my face.

"I don't know," I reply honestly. What is wrong with me?

"What's wrong?" he asks, bending over, his face now next to mine.

"I can't —catch —my breath," I say between heaves of air. "My heart's ... racing."

"Calm down." Dean slips into the role of caretaker, a knight in shining armor. With one hand on my arm and his other around my waist, Dean leads me over to the nearby cargo van. He opens the passenger door and instructs me to take a seat. "Okay, now I want you just to focus on taking a deep breath. Can you do that?"

I shake my head wildly, my chest growing tighter and tighter with each attempt.

His hands are on my cheeks now, gently tracing the lines with his fingertips. "Baby, close your eyes and just concentrate on taking one good breath for me."

I do what he says, squeezing them shut, and his hands never leave my face. I'm able to steal one breath, and then another. Soon, I'm breathing normally again. I open my eyes and find his looking back at me, the pools of blue full of concern.

"What's wrong with me?" I cry.

"I think you just had a panic attack."

"What?"

"It's okay," he assures me, pulling me close to his body, my head now pressed to his chest. Did I really just freak out over the thought of having sex with Dean? What is wrong with me? He's perfect. "We can take our time. I'm not going anywhere."

I say nothing, leaving my head buried. I close my hands, clutching the fabric of his shirt in my fingers, and, shutting my eyes, I focus on breathing. This new journey is going to be harder than I thought.

EIGHTEEN

"SO YOU'RE REALLY NOT GOING to tell me where we're going?" I press, leaning forward and adjusting the air conditioning vent.

"How about this ... you answer a question of mine, and I'll answer a question of yours. Sound fair?"

I think about his proposition for a moment, then nod. "Fine, but I get to go first."

"I can agree to that."

"Who are we going to visit?" I ask.

"My mom," he answers, keeping his eyes on the road. This surprises me, since I had assumed his mother was dead.

"But I thought your grandma raised you."

"Nope, you've had your question, so now it's my turn." He grins. "What was the deal when we were leaving the bus this morning?"

"I don't know what you're talking about," I lie.

"Oh, come on, I hang out with you every day, and I've never seen you bug out like you did back there."

"Honestly?"

"That's why I asked."

I glance out the window, biting my lip. I've shared with him, been vulnerable, so why hold back now? "I'm starting to freak out a little about us having sex."

"Mac!" he gasps. "I'm so sorry. Do you feel like I've been pressuring you?"

"No," I huff. "Just the opposite. I feel like you don't want to have sex with me."

"Oh God," he moans, leaning over and squeezing my leg. "You have no idea how much I want you. I've been trying to let you go at your own pace."

"I don't know what that is. Maybe I'm ready, but I don't know."

"Trust me, I'm happy to try."

I blush. "Okay, my turn. You said your parents were dead."

"No," he says, shaking his head. "I said my dad died when I was little."

"Right, and your grandma raised you."

"Yeah, but that doesn't mean my mom's dead. My turn. Why do you still wear your wedding ring around your neck?"

"I didn't get to ask my question," I protest.

"You need to learn to ask more clearly. You used your turn."

I huff and cross my arms.

"Come on," he presses. "It's the rules."

I think about it for a moment. "I don't want to forget."

"Baby, I can assume you would never forget someone you love."

"Not him." I look down at my hands, anxiously hooking my fingers together. "I don't ever want to forget that I'm cursed."

I can feel his eyes on me, looking from me to the road and then back to me. "You don't really believe that, do you?"

"I don't know, maybe. My mom dies, then I survive a crash that my husband and daughter don't. Oh, and let's not forget my dad dying recently. You tell me ... does that sound cursed?" I have to laugh to keep from crying.

"People die, but it's not our fault."

"If you say so," I say dismissively. He won't understand, so why bother trying to explain it to him. Nobody who hasn't been bathed in death could understand. "My turn," I say. "So your mom's alive—"

"She is," he says, slowing to take a turn onto a country road.

"But your grandma raised you?" I continue. "What's the story?"

"She did, because my mom wasn't around," he says, picking up speed. "It's not much farther."

Glancing around at the fields of grass, I take a deep breath. It's obvious his past is just as hard to talk about as mine.

"I miss Grams." His words are tender and sincere. I touch his arm, running my hand up to rest on his shoulder.

"When did she pass away?"

"It's been a couple years. That was the first time I saw Mom since I was little; before that, it was too much on Grams." The way he spoke of her, I could tell he loved her in a very special way.

"She meant a lot to you," I comment. I can see a smile tickling the corners of his mouth, and I wonder if he might be lost in a memory.

"I wish you could have met her," Dean continues, letting out a sigh. "She was a baker, just like my mom. She used to tell me a cupcake had magical powers that could cheer up anyone."

"I could see that."

"It never failed. If the kids at school would say something about my mom that upset me, she always managed to fix it with some sort of sweet treat."

"Did you grow up around here?"

"Mom did," Dean starts. "But I think it's time for another one of my questions."

"Fair enough."

"Would you ever consider getting married again?"

A breath catches in my throat. A bittersweet question such as his can only be answered with humor. I smile and tease, "Why, you asking or something?"

"Come on, I'm curious. After watching how much my mom and dad hated each other, I swore I'd never get married, but my views seem to be softening lately," he explains, the van slowing as he flicks on the turn signal.

To our right is a large concrete building, surrounded by barbed wire. It looks like a—

"Well, we're here," he huffs. I'm relieved I don't have to answer the final question.

My eyebrows lift as I ask, "A prison?"

"Yup." He doesn't look at me as he drives down the long dirt road toward the gate. I realize there is so much I don't know about this man, and the mystery that once seemed sexy has my stomach twisting itself into knots.

I consider what words to say next, but none seem appropriate. We're here to visit his mother, and something tells me that she isn't a guard. We slow to a stop, Dean leaning to one side to retrieve his wallet from his back pocket. He presses the switch to roll down the window, handing his identification to the guard.

"Visitors' lot is to the right, and you take the—"

"Doors on the left, yup, I know the drill," Dean interrupts. The young gentleman nods at him, then walks over to activate the gate.

"Are you all right?" he asks, glancing in my direction.

"Uh-huh," I say, though I'm so far from all right.

There are a lot of firsts Dean is bringing into my life. He gave me the experience of life on the road with a band, my first ride on a motorcycle, and now my first visit to a prison. I'm not sure if I can handle any more firsts from this man.

"You're going to love her," he comments, putting the van in park and releasing his seat belt. "And I know she'll love you."

"Wow, meeting the mom. This is so soon." As soon as the words come out of my mouth I want to smack myself in the forehead. Did I really think that was going to be funny?

He gives a soft laugh, opens his door, then makes his way around the front of the van, pulling open the passenger door. When he reaches to take the mac-and-cheese from my lap, I wrap my arms tightly around it. "I've got it."

"Afraid I'll steal credit? Don't worry; she knows I can't cook worth a damn. I might love food, but that doesn't mean I can cook."

He takes the handles of the stay warm pack from my arms and then, with his other hand, helps me from the van. *What are you doing? So his mom's in prison, you're not exactly the perfect package. He cares about you.* I realize what a complete and total jackass I'm being. Dean will tell me more when he is ready. He's patient with me, so the least I can do is be the same for him.

I link my arm around his elbow, and we cross through the parking lot. I notice there have to be a couple hundred other cars parked around us. The facility is out in the middle of nowhere, yet there seem to be so many people here. The landscaping is crisp and well done, and aside from the barbed wire it doesn't look like a scary place. There are trees along the perimeter, with gardenias planted all around them. To the far left I see a second chain-linked fence, and wonder what might be in that area.

"You sure you're okay with this?" Dean asks me again. "You can wait in the van if you don't want to do this. I'd understand."

I shake my head, even though I'm not sure, insisting, "I'm good."

We enter through the large doors on the left; a woman with two small children enters just ahead of us. I look at the little boy who appears to be around eight or nine, and I can't help but wonder if Dean had to see his mother like this when he was that age. We wait patiently at a window, and when it's our turn, a female prison guard greets us, handing Dean a form to fill out while we wait some more. She asks if we have items to be passed through security, and he slides her the carrier with my delicious meal inside. She takes it from him, moving it to a small table behind the counter where another guard begins searching the contents. Unzipping it and pulling out the mac-and-cheese dish, my heart sinks as I watch him place his latex-wrapped hand through the dish, mixing it all about.

"So much for presentation," I mumble.

Dean starts laughing, nearly roaring, and I feel my cheeks grow hot. "You're pretty damn cute, you know that?"

I shrug as we take our place along the wall, filling out the cards that were given to us. Relationship with prisoner, names, addresses. I hand him my ID, and he returns all of the items to the female guard. She instructs us to move into a processing room. In there we form a line and shift slowly through a security checkpoint, similar to what you would see at an airport.

"What about the food?" I whisper ignorantly.

"It'll be waiting for us," Dean explains in a whisper. "She's in minimum security now, but it still has to go through the back-room security."

"Really, just for mac-and-cheese?"

"When I was a kid she wasn't allowed any food, so this is an improvement."

When he was a kid? So he did grow up like this.

I'm not sure what I expected on the other side of the security checkpoint, but certainly something much more terrifying than what awaits us. Two gentlemen take our group through an outdoor cage area, and on the other side of the big heavy metal doors is a long concrete slab with picnic tables.

I sigh a breath of relief that the searches seem to be over. Immediately to our right is a table with all of the items that had to go through a more intense security check, including our dish. It's no longer in the warmer bag; instead, there is just the tray I cooked it in. Even the cover that was on it is missing. This does not seem to alarm Dean. He picks up the tray and starts looking around at the tables.

I see a woman standing and waving wildly in our direction. "Dean! Baby, over here."

He looks at me, slipping his hand around mine. "Ready?"

I nod, silently, my heart pounding in my ears.

We head in the direction of the table. The woman's frame is slight, her auburn hair cut off at her shoulders, sprinkled with gray. She has a smile that reminds me of Dean, but when we get closer it's the eyes that knock me back. Those pools of blue-gray—it's as if I am staring into his eyes. Placing the food on the table, he releases my hand for a moment and wraps his arms around his mother. I watch, still silent. She squeezes her eyes closed, and I suddenly feel like an intruder.

Dean lets go of her and takes a step back. "Mom, there's someone I want you to meet."

Her eyes shift to me, starting at my eyes and work their way down my body.

I reach out to shake her hand; her skin is soft and her touch slight. I can't imagine what in the world this woman has done to be in a place like this.

"Mom, this is MacKenzie."

"Hi, Mrs. Johnson," I offer quietly.

She shifts awkwardly when I say this, and I wonder if I've done something wrong. "Please dear, call me Patti." Her voice is as tender as her touch.

I nod and agree, "Okay, nice to meet you, Patti."

She motions to the bench in front of us. "Please, have a seat."

We do, and I watch as she leans over and takes in a huge sniff of the mac-and-cheese.

"MacKenzie made it," Dean says.

"It smells delicious, dear," she says.

I sit, quietly watching as the two of them interact, hoping for some hint of what I'm missing. Some hint that would help me make sense of the recklessness that brought this family to its knees. She asks how we met, and Dean is more than happy to tell her the story about how I rear-ended Christian in a parking lot, which then led to me applying for the chef's job. My mind begins to wonder until a question from Patti jolts me back to reality.

"You were married?"

I choke on my own saliva. "Excuse me?"

"Momma."

"What ... she's still wearing the ring around her neck."

My hand slips instinctively to the trinket, and I nod. "It's okay," I reassure Dean. "I don't mind."

"Widow?"

"How did you know?" My brow narrows.

"I doubt a divorced woman would want a reminder."

"I lost my husband and daughter a few years ago in a car accident." I'm proud I manage to get the words out without my voice cracking. I'm holding it together, that is, until Patti reaches across the table and touches me with her warm fingertips.

"Oh, honey, I'm so sorry. I can't imagine losing a child. I know a mother would do anything to protect her baby."

I feign a smile, looking into her eyes. There's more than pity in her look; there's a story I wish I could know and understand. Perhaps the entire story is in her statement. Is that why she's here? Was she protecting her baby?

"Okay, can we talk about something else?" Dean huffs uncomfortably.

"Did Dean ever tell you I potty trained him with mac-and-cheese?"

"Really, Momma? I tell you to change the subject, and this is where you go?"

Patti leans back, laughing wildly, a light in her eyes that makes me feel warm all over. There's something about her that mesmerizes me. I hope one day I get to learn her story.

I quickly join in the laughing. "No, he hasn't, but I'd love to hear the story."

We talk, and as she shares stories, I see a mother who cherishes her son, and a son who would do anything for his mother. Just when I'm getting comfortable with Patti, the guards announce visitation time is up. My eyes shift to

Dean. He's staring at his mother, and they nod to one another, an unspoken code. I imagine it's a way to tell each other to stay strong.

As we leave, a million questions are racing through my mind, but how? How do you ask someone what terrible thing happened to put your mother in this place? So, instead, I continue to walk next to him, silent.

———

NINETEEN

WE'RE only minutes away from the caravan when I ask him to pull over. I thought I could accept not knowing—waiting for Dean to tell me his mother's story—but as we've sat in silence the entire trip back, the anticipation has been absolute torture.

He nods in response; if his silence lingers any longer, I'm not sure I'm going to be able to contain myself. Why won't he say something? Anything. Dean pulls over into a parking lot of what looks to be a medical services building—a fitting choice considering I might cause him some bodily harm if he doesn't start sharing with me soon.

He looks at me, a sadness in his eyes that makes me regret my frustration. "Too much baggage?" He's nearly whispering.

"Weren't you the one who told me no baggage means boring?" I remind him, turning toward him. "I just don't want to have this conversation back at camp, in front of everyone."

"What conversation is that?" He reaches out, running his fingertips across the skin on my arm.

I expel a hitched breath, a shiver running down my spine. "How about, 'Hey sweetie, I forgot to mention—I have a mom, and she's in prison...'?"

"Everyone has a mom." Dean grins.

I pull away from him. I want him to know I don't think now is a great time for him to show his keen sense of humor. "Don't do that."

"Do what?" He shrugs.

"This is serious."

He huffs a heavy sigh, and I sense his sudden frustration. "Why does this have to be serious?"

I pause; I'm approaching this in the wrong way. "I don't mean serious, I'm sorry. All I mean is, I don't want there to be any secrets between us."

"So this is about my mom."

I want to tell Dean never mind, that he doesn't need to tell me anything, but I can't. I'm starting to feel something for this man. I'm putting myself on the line, and I need to know him—know what has gone into making him the kind of person I'm falling in love with.

I take a deep breath, swallow, and try my best to be honest without upsetting him. "I have no idea how to approach something like this, so I'm just going to be honest. I've been happy these past few weeks. That's not something I've been for a very long time."

"So what does my mom have to do with us being happy?"

"It has to do with your past. You want to be there for me, let me do that for you."

He shifts in his seat uncomfortably. I lean forward, clasping my hands around his forearm, pulling him toward me. "Don't shut me out," I plead.

"I'm sorry, that's not what I'm trying to do. I guess I'm

just nervous. I'm torn, because I want to share this part of my life with you, but at the same time I don't want you to see me differently," he says.

I fall onto my knees in the empty space between the seats, and, lifting my hands to either side of his face, pulling his forehead to my lips, I kiss him. My fingers wrap around the back of his head as it lowers to rest on my shoulder. "Dean Johnson, I see you for exactly who you are. Nothing from your past will ever change that."

He shifts his head, pressing his mouth against my neck. I quiver slightly as a chill runs through my body. "Okay, I'll tell you," he whispers against my skin.

I wait for him to pull away, my eyes staying locked onto his the entire time I return to my seat. I sit on the edge, keeping the distance between us small so that I can keep a hand on his leg. This is odd for me, but strangely empowering. For the past three years, everyone has been trying to be strong for me, to help piece me together again. Here I am being that for Dean, or at least trying to be.

"I don't remember everything," he begins. "There's details that get cloudy, you know? Like I could have sworn I was wearing a red T-shirt that day, but other times I remember it as blue. The important stuff doesn't change, though."

I nod, swallowing hard, telling myself that no matter what he tells me, I need to make him understand this doesn't change anything between us.

"I was six years old, and it was a Saturday. I know because Saturday was when my dad would go hunting with his buddies from the precinct."

"Your dad was a cop?"

"Oh yeah, he and his buddies used to always say they bled blue," he continues. "He wasn't always scary; in fact, sometimes he actually was a good guy. He taught me to ride a bike, took me fishing, he'd bring home flowers for my mom, but all of that was usually as a way to say he was sorry."

I can feel my jaw clench. I know where this is going, and it twists my stomach into knots. I was given parents who cherished me; the idea of them hurting me is unimaginable.

"Dad liked to drink, and after one or two he was actually kind of fun, but he wasn't the type to stop at one or two. No, he had to keep going until he transformed into one of the meanest son of a bitch drunks I've ever met." Dean falls quiet, staring into a void only he can see.

The quiet is so painful, I have to break it, "I'm sorry you had to deal with that."

"That's life, right?" He laughs uncomfortably. "Bad shit happens, you deal with it, and move on."

"So did you and your mom leave?"

"We tried," Dean continues. "There was a party, a cookout at one of the neighbors' houses, the night before. It was one of the guys on the force—Mom called him Teddy. He was friends with dad, but things always got weird when Mom was around. I never understood why until after it all happened."

His eyes shift around the parking lot, then back at me, as if he expects someone to be watching. "She loved Dad. His paranoia was just that; she swears they weren't messing around, but he wouldn't listen."

"Who?"

"My mom. Dad thought she was sleeping with Teddy. Jesus, the guy was married too. They dated in high school, but that's all it was. That night, he had too much to drink and practically dragged my mom home by her hair. Teddy offered to have me stay the night with his kids, which I'm sure he was just trying to be nice and save me the hell he knew we were in for, but that only pissed Dad off more."

Deans sucks in a nervous breath, and I can tell he's struggling with the memories. I know I need to hear this so I can be there for him, but I hate putting him through it again.

"He only ever hit Mom ... that was his pattern—until that night. When we got home I begged him to leave her alone. He backhanded me so hard I went flying across the room, shattering a living room lamp. I don't remember too much more from Friday. Most of it's from the day—" His voice cracks.

"Baby, you can finish telling me later," I offer, wanting his pain to stop.

"No, you're right; you need to know," he insists, then continues. "I was watching Saturday morning cartoons when she came out with the bags. She told me we were going on an adventure. I think I knew because I asked about Dad. She told me he'd have to join us later. On hunting days, Dad was always gone until late in the afternoon. Always. He forgot his back-up rod and decided to come back for it. Maybe he was suspicious; maybe he thought Mom was planning something. Who knows? Mom was getting me in the car when he pulled up. Most of the argument happened out of earshot. He dragged her in the house, kicking and screaming. I just froze. I always went to protect her, but after the night before I was terrified."

"That's understandable," I offer in a soft tone. He looks at me, and his eyes make my heart ache.

"The next thing I heard was a shot," Dean says almost coolly, as if he's separated all emotion from the event.

"What happened?" I gasp.

"Mom staggered out of the house; her hair was a mess,

there were red marks all around her neck, and her lip was bleeding. The gun fell from her fingers onto our perfectly manicured lawn. And that was it. She'd killed him."

"Your mom shot your dad?"

"Yup, and she got twenty-five to life for it," he answers solemnly.

I shake my head wildly. "No, that's impossible. She can't. It was self-defense."

"You'd think so, right?" Dean scoffs.

"I don't understand."

"I told you—he and his buddies all looked out for each other. She shot him in the back, so they said there was no way it could be self-defense. She claims he was going for his service weapon, but she had already hidden his back-up piece in her sweater pocket. She says she shot him in the back to stop him from reaching for his gun. The prosecutor claims having the other gun on her body meant it was premeditated, and shooting him in the back only proved he was running away. They said she was in no immediate danger."

"No jury would convict."

"Oh, by the end of it they had made her out to be a whore, an unfit mother, and a cold-blooded killer. I went to live with Grandma, and we visited at first, but then it was too hard on Grams."

"I don't know what to say, but this is possibly the most terrible thing I've heard in my entire life."

"So do you think I'm totally screwed up now?"

"What?" I'm back on my knees, pulling his hand close to my chest. I lift a hand up to his cheek, touching it softly with my palm. I wonder how someone so amazing could have been born of such a violent past. "Baby, if anything, I love you more."

"You love me," he says quietly.

"I—You—I mean ... you know what I mean, I like you a lot," I stammer. "You're so amazing. To find out what you've been through, it just..."

He leans forward, stealing away my words as his lips press firmly against mine. It isn't like any other kiss we've shared. There's a pain behind the tenderness. A vulnerability that shows we have no more secrets, no skeletons, and we still accept each other for who we are.

We break from each other for a moment. He's looking into my eyes, and I into his, and I can see a smile tickling at the corner of his lips. "I like you, too, Macaroon."

I laugh. This man drives me crazy, and it's clear he loves it.

———

TWENTY

I'M STANDING off to the side, a black floor under my feet, black curtains to my left and right, the band directly in front of me. My eyes are locked on Dean, but he doesn't notice me. He's instructing the person in the sound booth to adjust the settings.

Looking at him, one would never know the tragedy he emerged from. I can't even believe that he could be so tender and loving. For a child to experience what Dean had to go through must have been an unimaginable torture. Yet there he is confident and sexy. No monster lurking, waiting to burst from him. I can see the tenderness in him when I look in his eyes.

"All right, I think we're good," Dean shouts to the faceless man off stage. Suddenly there is the sound drumsticks clanging together, the hum of guitar strings as they are shifted, and the pop of an amp shutting off.

I sigh then walk out on stage to make my announcement. "Hey guys, food's ready."

They waste no time. A clatter fills the space around me as the three men exit to the left and right of me, in the direction of the green room. Dean is the only one not rushing off. He's standing, looking at me. The spotlight is still on him. The other guys are gone before he moves toward me.

I'm frozen, as if his eyes have somehow locked me into my exact position. He's walking closer. I don't look away, and neither does he. He closes the space between us until he is gripping my upper arms and pressing his lips against my forehead. "Hi beautiful," he says in a near whisper. My stomach flutters.

He gently nudges my arm and turns me in the direction the guys went. We walk toward the stairs, but then he suddenly stops and looks over his shoulder. I'm watching him, wondering what is going through that gorgeous head of his.

When he reaches out a hand in my direction, I instinctively grab it and he pulls me to the side, weaving between the curtains until we are against the back concrete wall of the building. I'm breathing heavy. My heart is pounding. And I can barely make out the features of his face in the darkness.

"What are you doing?" I whisper.

"I wanted to be alone with you," he answers. I can feel his breath on my cheek and the heat coming off his body. I swallow hard, no idea what to expect next.

"How was practice?" I ask, trying to mask my nerves.

"Fine, but that's not really what I want to talk about," he nearly growls as he speaks the words.

"What do you want to talk about?" I'm now practically shaking.

His lips graze my cheek and settle on my ear. "Well, to be honest, I don't really want to talk. I'd much rather be doing other things."

From the hard bulge pressing against my leg, I know

exactly what he would rather be doing. I don't resist when his hand slides up my waist.

"Oh yeah," I taunt. "And what exactly did you have in mind?"

His lips touch my neck at the point just below my ear. He pulls away a little. "I think you know."

I do know. I've been thinking about it since we got together. I press my back against the cool wall to try and steady myself, my legs growing weak. He doesn't allow the distance between us to grow and quickly closes the gap.

"Umm..." I begin. "Let me see if I can guess. You want to go see a movie with me?"

He leans in, his lips delivering a soft and wet kiss. Pulling away, he whispers, "No, guess again."

I swallow and wonder if it was as loud as it was in my head. "You were hoping we could play a board game?" I squeak out.

A hand slides around my body, settling on the small of my back as another kiss is delivered, but this time a little lower down my neck. "No, not a board game." His lips are so close to my flesh I can actually feel him grinning.

"Hmm," I moan. "I don't know. I'm not sure what else there is."

"Let me show you." He sighs, bringing his lips up to meet mine.

He parts them without resistance from me. His tongue explores the inside, entwining and dancing with my own tongue. Even though we are shrouded in darkness, I close my eyes, but I can see little pops of color on the back of my eyelids as he kisses me. God, he smells good.

This gorgeous guy is kissing you. You are being kissed by him. He wants you. Jesus, this feels good. How is his tongue so soft and smooth when it moves? Travis was not a great kisser; it always felt like a hard, wet probe repeatedly sticking itself in my mouth. Jesus! What's wrong with you? Quit thinking about your dead husband.

Our lips part only long enough for me to catch my breath, then Dean is right back in there. I love that he has taken the lead. I'm not sure I could have done this. I couldn't have been so bold to simply take something I want.

You know you're a terrible person. You are making out with your boyfriend while thinking about what a terrible kisser Travis was. Who does that? That really isn't fair; Travis made up for his lack of anything orally pleasing with his—Stop it! You're doing it again.

Dean pulls away. "Are you okay?"

I nod frantically. "Of course, I'm great. Why would you ask that?"

My eyes have started to adjust to the darkness. I can see him pressing his lips together in concern. He sighs and takes a very small step back, still holding my waist. "You seem distracted."

Do I lie? Do I tell him what I am really feeling? Will it terrify him? Tell him.

I shake my head. "I'm nervous," I admit.

I can see his mouth form into a grin. "I'll be gentle," he promises.

He doesn't return to kissing me, but I can feel his eyes on me. What is he looking for?

"What's wrong?" I ask, afraid I've ruined the moment.

"Nothing," he starts, before adding, "I'm just getting the vibe you're not ready."

"I'm totally ready!" I exclaim. "See, this is me, totally ready." I press out my lips in an exaggerated attempt to kiss him.

"I tell you what ... how about we go grab a bite to eat?"

"What?" I gasp. "No way, we were totally going to public sex this up."

Dean laughs. "Wow, that sounds so romantic when you put it that way."

"I'm serious. I want to make sure you understand how much I want you." I'm squeezing his arms.

His hand reaches around and grips the back of my head, his fingers entangling with my hair. Tilting my head back, he moves in for another kiss. This one is slow and soft. One, two, three motions, and then he pulls away, his lips pressing against my cheek.

"Let's take it slow," he says at last.

My face is hot in an instant. "Did you just use the 'go slow' line on me?"

"Whoa, baby, calm down. It's not like that."

"Do you not want to have sex with me?" I question, my voice squeaking.

He takes my hand and presses it against his hard bulge. "What do you think?"

"Then why not?"

He doesn't respond. Taking my hand, he leads me back over by the stairs. He lowers his lips to my ear and whispers in a breathy voice, "Because the first time I'm inside of you —screwing your brains out—I want it to be all you can think about."

I squeeze his hand. I can't help myself. If I don't, I might actually fall to the floor from the weakness that is rising up my legs. He sees inside you. He knows you're terrified, and he knows more than you do that you're not ready.

"Promise?" I ask, smiling playfully.

"You can count on it," he answers, before leading me to the green room, his hand secured safely around my own.

TWENTY-ONE

THE PAINTED ladies tower above me, each one a more dramatic display of flamboyancy than the next. It's obvious that care has been taken to keep them in pristine condition.

I look down at my feet and study the bits of spongy moss peeking between the cracks of the sidewalk. Just on the other side of the sidewalk is a shared white picket fence extending the length of the street.

Dean steps over to one of the gates and pushes it open, waiting for me to enter first. He's smiling at me, and I feel my stomach flutter. I love that every time he smiles at me my body reacts this way, I hope it never changes.

"Shall we?" he asks, using his free hand to lead the way.

I give a playful scowl "You sure you want to go through with this?"

He lets the gate fall shut, taking a few steps forward and scooping my hand up into his. When he touches my flesh, I feel that familiar flutter. Jesus. It's amazing when you touch me.

"Day in and day out you're cooking and serving me and the guys. I'm excited about doing that for you."

I glare at the oversized bright red door at the top of the stairwell. "So you do know what I do for you every day doesn't even compare to this." I happily correct him.

"Okay, okay," he says, releasing me and shaking his hands in the air. "It's absolutely not the same thing, so how about this: I wanted to create an incredible food experience for you. One where instead of considering the ingredients or timing or prep work, you instead sit back and truly enjoy every single bite."

"I get it," I concede. "I just think it's dangerous."

"Oh yeah?" His inflection as he speaks is clearly flirtatious. "And how is it dangerous?"

"You want to give me a special night, you want me to enjoy a meal, but this is my passion. Aren't you worried I might be overly critical of any restaurant you take me? Doesn't a painter scrutinize when he sees other artists' work?"

He leans in; his lips graze my cheek and settle inches from my ear. He whispers, "I think you'll pleased."

I lick my lips, unsure if I'm salivating in a desire for him or the promised food. Perhaps it is both. He moves away, and I nod in his direction. Once again he guides me through the gate and up the small concrete path, lined on either side with green bushes and bursts of color from various flowers. I want this to be amazing, and no matter how hard I make it on him, I have a feeling it will be with him as my companion.

"How did you find this place?" I inquire, stopping at the top of the stairs for him to join me.

"That's my little secret," he taunts. Dean has assured me repeatedly that I am in for a treat. He knocks on the door, his eyes soft and wide as he eagerly waits. I stare at him and can tell he wants tonight to be perfect.

An older woman, wearing a flowing navy blue dress paired with simple flesh-toned ballet flats, opens the door. From her appearance, I would not assume she works at the restaurant, but perhaps a patron, though why would she answer the door? Why would anyone answer the door? Why wouldn't we just walk in? Why kind of place is this?

"Hello," the woman nearly squeals in a high-pitched voice. She steps to one side allowing us room to walk through the doorway. "Welcome, you must be Dean and MacKenzie, am I right?"

"Yes, we are," Dean answers, taking my hand and guiding me through the open door. I am even more confused than before.

I see there is no hostess table. No obvious kitchen or wait staff. Immediately in front of us, to our right, is an old wooden staircase. The wall leading up to the second floor is lined, floor to ceiling, with oil paintings in ornate gold frames. Perched above the open stairwell is a massive chandelier, and I suddenly feel as though I have been transported back in time.

"We have you in the green room," the woman explains, as if I should understand what this means. I want to ask Dean a million questions but decide I will wait until we are seated. "Right this way."

The woman does not retrieve any menus; she simply begins moving around the corner and through what I initially thought was a living room. We follow silently. In the first room I discover my assumptions were wrong. There are three round two-person tables. The room is a bright color, and I wish this were where we would eat.

I'm soaking in the decor and nearly fall behind. Catching up with the woman, we enter into what I can only assume is the room she had referred to as the green room.

The walls are covered in textured wallpaper that has various sizes and shapes of green leaves. It's lush in its quality, and I fight the urge to run my fingertips along it. A couple is perched at one of the tables, but they are staring longingly into one another's eyes and do not notice we're even here.

The woman seats us, and in the light of the new room I notice more than her stout figure. Her skin appears almost translucent, and heavy rouge marks on her cheeks attempt to add a small piece of color to her nearly pigment-less face. Her hair is silver and gathered in a tight bun at the nape of her neck. She reminds me of my Nana—my mother's mother.

I sit, trying to see if the diners at the table across from us have a menu. I see neither menus with them nor any sign of food.

"Will it be field or ocean this evening?" she asks, looking back and forth between us.

"Field for me," Dean answers, and suddenly I feel like I am missing something very important. My eyes widen in his direction, and I shrug my shoulders. He grins, very pleased I am still clueless by his surprise. "Do you want a protein that was raised in a field or in the ocean?" he clarifies.

"Oh," I gasp. I can feel the woman's eyes staring at me, waiting for me to make a decision. I have no clue what is happening, but I can provide an answer. "Ocean?" I say more as a question.

She nods and disappears.

Leaning across the table and staring into Dean's eyes, I ask pointedly, "What in the hell is going on?"

"So I have you stumped?"

"Yes, completely." I laugh. "Now will you please tell me what is going on?"

"It's called The Experience," he begins.

I look around the room. "Oh, it's an experience all right."

"You hate it." He frowns.

My voice rises when I say, "I don't even know what the hell it is yet."

"Okay, so they have converted this old house into a lot of small dining rooms. Each table can only be booked twice a night so that diners can slow down and really enjoy the dining experience."

"Seriously? How can that be profitable?"

"Trust me, it is," he jokes.

"Dean, how much did you spend on this?" I huff.

"Don't worry about it ... I want tonight to be special," he insists.

"So there are only two menus?" I ask for clarification.

He nods. "One from the ocean and one from the field. They plan each course based on that initial choice."

"That's different."

Dean and I glance at one another, smiling. My eyes shift around the room uncomfortably, but I can see from the corner of my eye that he doesn't look away.

"What?" I ask, looking him directly in the eyes.

He shakes his head and delivers me a long blink. "I don't think I will ever get used to your beauty."

I blush. What do people say in response to such amazing declarations? I've forgotten how to interact.

The same silver-haired woman approaches our table with a set of wine glasses and a bottle with deep red liquid inside. I glance at Dean, puzzled.

"I hope you don't mind, I reserved us a Malbec. I don't really drink, but this seemed like a special occasion."

"An anniversary?" the woman asks, clearly eaves-dropping.

"Oh, no," I quickly respond.

I look down at my lap, embarrassed by my quick response. "No," Dean jumps in, saving the day. "We are celebrating the fact that one of the most intelligent, beautiful, and tender women I have ever met somehow has become my girlfriend."

He might never get used to my beauty, but I know I will never get used to him calling me his girlfriend. "Dean." I smile, not looking up from my lap.

"It's true!" he exclaims.

"Seems like a perfect reason to celebrate," the woman says, pouring a glass for Dean and waiting for him to taste. He sips, then nods. She pours us both a serving, then takes off back through a side room.

"So, honestly, what do you think so far?" Dean asks when we are alone again.

My eyes scan the room once more. "So far it seems amazing."

"Fair enough," he relents. I stare at the glasses in front of us, and, without thinking, say what pops into my mind. "You know, I don't remember ever seeing you drink."

I peer up at his face; his lips are pressed together, his brows narrow, and I wish I hadn't said anything. "I guess I know history can repeat itself, and I don't want to become my father so I'm cautious."

"Really?"

"I'm not saying I would be an alcoholic if I drank more, but with a family history of it, why press my luck? I would never want to treat someone I love like my father treated my mother."

My heart aches. His wounds are so deep, I wonder if they can ever fully heal. I'm relieved when a young man appears at our table carrying a bread bowl in one hand and two salad plates on his other arm.

The lanky blond boy seems nervous as he places the bread in the center of the table, and I wonder if he's new. "Yeast rolls for your enjoyment," he says softly.

I realize how quiet the room is when he speaks. The lighting is dim as well. "For the ocean course, we have a citrus-inspired salad, and for the farm course, we have what our chef calls the earthen salad. Can I get you anything else?"

We both shake our heads, and the waiter retreats to the kitchen.

I pick up the fork from the table and dive into the layers of spinach, strawberries and tangerine slices, dried cranberries, and candied walnuts. I slide a bite into my mouth and moan as the vinaigrette mixes with all the flavors.

"Good?" he asks, watching me eat with a smile on his face.

I nod, chewing my bite and swallowing. "Oh my God, gorgonzola, what an awesome surprise."

He laughs.

"What's so funny?" I ask, shoving another heaping bite into my mouth.

"I think I love watching you eat even more than I love watching you cook."

I raise a napkin to my mouth and giggle. "Creepy much?"

"I'm serious. You light up around food," he insists.

The courses continue, one after the next. We marvel at the dishes, each one more delicious than the last. The forty minutes I expected stretched into two glorious hours of delectableness.

As we wait for our dessert, my head is swimming. I'm

not sure if it's the wine or the blissful high of the incredible food. "Thank you."

"For what?" he asks, but his smile and his eyes tell me he knows exactly what I am thankful for.

I look down at the tablecloth in front of me, splattered with drippings from the evening meal. My cheeks flush. How do I tell him? How do I say, 'For getting me,' without seeming like a total dork?

"For tonight," I say at last.

"Thank you for joining me," he replies. "I hope you've enjoyed it."

"Are you kidding? This place is amazing." My voice trails off when I see the waiter approach with the final course.

He places a hearty slice of chocolate melting cake in front of Dean, and in front of me a dish of crème brûlée topped with a sprinkling of fresh berries. I bite my lip to contain my excitement.

The waiter leaves us and immediately Dean asks, "Are you okay?"

"This is my favorite dessert," I whisper, practically vibrating in my chair.

He responds with a deep belly laugh, and I feel my face go hot. "You might be the most adorable creature I have ever met, Macaroon."

Tapping my spoon on the sugary crust of the treat, I scoop out a bite of the creamy goodness. I close my eyes and allow the explosion of sweet to hit my tongue. "Oh my God," I moan. It's the only reaction I can have.

I open my eyes, and see he hasn't touched his dessert. "Aren't you going to eat?" I ask.

"Just savoring the moment."

I huff. "Okay, enough with the googly eyes. We like

each other, I get it, but is that any reason to let that melting cake get cold?"

He picks up his fork, laughing. Cutting into the center, a perfect molten chocolate seeps from its no-longer-secret hiding spot. He cuts off a piece of cake, drenches it in the liquid heaven, then leans across the table, extending the fork in my direction.

I think I might throw up from all the food I've eaten, but how can I turn away this new thrilling taste in my mouth? The fork slips past my teeth, and he lingers for a moment. He's not laughing anymore; no, he's staring. I press my lips around the fork and slide back. I don't look away from him. The flavor in my mouth is delightful, but the lustful look in his eyes is making me tremble.

"Let's get out of here," he suggests.

I nod as he lifts his finger, motioning to the waiter for the check. I can't imagine this evening could get any more perfect.

TWENTY-TWO

IT'S a moment I've been waiting for. A moment we both have been waiting for. And now it's here. Dean steps into me, his skin pressing against mine. One of his denim-clad legs slides between my thighs, parting my legs. My arms wrap around him instinctively.

"So Storm isn't coming back?" he whispers against the skin of my neck, his warm breath causing me to shudder.

"She said she's staying with Pete."

"Good," he moans, and I feel a bulge pressing against me from the other side of his jeans.

He takes my hands, entwining my fingers into his, and kisses my neck, then my jaw, and my chin. I can't take the anticipation, so I turn my face, forcing our lips to meet. I can feel the smile on his mouth. He pulls back from me, lifting his shirt up and over his head.

I blush and mumble, "Oh shit." I'd seen him shirtless before, but to be this close to him, touching his firm stomach, gazing at his tatted biceps, I'm not sure I'm actually prepared for the perfection of him.

He laughs. "What?"

I peer into his eyes as the backs of his fingertips trace the bare flesh of my arm. "Nothing, I just ... I can't believe this is actually happening."

"Do you want me to stop?" There's a smirk on his face when he asks me; it's obvious he already knows my answer.

I ignore his question, instead running my finger along the detail of the ink on his arm. "Why a ship?"

"Why not?"

"Really? There's no special meaning?"

"It has to do with never being afraid to take a journey, but do you want to sit here and discuss what my tattoos mean, or did you have some other things in mind?"

"Like what?" I tease.

"Well, I know I have a few things going through my mind," he begins, pulling me close to him, wrapping his strong arms around me, cupping my backside through the fabric of my mini dress and squeezing. I am still self-conscious about how I look in the revealing outfit, even now that I've lost weight, but he doesn't seem to mind how I look.

He's searching the back of my dress with his hands. "Where in the hell is the zipper on this thing?"

"There's not one ... it goes over my head," I explain.

He smirks at me. "Well then, let me help you with that."

Bending down, he grips onto the hem of my dress. My knees feel week. I reach out and steady myself with a hand on the wall of the bus. He takes his time as he lifts the fabric, his fingers sweeping over the flesh of my thighs and stomach as he moves upward. Lifting the dress over my head, he doesn't take his eyes from me as he allows it to drop to the floor.

I'm standing here—a pair of black lacy boy shorts and a black bra with lace along the cups the only thing between our bodies. My hands grasps my stomach; I'm suddenly self-conscious about the stretch marks, faded scars of motherhood.

He sees me, his head tilts, and I wish I knew what's going through his mind. He grips my wrists and pulls them away from my stomach. Dropping to his knees, I feel his soft lips press against the flesh of my tummy. His hands move around my skin, leaving a trail of fire as they dip under the waistline of my panties and grip the fullness of my bottom.

I realize I'm moaning and quickly close my mouth to prevent any further noises from escaping my lips. He pulls his head back, looking up at me. "God, you're beautiful," he groans, before standing up and looking into my eyes. My breath hitches; no matter how hard I try, I can't hide what he does to me.

"I want to see you naked," he says, and I nod, shocking even myself that I'm so quick to comply. Though I'm pretty sure at this point I would agree to anything Dean asks of me. He wastes no time, gripping the waist of my panties and tugging, letting them fall to the floor. I step out, kicking them to one side while reaching back and unsnapping my bra. But I don't remove it. I leave that task for him.

His gaze shifts from head to toe, and one of my legs crosses over the other awkwardly, as if I'm somehow trying to shield myself. He bites his lip as he looks at me, and I feel the inside of my thighs go hot. Moving closer, Dean brushes the straps from my shoulders with ease, watching as the bra falls to the floor, revealing the roundness of my breasts.

"Jesus Christ," he gasps. "You're so incredible."

He closes the space between us, his hands resting on my hips, his lips exploring my neck, then lower, his mouth finding the flesh of my breasts. I'm breathing heavy, heaving in and out, trembling. I begin to lose my balance and stumble backward, catching myself on the bunks.

"Are you all right?" he asks, grinning with satisfaction.

"Uh huh," I gasp, sitting down on my bed and reaching out with a single hand to grab his belt loop and pull him close. My finger curls around the jeans, releasing the button. I start to shimmy them down over his muscular thighs, but he grows impatient, rapidly moving his legs up and down to remove them from his legs.

"Boxer briefs, huh?" I ask with a smile.

"Do you approve?" He lowers himself on top of me, the only thing between us now that thin layer of fabric.

"Oh yeah, very much so," I answer.

"Lie back," he instructs me, and I instantly do what he says. His tongue wraps itself around my hard nipple, and my back arches in response. He's not content with this though, and he continues moving down my body, exploring all the curves and grooves with his lips and tongue.

"What are you doing?" I moan, reaching down and grasping his hair with my fingers. The lower he moves, the tighter my grip, but he's not answering me.

His kisses pepper my stomach, then my pelvis, and suddenly, with a firm grasp, he parts my legs, kissing the inside of my thighs. His tongue slides up the crevice of where my leg meets my hip, and I'm nearly convulsing as my muscles twitch wildly. I haven't felt the intimate touch of a man in so long, I'd forgotten what it can do to you.

First, there is a gentle kiss at my entrance, then a more powerful one, and before I can protest, before I can say I'm not sure I'm ready, he silences me with the pounding force of his tongue, parting my lips. It flicks wildly against my clit, and before I know what I am doing I find myself drawing him in deeper.

With a forceful hand, he presses my thighs back against the bed, hooking his arms around each leg. His tongue broadens and begins circling. I feel an energy building inside me, one that feels like at any moment I might lose all control. Stay calm, I tell myself silently, but it does no good.

Travis never enjoyed oral sex, and he never pleasured me in such a way—no man ever had. He'd tried, but it was always fast and obviously not something he took enjoyment in. I assumed it was something we did for them, not something that was ever done for us. It's a confusing pleasure. Part of me wants to release myself into the bliss of it, but the other part of me fears I can't handle the pleasure, and wants to pull away. Dean doesn't let me, though. He can sense the pleasure it's bringing me, and he has me locked into place.

As his tongue moves up, down, side-to-side, and even in and out, time loses meaning. A blur begins to leak into my vision, all around the edges, and there is a soft hum surrounding us. I want to envelop him, never allowing this moment to end. He can feel it building in me; I can tell because he's increasing the intensity with each wave that flows through me.

Travis. His name is in my head again. Why didn't he ever do this? Did he think something was wrong with me? Is there something wrong with me? If I let Dean stay down there, will he find out whatever Travis saw wrong with me?

"Take me," I beg, wanting to think of anything other than what my dead spouse didn't do in bed.

I only have to ask once, and releasing my thighs, he climbs up my body. He hesitates at my breasts, taking a nipple into his mouth again, pressing down slightly with his teeth, and I hiss in delight.

He rises higher, and I run my hands down his back. I'm gripping his flesh, my nails digging in, and he doesn't seem to mind. When he shifts completely into place on top of me, I suck in a breath of shock, realizing at some point he has removed his underwear without me noticing. His lips are tracing the line of my neck, leaving a trail of kisses as he makes his way up to my face.

He holds himself up with his arms, over me, highlighting the muscles in his shoulders, and I feel myself growing even wetter. He shifts his weight to one arm, his shaft pressing hard against my inner thigh. Leaning over the bed, he grabs his jeans with the other hand. From the back pocket he wiggles loose a condom, slipping it between his teeth, returning to his position over me.

Reaching up, I take the condom from his mouth and tear it open. He doesn't have to ask for my help—I want this to happen as much as he does. I reach down and grab the warm flesh of his length with one hand, placing the condom on with the other. Rolling it into place, I hear him moan from my touch. I smile longingly.

Returning my hands to the sides of his torso, guiding his weight into place, I widen the gap of my legs. He's looking into my eyes. There's intensity in his, a lust that says he has to have me. I need him just as much. I need to feel that connection, the closeness of intimacy at this level with another human being.

I'm afraid. It's been years. Will it hurt? Will it be like losing my virginity all over again? He lowers himself to his forearms, pulling up on his hips to bring himself into the perfect position to enter me.

He licks his lips. "Are you sure?" he asks one last time.

This question startles me. Have I given some indication I'm not? "Yes, please," I beg in a whisper. But his words already have me questioning myself. Perhaps I'm not ready. Maybe he senses it in me.

You're here, you're doing this, I tell myself, wrapping my legs around Dean, preparing myself for him. I take in a breath, tilt my head back, and close my eyes, waiting. He begins pressing forward with light thrusts. They're controlled at first, but then they begin to pick up pace and intensity as he moves deeper into me.

When his mouth is pressed into my neck, his hot breath makes me ache. The pain isn't the same as my first time; it's intense, but then passes. He's rocking into me, and when I get used to the rhythm, he changes it. He's driving me insane.

The same explosion I felt building when his mouth was below the waist begins building again. When I arch my back in pleasure, he slides an arm behind me, pulling me up, closer into him.

"I love you," he whispers.

It's like a sucker punch to my stomach. All of the air escapes me, and my world is spinning out of control. Every time Travis would get ready to climax he would whisper that same thing. Travis's faces flashes through my head, and I open my eyes wide, trying to escape the image of him. But he's there, locked into the moment with me and Dean.

I'm past the point of return—we both are—and I feel the climax, on the verge, ready to release, and behind that is a struggle. A struggle brews inside of me because each time I think of Dean, Travis' name isn't far away. I feel Dean begin twitching inside of me, and he moans, pulling me into him even tighter. So tight I wonder if he could break me. His orgasm sets off a chain reaction, like an avalanche inside of me.

I moan as the climax overtakes me, and, in an instant, it's like a beam of light is shooting out from my core, extending out from all of my entry points, and even out my fingertips. I'm floating now, a blur of reality and uncon-sciousness mingling around me. There are tiny golden diamonds in my mind, sounds are muffled, and I'm in a place of ecstasy like none I have ever known.

Then I hear him—Travis—heaving in and out, and I open my eyes wide. Jesus! Dean. Did I think for a moment at the end he was Travis? He rolls off me, his panting mixed with laughing.

"Wow, that was insane," he huffs.

I sit up, pulling a pillow to my stomach. "Yeah, it was," I agree. I don't want him to see me ... he won't understand. I can't stop it; the water has filled my eyes, and I'm going to start crying. No matter how much I fight it, the tears will win.

TWENTY-THREE

HE TIGHTENS his arms around my waist, shifting his body, resting one leg on either side of me. My back is pressed to his torso, and we're both forced to sit slightly slumped over on the bottom bunk. He rests his chin on my shoulder, and asks, "You okay?"

I glance at him briefly, force a tight-lipped smile, and say, "I'm fine."

He isn't buying it, that's obvious. Leaving his legs wrapped around me, he releases my waist and leans to the right side, resting on his elbow and forearm. This makes it harder for me to avoid looking at him.

I feel his other hand slide against the skin on my back, and I tense up for a moment. He softens his touch, his fingertips now dancing across my flesh. "Are you going to tell me the truth?"

I hesitate, running through things I can say in my head. How can I possibly tell you the truth? How can I tell you that, for a split second, when I climaxed, my mind tricked me into thinking I was with Travis? I'm pretty sure the last thing you want to hear after having sex with me is that I was thinking about my dead spouse during it.

I turn toward him, with only a sheet between our bodies, and lean in to kiss him. My lips press against his, and I pull his bottom lip into my mouth with my teeth, letting it slide slowly back out between my lips. I pull away slightly and open my eyes. He's smiling.

Sitting up, I feel relief wash over me. I'm sure the last thing he's thinking about now is—

"That was nice," he interrupts my thoughts. "But are you going to tell me what happened?"

"What do you mean? What happened when?" I play dumb. My heartbeat quickens, my palms start to sweat, and I can feel his eyes fixed on me.

He moves his legs, and lies down completely on the bed, motioning for me to join him. I bite my lip, nervous I'm going to say or do something to ruin this great thing happening in my life. I comply, yanking on the sheets, and, making my way underneath, I hook my right leg across his body, resting my head on his shoulder and hand on his chest.

"I want you to be able to trust me," he says at last.

I don't move my head. "I do."

"Then tell me why you were crying."

"I—" I'm about to lie. Why am I going to lie to him? Tell him the truth. "It's about Travis."

I can hear him breathing, in and out, but he remains calm when I confess what brought me to tears. I can't tell if he's upset. I'm silent, waiting for him to respond.

"That's it? That really doesn't tell me a lot, sweetie. What about Travis made you cry?"

"I don't want to upset you."

"Do I really seem like that unreasonable of a guy?" he

asks. I'm glad I'm lying on his chest, because I doubt I can have this conversation face to face.

"No, of course not," I quickly reply. "I—I didn't mean for it to happen, but right at the end I got overwhelmed, and I—"

"You what?"

"I thought you were Travis." He laughs softly, and I ask, "You're not mad?"

"Am I excited you're thinking about another man when I give you an orgasm? No, but I also get that this isn't going to be easy. I'm just amused you thought I'd be so upset."

"I'm so sorry."

I feel his lips press against my forehead. "I'm willing to make love to you as many times as it takes to put this behind you."

I give him swift slap to the tummy, and he folds in half for a second, a gust of air blowing out. "Yeah, is that right? You're so giving," I taunt.

He laughs, clutching his stomach and moaning, "I do what I can."

I shift my tongue in my mouth, a sour taste overwhelming me. Closing my eyes, I try to be content in the moment, but sadness is finding its way into my mind. I breathe in a deep breath of air; it shakes as I exhale.

"Are you sure you're going to be all right?" he asks, his arm around me tightening.

I turn my face into his rib cage, shielding myself, fighting back the flood emotions that are threatening to erupt. Don't let him see how unstable you are. Who in their right mind would want a complete basket case?

"Come on baby, tell me," he pleads.

"I guess I just feel like an idiot. It's been three years. I should be past this."

"Who says?"

"What?" His question surprises me.

"Who in the hell says you should be over this?" he asks again.

"Everyone," I reply.

"Then everyone should shut up because they don't know what the hell they're talking about," he huffs defensively. "Until they've been in your shoes, they should keep their mouths shut. People tried to tell me how I should feel about my mom, and I figured out real quick that they were all idiots."

"Thank you," I whisper softly. My heart hurts so much it's the only words I can manage to say. He understands, he gets that life is full of pain, and the ghosts that haunt me do not threaten him.

He smiles that grin I love so much, then takes my hand into his and nudges me toward the edge of the bed. "Come on, I wanna take you somewhere."

I slide out of the bed and begin to search the floor for my clothing. "Where?"

I pause when he stands up, the full sight of him coming into vision. He sees me staring, and a smirk appears on his face. "Yeah, I'm a grower."

"Huh?" I gasp, my face flushing red.

"Keep staring at my cock like that and you'll see what I mean pretty quick." He laughs. Catching a glimpse of his underwear, I snag them and toss them in the direction of his firm body. As he slides them on, I can already see what he meant by his now partially hard penis.

I slip on my panties, then bra, and ask, "So where are we going?"

"What's with the flower tattoo along your shoulder?" he asks, avoiding my question.

"Huh?" A stitch sews its way across my brow. "They were my mom's favorite flowers. I got them when I turned eighteen." I laugh to myself as I remember the event. "My dad had warned me not to defile my body with a tattoo, but when he saw them, he cried and told me how much she would have loved them."

I'm not looking at Dean as I recall the memory, but I can feel his eyes on me. I grab my dress off the floor and pull it over my head, and by the time I have it pulled into place, Dean is fully dressed and staring at me again. "What?" I cock my head, asking self-consciously. I don't look away from him, though, a challenge in my eyes.

He walks over, wrapping his arms around me. My arms are pulled into my chest, and I can't help but be impressed by the way he can still envelop me. His chin is resting on the top of my head, and I'm scared to move, breathe, or even blink for fear of the moment coming to an end.

"You're amazing. Just when I think I have you figured out, you surprise me."

"Just trying to keep you on your toes," I say with a smile. My heart sinks when he releases me from his grasp. He slips his hands up my shoulders, caresses my neck, and moves his way up until he is gripping my cheeks. Gently, he pulls me closer, our lips finding one another. My head is swimming, and I release all of myself into the moment. He kisses me in a way that makes me curl my toes and lose all feeling in my fingertips. If fireworks actually could erupt from a kiss, it would be this one. His lips linger a moment, then the kiss ends.

"Come on, we should probably ask around at the club for some of the best places to go," Dean says, releasing my face and grabbing hold of one of my hands.

"A place for where?"

"Tattoos," he answers casually.

"You're getting a tattoo? Oh God, don't tell me you're getting a tattoo of my name or something," I mock.

He laughs. "No, but you are."

"Excuse me?" I gasp.

"Well, not of your name, but not of my name either," he continues with a chuckle. He turns and faces me. "You're the bravest woman I have ever met, and I want you to always know that it's okay for you to miss them."

"So ... what? I'm supposed to get a tattoo of Travis and Katie?"

"Something that makes you think of them."

Instantly, I remember the nickname I used to call my daughter, and I whisper, "Katie Bird."

Dean shakes his head. "What?"

I swallow hard. I haven't felt her around me in so long, but as I say her nickname, it's as if she is right here with me. "I called her my Katie Bird."

"That's nice," he says in a low and smooth tone.

"You don't think it's weird? To get a tattoo for them?"

"I suggested it, so why would I think it's weird?"

I smile. I have to look away before I burst. "I want to get a bird tattoo."

"That sounds perfect." He squeezes my hand. "And for Travis?"

"You really don't mind?"

"Half my tattoos are about ex-girlfriends ... how could I mind?"

"Seriously?" I gasp, my head swooping in his direction, mouth hanging open wide.

He laughs wildly, then stops, focusing on my eyes. "No, silly. I'm messing with you. And I'm beyond okay with you loving him as much as you do. I hope one day you might love me that way."

"Dean—" I say, my voice cracking. Don't ruin it. Don't tell him you don't have enough love left in you for that.

"I know." He nods. It's in his eyes. He already knows I'm half empty in the love department. "So what are you going to get for him?"

I think about it for a second, and the answer is easy. "I like to think they're together, so I'm going to get two birds."

I fear I might run from him, from this selfless gift of caring he's offering me, but I know I can't. Deeper than that fear is the one that tells me if I did run, then I might fade from existence altogether. Instead, I tighten my grip on his hand and let him lead me from the bus. I'm about to get a new tattoo.

TWENTY-FOUR

I STARE INTO THE MIRROR; the smile it's reflecting isn't recognizable. Who are you? I take the time to do my hair and makeup, I eat a healthy and well-balanced diet, and I even go for walks. Dean has had a tremendous effect on me.

Pulling out a hair clip, I twist one side of my chestnut hair and pin it up. I remove the tube of plum-colored lipstick from my purse and reapply. With widened fingers, I carefully smooth out my shirt, ensuring it lays properly over the waistline of my slim fit jeans. I smile, pleased with the way the ensemble complements my curves. I'm confident Dean will approve.

This new life has completely removed me from my comfort zone, and the things I was once terrified of are now exhilarating. Had someone told me only a year ago that I'd be this happy again, I would have told them they were crazy. Had they told me I was going to find this happiness with a rock star, I think I may have even suggested they seek professional care for their madness.

Here I am, though, living this life that sometimes seems

like at any moment I could wake up from. Tonight's show was late so the band ate in advance. This means Dean and I will get to go out after the show. I prefer it this way. Night riding on the back of his motorcycle through new and exciting cities is an adrenaline pumping experience.

Tonight I managed to finish up my after-show snack preps early enough to slip in for the last half of the show. It's fascinating to watch Dean on stage; he slips into character. He's always confident, but with me he's vulnerable. On stage he comes off as arrogant, but oddly enough in a sexy way. When he moves across the stage there's no hesitation; he owns every step and every note. He's beautiful.

Eagerly, I press the button on the face of my phone, checking the time. I've never been a patient person, but waiting for Dean is agonizing.

"Finally," I start, leaning out of the small travel size bathroom when I hear footsteps on the rubber-covered stairs.

Storm freezes, staring at me with a puzzled look.

"Oh, I thought you were Dean," I explain.

She grins mischievously. "Sorry to disappoint you."

"No, I wasn't saying that," I argue, walking out of the bathroom and flopping down onto my bunk. "Shouldn't you be with Pete, I don't know, with your tongue stuck down his throat or something?"

"Ugh," she huffs. "Don't get me started." She moves into the kitchenette area and pulls out a jar of Nutella and bread. Storm amazingly always eats like a twelve year old, when she eats at all.

"Uh oh, trouble in paradise?" I inquire, shifting on my bunk so I can maintain eye contact.

"What's wrong with men?" she growls, before continuing with her story in the very next breath, wildly waving the Nutella-covered knife as she relays her frustrations. "I mean, really? At what point in life do you grow a pair and start acting like a man? It was hard enough to get Pete to admit how he felt about me, but when my brother says something, he tells me he needs to think about things."

"I'm sorry, sweetie," I answer sympathetically, making sure I'm not smiling from my lingering Dean buzz.

"There's nothing to think about. He knows how he feels; he's just too much of a damn coward to own up to it. And who the hell does Andrew think he is? He has no right," Storm snaps, dropping the knife into the sink and pressing together the slathered slices of bread. She rips off a chunk with her teeth, releasing a deep moan.

"He's your brother, and he loves you, that's all," I attempt to reassure her.

"Please," she huffs with a full mouth, shifting the food into her cheek. "Do I stick my nose into his business? How about the fact that he has slept with about three-dozen different women on this trip? Nope, I keep my trap shut, even though that is absolutely disgusting."

"That is disgusting." I crinkle my nose. Storm starts laughing, and I quickly join her. "Just give Pete some time, he'll come around. Some men are scared to admit their feelings ... I don't get it either."

Storm tears off another monstrous bite of her sandwich, chews and swallows, leaning against the wall of windows across from my bunk. "You're lucky, you got Dean."

I smile and sigh. "I am pretty lucky, aren't I?"

Storm and I both turn our heads immediately toward the tinted windows, a commotion stealing our attention from the conversation. She heads for the door, and I'm on her heels in only a moment's time.

"What the hell is going on?" she yells to one of the roadies running by.

He shakes his head and raises his hands in bewilderment, continuing in the direction of the crowd gathering at the street. "Some sort of accident."

Storm steps off the bus completely, and I'm now standing directly next to her. "Do you see Dean anywhere?" I ask, my heartbeat quickening.

Storm looks around wildly. "No."

I look back in the direction of the crowd. Christian is running toward us, and he's yelling something, but I can't make it out.

"What?" I plead. I can feel vomit climbing up my throat.

"Call 9-1-1," he yells again, pausing and looking to us for confirmation of his instructions.

"What do I tell them?" I ask, the phone already in my hand, dialing.

"There's been an accident with a motorcycle," he replies, and then he's gone. Before I can process his statement and ask any of the million questions in my mind, he's gone.

This isn't happening. This isn't real. Everything is okay. It's someone else. It's not him.

"Mac!" Storm yells. "Mac! They're on the phone." Her words are not registering. I feel the phone in my hand one moment and then not the next. I see Storm talking on it, but I can't hear what she's saying. The blood is surging in my ears, drowning out all other noises.

I'm shaking; my legs feel as though they might give out on me at any moment. I sit down at the foot of the bus steps, directly on the gravel of the parking lot. I place my hands on the ground, hoping for a comforting coolness, but the grit of the gravel gives me no relief.

My entire world begins to shift violently. He's late. He should have been here by now. Motorcycle accident ... you know what that means. You're cursed. You killed him.

I let out a strangled sob; the scene around me is a total blur. I see glimpses of Storm in my face, waving her hands. She's saying something, but it's making no sense. I can feel her shaking my body, but I can't seem to will myself to look at her.

I can't do this again. The pain nearly killed me the first time. How can God be this cruel?

"Baby?" A voice breaks through the panic. "Come on, look at me. Macaroon? Are you in there?"

Pressing my eyes shut for several moments, I try to pull myself out of the haze. When I reopen them, Dean is looking into my eyes. I can't speak; all I can do is pull him into my body. His arms are wrapped tightly around me, and as he rocks me, I dig my fingers into his back, too scared to let go.

I watch him as he looks up at Storm. "I was in the shower ... what's going on?"

"Christian said it was a motorcycle accident, and I just called 9-1-1," she explains as Dean helps me to my feet.

"What? Pete—" Dean gasps.

Storm looks at Dean, her eyes wide and crazy, and asks, "What about him?"

"I lent him my bike." He doesn't even finish getting the words out before his hands release me and he takes off at full speed in the direction of the crowd.

"What did he say?" There's a panic in Storm's voice that I know all too well.

"I'm sure it's not—" She doesn't wait for me to reassure

her. She is now running after Dean in the direction of the chaos. I do my best to keep pace with her, and with every step praying for her that it's not him.

The other car comes into view first. A shattered windshield, a dented hood, and what's left of a motorcycle under the tires. There's an older gentleman with salt and pepper hair standing next to the driver's side door, clutching a bleeding wound on his forehead. People are talking to him, keeping him occupied, but the scene fifteen feet away distracts him.

I push my way through the crowd, staying close to Storm, my chest tightening around my heart as I hear her repeating the words, "No, dear God no, not him." I know those words; I've said them too many times in my lifetime.

Breaking through the front of the crowd, I see the lights of an ambulance coming in the distance. Storm screams, I grab her arm, pulling her close to me, and the horror comes into view for me as well.

We see glimpses of Pete's body between the circle of people. Christian and Dean are at his side, along with a smattering of people I don't know.

"We have to stay here," I tell her. "He's going to be all right." I feel like I'm lying. In my experience, people are never all right. Dean looks over his shoulder and sees me struggling to hold onto Storm.

In an instant he's at our side, pulling Storm into his arms, squeezing her firmly. Gripping her cheeks, he pulls her red and swollen face upright so their eyes meet. "I'm not going to let anything happen to him. He needs you, all right?"

Storm nods, and I watch in awe as Dean takes control.

"I need you to go with Mac, okay? You're going to take one of the vans, get some of Pete's things together, and you're going to meet us at the hospital. I'll go in the ambulance with him."

"But—" Storm starts.

"Shh," he hushes her, "trust me."

She pushes the tears off her cheeks with the heels of her hands, acknowledging him again with a nod before turning to me.

"Ready?" I ask her.

"Yeah," she breathes.

Dean squeezes my arm, and then he's back at Pete's side. I take Storm's hand into mine and guide her through the crowd to do exactly as Dean instructed us to do.

———

TWENTY-FIVE

I KNOW, firsthand, that hospital waiting rooms are hard. I'd been spared the wait when I lost my Travis and Katie Bird, but the hours leading up to my mother's death were long. My father lived on machines for three days after his heart attack, but he never regained consciousness. There are different kinds of waiting. There are the people waiting to find out what might be wrong with them, there are the people waiting and hoping their loved ones will be all right, and then there are those who know nothing is going to be all right, and they are waiting for death to take their loved ones.

There was a reason Dean gave me this job. He entrusted me with the responsibility of keeping her focus anywhere but on the fact that the man she loved was probably dying. We start at his bus, pack his belongings. While there, Andrew finds us, but Storm is in no shape to deal with the feelings she has about everything. I assure him I'll take care of her.

When we leave, the ambulance is already gone. Storm panics, wanting to be at his side. I convince her he will want comforts when he wakes up, and that we should stop by the store to pick up some of his favorite treats, perhaps a magazine. The idea of him being conscious enough to read seems to calm her.

But now I've done all the stalling I can. Our purchases are made, and she demands to be taken to the hospital. She knows I'll comply. I rush in behind her, but I know there is no reason to rush. No matter how bad you want answers, they take forever to come.

We walk into the main room, where there is a huge desk in front of us with two nurses sitting behind it. One is on the phone, while the other is speaking to a mother who is rocking her sleeping toddler in her arms. Storm is pacing in short strides. I place a hand on her back, trying to comfort her, but I know nothing can comfort you in a time like this.

As the woman on the phone hangs up, Storm rushes to her, pleading for information. She is told there is no news and to take a seat in the waiting room. This flusters her, but we have no choice. We choose one of the large rooms full of other waiting people and sit down. Storm fidgets, and I wish more than anything I could make it easier for her.

From where we sit, we can see directly into the emergency room every time the doors swing open. When this happens it's impossible not to hold your breath and prepare yourself for a glimpse of the worst. There's a bustle of activity, doctors and nurses in their various colors of uniforms moving around, in and out, all with an important mission on their mind.

"Why won't they tell us something?" Storm whimpers.

"I'm sorry, sweetie. They'll come tell us when they know something, I'm sure."

"If he's dead, just tell me," her voice cracks.

"Don't!" I exclaim. "Don't think like that." Though I already am.

The door swings out again, and Dean emerges. He's looking around the room, a worn and weary expression on his face. Storm hops to her feet, and I next to her. He sees us, rushing across the room to join us.

Scooping Storm's hand into his own, he guides her back to a seated position.

"What's going on?" she cries.

Dean stares at Storm, and, squeezing her hand, he tells her, "Pete's going to be fine. His hip is pretty messed up, some cracked ribs, but he's lucky."

"Oh thank God," Storm moans.

Dean keeps talking to her, but I'm no longer paying attention. He's going to be fine? People are never fine. His words make no sense to me. When people get hurt or sick, they die, that's just how it is. Or perhaps that is just how it is when it comes to me. Had Dean been the one in that accident, he wouldn't have survived, simply because I love him. Dear God, I love him. I can't ... but I think I do ... and people I love die.

TWENTY-SIX

ALL THE DATES for the next week have been rescheduled while Dean and the rest of the band audition replacements for Pete. There's no way he will be able to rejoin the tour. Storm was next to him when he woke up, and like a lightning bolt of clarity, Pete didn't have any more thinking to do about them. He professed his love instantly. She'll be staying here, helping him with his recovery, until he's strong enough to head back to his home in Atlanta.

Dean's time has been filled with tour details and visiting Pete as often as possible. I don't mind; it's given me a chance to think about everything I almost lost—time to think about what would happen to me if I did lose Dean, like I lost Travis. Most importantly, time to make one of the hardest decisions I've ever made in my life.

I slip the letter into the envelope, lick the flap, and press it shut. In it, I thank Dean for helping me heal. For caring so deeply about me and letting me be there for him as well. And then I tell him I have to go. I've learned I'm capable of being happy, but I've also learned I'm still searching for what I want my new life to look like. I close with the line I hope you understand. Which I know he won't.

I pull out my phone and dial Monica's number. The taxi is already on its way.

"Hey!" she exclaims as she answers the phone. "I was just thinking about you. How's your friend doing?"

"Good, he should make a full recovery," I reply.

She sighs in relief. "Thank God."

"Yeah," I add in a whisper.

"What's going on?"

"Is there still room in your apartment for me?"

"What?"

"I want to come home," I answer firmly.

"What about Dean?" she asks.

"He'll understand."

"I don't. Why are you coming home?" she presses.

"The tour ends in a month anyway," I say defensively.

"So why come home now? Did something happen with Dean?"

"I made a mistake." My voice cracks. "I'm not ready for this." I don't hide the fear in my tone; I want her to know how much I need to come back.

"You know you're always welcome, but I think you should talk to Dean first."

"I will," I lie to her. I have no intention of talking to Dean. "Can you pick me up from the bus station tonight?"

"Yeah, of course, just call me when you're getting close."

"Okay, I will. Love you."

"Mac," she quickly adds, "are you sure about this?"

I swallow hard. "Positive."

THERE'S a honk outside of the bus. I grab my suitcases and drop them at the bottom of the stairs. Turning around, I prop two envelopes against the steps so they are visible when you enter; one for Christian and the other for Dean.

"Where are you going?" I hear behind me. My heart catches in my throat. I turn and see Christian looking back at me, his eyes shifting from the cab, to my bags, to my face.

I lose control at the look in his eyes; the tears I've been fighting back begin to fall. "I have to go."

He shakes his head. "Go where?"

"Home."

"Did something happen?"

"I made some meals. They're in our kitchenette fridge," I say, handing my bags to the cab driver.

Christian moves closer. "You didn't answer me ... why are you going?" I see his eyes connect with the envelopes. "You weren't going to say anything?" There is so much hurt in his voice I feel sick to my stomach.

"I can't do this anymore." My voice is shaking.

"Mac, this will kill him."

"No—I'll kill him."

"What are you talking about?"

"I'm not ready. I thought I was, but I'm not," I plead.

"He deserves to hear it from you."

"I can't. If I talk to him, he'll persuade me to stay," I explain.

"Maybe that means you shouldn't be going."

"When Pete was—I—" Swallowing hard, I try to think of the words to tell him the way my world almost ended again. The way everything began to spiral out of control.

"Dean's fine. Pete's fine. I don't understand."

"This time!" I shout.

"So you're leaving because you're scared of what might

happen?" Christian argues. "Do you know how crazy that sounds?"

"Please, just trust me, I have to go," I reply.

Christian looks over his shoulder. I wonder if he is contemplating running for Dean. He looks back to me. "Are you sure?"

I nod. "Yes."

He opens his arms and pulls me in for a hug. "I wish you'd stay. I think this is a mistake, but I love you, and I know you wouldn't do this to him if you thought you had a choice." I think his words are meant to make me realize how selfish I'm being, but I've made up my mind. Nothing will change it. Love doesn't set you free ... it only complicates things.

Dean may deserve to know that I'm leaving, and he also may deserve to know why, but I can't tell him. I'm not strong enough to face him. "I better go ... I don't want to miss my bus."

"Call us?"

"I promise." I smile, squeezing Christian close to me before slipping into the cab and watching my new life disappear behind me. I'm going home, back to where it's just Buttons and me, my comforting recliner, and a familiar pain rather than a new one.

TWENTY-SEVEN

"ONE TICKET TO CINCINNATI, OHIO PLEASE," I say to the woman on the other side of the glass window. She chomps on her gum, somehow making clicking noises between motions. I've been staring at the bulky red rims of her glasses since I got in line. The way she peers at me over the top of the lenses, I'm certain she knows all of my secrets. She knows what a terrible person I am. She knows that I just left, without so much as a goodbye, the only man who has loved me since my husband. I want her to judge me; she should. I deserve it.

"One way?" she asks with a nasal pitch.

I nod, sliding her a credit card before she tells me the total. It doesn't matter what it costs. I need to be anywhere but here, in the same city as Dean. Distance from him will make me stronger. Distance from him will keep my heart safe—will keep him safe.

She mutters the total and a few pieces of information I should know during my travels. I sign the receipt, sliding it back to her. She returns to me my card and ticket. I look at the face of the ticket, staring at the words: Cincinnati, Ohio. I sigh a breath of relief. I'm going home.

Smiling, I say thank you and turn toward the signs on the wall of the bus station. My connection isn't loading yet. Glancing around the lobby, I see a number of hard plastic chairs to choose from. I find one with a comfortable number of buffer seats between myself and anyone else. Dragging my suitcases behind me, I take a seat in one of the chairs that has been bolted to the chairs around it.

I half-smile at a teen girl sitting diagonal from me. Shifting in my chair, I turn my body in the opposite direction of her prying eyes. The entire station smells like a stale gym locker. I can feel my hair sucking in the moisture from the air, and my skin feels dewy.

I click the screen on my phone to check the time. I silenced it in the cab when I saw Dean was trying to call me. I'm not sure if Christian told him I was leaving, but based on his repeated attempts, he knows I'm gone. The bus is scheduled to leave in thirty-five minutes. I'm surprised they haven't started boarding yet. I glance back at the sign, but still no change.

The last thing I want to think about right now is Dean. I'm leaving ... this had to end eventually. I'm making it easier. But going home means I have more choices. I still don't want to live with Monica's roommates or Percy. Maybe I should return to culinary school; I only had one semester left. Once I finish, a job in a restaurant I would actually enjoy cooking in shouldn't be too hard to find.

You'll work. You'll get a job, you'll get an apartment, you'll work, and you'll survive. You're a survivor. I silently tell myself all of this.

I watch as the girl who has been staring at me stands and chucks her empty soda can into a recycling bin. From the expression on her face, I can tell she is no stranger to unhappiness. I can't help wonder what has made her look such a way. Her eyes shift in my direction, and I quickly look away. Does she see the same sadness when she looks at me?

The girl walks across the room, and I watch her. I shift, trying to keep track of her, but someone passes in front of me, blocking my line of sight. He doesn't move; in fact, he stops directly in front of me. I lean to the side, not taking my eyes from the girl. She is talking to a couple other teens now, another girl and two boys.

"MacKenzie."

My heart stops beating, my head begins to spin, and in that moment I am certain time has stopped. The world is no longer turning, and at any second we will lose gravity. My eyes shift to the person standing in front of me—Dean. He's looking at me; his eyes are red, bloodshot, his face sad.

I stand and gasp for air. Oxygen is key to making it through this conversation. "You shouldn't be here."

"I shouldn't be here?" he repeats, his voice heavy with disbelief. He pulls out the letter from his pocket.

I shake my head. "I meant to be gone by the time you found that."

"Wow, that makes me feel so much better," he snaps, his jaw tightening.

I lean down, taking my suitcases in hand. I can't do this. "I have to go," I say, unaware if we are even boarding yet.

He grabs my arm. "No, you're not leaving."

"You're hurting me."

He loosens his grip but doesn't release me. "Like you're hurting me?"

"Don't do this," I whisper, certain everyone is staring.

"You're not leaving like this," he informs me.

I yank my arm sharply from his grasp, gripping my bags and making my way around the seats. I drag my luggage to an area just before the doors that exit to the loading area. I can feel Dean close behind me.

"You have to talk to me."

I turn and face him; he's not going to make this easy for me. "The letter says it all."

"This letter doesn't say shit," he huffs, crumpling it into a ball.

"I was going home in a month anyway when the tour was over. I'm just ending it a little early." I try my best to explain.

"Are you calling your job it or our relationship it?"

I shrug. "Both."

He throws the paper in a nearby trashcan, then runs his hands through his hair. "I don't even know how to react to this."

"I knew you'd be this way ... that's why I wrote it all down."

"You knew I'd be upset that my girlfriend is walking out on me." When he calls me his girlfriend I feel my heart wither.

"Pete's accident got me thinking..." I don't tell him what it actually got me thinking about. "I have my life in Ohio. When this tour is over, you'll go back to Georgia so you can visit your mom."

"And you just decided that?"

"Dean, you know she needs you. You have to go."

"Fine, let's say she does ... haven't you ever heard of a long distance relationship? We can make it work," he argues.

I step forward, take his hand into mine, and muster all my strength to say, "I'm just now dealing with the idea of dating after being a widow. The last thing I can handle is a long distance relationship."

"Aren't I worth trying?" he asks, his eyes full of hope ... or maybe it's desperation. I can't be sure.

"It's not that easy," I insist. God, why can't you just let me leave?

"Then maybe you're right ... maybe we should be done, because it's that easy for me. I love you, and I'd do anything to make it work." As he speaks, I feel like if I move, my entire body might shatter into a million pieces.

Stop saying you love me! I want to shout. You're making goodbye so much harder.

"We're now boarding for Cincinnati," a gentleman calls from the double doors to my right. I glance over at the sign and see the update.

"Don't go," he pleads.

"I can't do this ... not right now," I say, trying to convince myself as well. I know this makes sense. This relationship is far more complicated than anything I can handle in my life right now.

"What if I gave you a reason to stay?"

"Don't do this, please. I'm not going to change my mind."

"What if I told you that when I met you, I decided you were it? I married you in my head, we bought a house, we had kids, and both were blessed with your beauty. In an instant, a blink, I lived our whole lives. We grow old together, I promise, I've seen it."

"You're crazy," I whisper, secretly wishing he were holding me.

"Crazy about you. Let me love you."

I'm physically shaking. I want to fall in his arms and kiss him, tell him I'll never leave him, but he can't make those promises. A daydream he saw in his mind isn't reality. Reality is full of broken promises, and death, and loneliness.

"Stop!" I shout. I know people are staring now. I grip my bags tightly. You can do this. You're strong enough. Just take that first step. I turn and walk to the doors. Don't look back. Don't look back. Don't look back.

"Macaroon," his voice is tender as he calls after me. Don't look back, I tell myself again.

I pause, but I don't turn around. I take a deep breath and walk forward. I'm going home, knowing a little pain now is better than an agonizing pain later.

TWENTY-EIGHT

IT'S BEEN two weeks since I came home. Monica's room-mates aren't hiding the fact that they want me gone. I even heard Claire grumbling about how I keep milking this widow thing, and someone needs to tell me to get over it. God, I hate them.

I almost broke down a couple nights ago and called Dean. I know he's the last person in the world I should be speaking to. Maintaining clarity when it involves him is next to impossible. I avoid the grocery store where I met Christian because that led me to Dean. I don't even drive near the Brewery District, because that's where I inter-viewed with him. Yet no matter how hard I've tried to avoid these memories, they seem to keep finding their way in.

I started working on my application to finish culinary school. It's a welcome distraction. Sometimes I think life is normal again, but then I realize I've never had what one could call a normal life. There has always been some disaster lurking around the corner.

I can tell when Monica and Percy look at me, they can see there is a new brokenness inside of me, but they don't ask. I think they're afraid if they do, I might leave, or come completely unraveled and turn back into the shell of a person I was before. You're home now. Breathe. Slow down. Take the time to figure who you are now, what you want, I tell myself.

Pulling into the parking spot in front of the downtown office building where Monica works, even the wrecked state of my car leads me back down the road to memories of Dean. Shaking my head, as if I'm trying to shake away the past, I step out of my car and feed the meter. Monica thinks I'm here to have lunch with her, but the true reason I've come is to tell her I'm moving in with Percy.

I never thought that was something I would decide to do, but the distaste I once had for her has begun to fade. I know if my dad can see me from wherever he is, it would mean a lot to him if I made an effort in developing a relationship with my sisters. I love Mon, but this is something I have to do. Plus, I would use any excuse to get Buttons and me away from her wretched roommates.

"Hey beautiful," I hear my friend's voice call out from behind me. Spinning around to face her, I beam the best smile I can.

"Sorry I'm late," I offer.

"You wouldn't be Mac if you weren't late." I grin, knowing the reputation is deserved. Her pencil skirt accentuates her slim waist, and the sheer blouse reveals just enough of her neck to show off her creamy and perfect skin. "How about Tom and Chee?"

I look at her, as if shocked by the suggestion. "Are you feeling okay?"

"What?" she defends.

"You never suggest anywhere that isn't extremely fancy."

"Sometimes a girl needs a grilled cheese doughnut sandwich."

I laugh. "So true." I'm the last one who could ever judge someone for needing a little comfort food.

We turn to walk around the corner to the grilled cheese and soup franchise. I can feel Monica looking at me.

"Okay, what's up?" I ask.

"Are you ever going to tell me what happened?"

"What are you talking about?" I question, even though I already know the answer.

"Oh, come on, it's been two weeks since you came home, and you've barely said a word about what happened. Was it all crazy rock-and-roll drug scene or something?"

I'm laughing again. "No, they were all really great."

"Then why leave?"

I pull open the door to the restaurant and wait for my friend to lead. It had been so clear when I left why I'd made the choice, but now that seems less and less clear to me. "I was coming home soon anyway, so I don't see what the big deal is."

"Oh, you must think I'm pretty stupid. That's exactly why I know something happened; you would have finished out the last month otherwise," she presses, moving into line and glancing up at the chalk menu on the wall.

"I don't know, I guess I realized that the sooner I got back here, the sooner I could actually restart my life."

"Restart your life ... what in the hell does that even mean?" Monica scoffs, then leans in and places her order.

"It means that things started getting a little too intense out there. If I had stayed, it would have been even harder when it was time to come home."

"That's what I figured," she grumbles under her breath.

"What's that supposed to mean?" I snap, signaling to the man who is ready to take my order to wait a moment.

"Just order," she huffs. I turn and look at the now terrified looking man. I rattle off my order, hand him my payment, and move down the line. We pick up our number and, after a moment of searching, find a small booth to wait for our orders to be delivered.

I sit down, and stare intensely at her. "Now will you please tell me what you meant?" I ask through gritted teeth.

"I kind of thought it was about Dean, but I wasn't sure until just now."

"You think you know everything, don't you?"

"Am I wrong?"

I pause. "Well, you're not exactly right."

"So tell me, what exactly happened?"

I bite my lip; I need to talk to someone about this. "I told you about Pete and the motorcycle accident, right?"

"Yeah, but you said Pete was fine."

"He is," I continue. "But it started me thinking."

"We know that's always dangerous."

"Ha ha, now shut up. When the accident first happened I thought it had been Dean who was on the bike. I was certain he was dead. It was like I was right back there, the night of the accident with Travis and Katie."

"But sweetie, it wasn't him."

"Well, I know that now." I sigh. "That's just it, though; that panic I felt got me thinking. What if something happens to Dean ... will I be able to handle losing someone again?"

"So what? You're going to be alone for the rest of your life?"

"I don't know, maybe. It's not just that, Mon. I was heading home in a month—my home, the place with my friends, my family, my life. Was he just going to abandon his mother, his friends, his entire life, and come live here? Was I really going to tackle a long distance relationship? It made me start asking the really tough questions."

"Like what?"

"Like what do I want to do with my life?"

"And?"

"And what?" I furrow my brow.

"What do you want to do with your life?"

"Oh—truthfully?" She nods. "I've been thinking a lot about that the past couple weeks. Some of the happiest times of my life were when I was working in the kitchen of our family restaurant. I want to get a job as a chef so I can save up enough money to open up my own place."

"Are you serious?" I can't tell from her tone how she feels about the idea.

"What? You don't like it?"

"Mac, this is exactly what I've been hoping for the past three years."

My heart nearly leaps out of my chest. An older woman with a tight blond ponytail comes around to our table and exchanges our numbers for baskets of food. I take in a deep breath; the guilty pleasure sitting in front of me is practically calling my name.

I take a monstrous bite of the grilled cheese sandwich, chew, and swallow. "I've even come up with a name ... Katie Bird's."

Monica tilts her head, and I see her eyes begin to glisten. "I love it." Her voice is nearly a whisper as she takes an extra long blink.

"So what about Dean?" she asks, ripping off a bite of her food.

"There's nothing to say about him. I made my choice

pretty clear to him. Besides, I'm starting to think we get one shot at this love thing. I had mine and that's that."

"I hope you change your mind one day about the love part, but I am super excited about the restaurant idea. I'll even be an investor."

"What?" I gasp.

"Sure. You grew up around the business, and you're the most amazing cook I've ever known, so I'd be foolish not to get in on the idea."

"I don't think we're anywhere near that, but thank you." I smile at her. If it weren't for my sticky fingers I would give her a huge hug right now.

"How much will you need?"

"Best guess, if I want to open up in the Gateway District ... $150,000 ... maybe a little less." I shrug.

"Holy shit," Monica gasps.

"That's if they will finance the build-out over the lease too."

She's thinking—thinking hard. At last, she looks at me seriously and says, "I can get you $35,000."

I laugh. "What? Don't be silly. I won't be able to do this for years. It takes planning and money, and a lot of work."

"I bet we can find other investors."

"Where?" I inquire sarcastically.

"I don't know, but you'll see, I'll figure this out."

"Eat your grilled cheese doughnut sandwich, freak."

"You'll see," she reassures.

TWENTY-NINE

I NIBBLE on the corner of the bacon and avocado sandwich I made for myself. Percy is busy moving around the kitchen, sweeping up the crumbs from my prep work into her open palm. I watch her intensely, wishing she would sit down, or leave, or anything but the constant pacing she has been doing all morning.

"I'll get it after I eat ... leave it," I offer.

Her back stiffens, she looks at me, and smiles. "I don't mind."

I sigh. I squeeze out a smile and take a bite of my sandwich, careful to make sure the plate catches the crumbs. She's looking at me. Something's eating at her, that much is clear. I've been living with her a few days now, and I can already tell something is different. She still has many of the annoying habits I've always hated, like her incessant need to clean, but there has been a distinct shift in her attitude. She's confident in a different way. When I see her talk to my sisters, she's a leader. I can see that she has picked up strength in a tragedy that caused me to fall apart. Of course she had living children to go on for; when I lost my life, I lost all of it.

"Have you heard back from school?" Percy asks, resting on her forearms in front of me.

I shake my head. "No, but I doubt I will for a few weeks."

She nods, then asks, "So, how did Monica take it?"

"Take what?"

"When you told her you were moving back in here."

I think about my friend's expression when I broke the news. There was no arguing, no trying to persuade me to stay; I even think I saw the hint of a smile. "Surprisingly well. My guess is she's tired of all the grief her roommates are giving her."

"The more you tell me about those girls, the more I can't stand them. I do not understand why someone as sweet as Monica continues to live with them."

"Because she insists on living in a downtown condo, and those bitches are the only ones who can afford to live with her," I explain confidently.

Percy laughs. "Doesn't seem worth it to me."

"Me neither," I agree.

"The girls and I are really happy you're here, you know that, right?"

I nod, remaining silent. I give another half-smile, popping a fallen slice of avocado into my mouth. I wouldn't admit it to her, but it's actually not been that bad. Last night we even sat around playing Cards Against Humanity. I never realized just how much my sisters were like me.

"You know, Monica told me about your restaurant idea," Percy says with a huge grin, eyebrows raised. And suddenly the pacing becomes clear. This is what she has been wanting to talk about and has been waiting for the perfect moment to bring up.

I swallow the dry bite of food, take a gulp of water, and ask, "She what?"

"Don't be mad at her, she's excited for you. I am too."

"For what? There's nothing to be excited about," I insist. "It's a pipe dream. It'll probably never even happen."

"Why would you say that?" Percy asks, maneuvering around the counter and taking a seat on the bar stool next to me.

"Money, for starters; I need to finish culinary school if I want a decent local restaurant to hire me. And then, after years of sweat and tears maybe I will save up enough to put a down payment on a place and go beg an investor to chip in the rest, but it rarely happens."

"That seems silly to me."

"My dream?" I gasp in disbelief.

"No!" she exclaims. "That you would have to go through all that to bring your food to the world. I mean, you know how to cook. You're better than anyone else I've ever known. You already have a lot of schooling, and you have real life experience."

I shake my head at her naivety. "It's not that easy, and it takes a lot of money."

"Well, I think we can help you get there much faster," Percy says, trembling with excitement. I think she may burst into a million pieces at any moment.

I laugh, and ask, "What are you talking about?" Then I shove the last bite of my lunch into my mouth as I wait for her to explain.

Percy raises her hands up, waving them wildly as she talks, "When Monica told me about your idea we started talking. She thinks she can come up with another $5,000, so she would be in for $40,000."

My brow wrinkles. "Yeah, I really appreciate her saying that, but that's not nearly enough. Even if I found a space ready to roll, I would need some runway cash to keep things running. There's all kinds of stuff to consider."

"Like what?" Her eyes widen in anticipation. I decide to humor her.

Taking another swig of my water, I suck out the food particles stuck between my teeth, then turn to face her. "All right, I would need industrial cooking and ventilation equipment, refrigerators, freezers, not to mention, tables, bar stools, shelving, counters, prep stations, stock the kitchen, and who knows what else depending on the space; that's also not including licensing and inspections."

"Would $105,000 be enough?" She looks away as she asks me.

Rolling my eyes, I scoff, "It might as well be a million."

"Would it be enough, MacKenzie?" she presses.

I huff, "Fine, sure, yeah, if we really tightened the budget and maybe found a place with a little higher rent that already had some of the equipment we need, we could probably pull it off."

"I have a buyer for your dad's car..." She's watching me, her mouth hanging open, waiting for my reaction.

"What?" The word slips out as a near whisper. I think my heart may have quit beating.

"Apparently a 1960 Corvette Convertible that's been fully restored to original condition goes for quite a bit on the classic car market," she continues.

"No, you can't be serious." I push myself back from the counter and stand up. I need to stand before I fall off the stool.

"I am. When Monica told me about your idea, all I could think about is how much your dad would have loved to see you do that. Then I thought about the car and asked a friend to look into it for me. He said he found a buyer willing to pay us $65,000."

"No, you can't," I argue.

"Why can't I? You and I both know that it's just going to sit in that garage gathering dust," Percy pushes back.

"But ... you need that for the girls."

She reaches out and grabs hold of my arm. "Mac, I had a small life insurance policy on your dad; it's not much, but we're getting by for now, and besides, I'm going back to get my real estate license."

"You are?" I tilt my head, shocked by this information.

She nods with a slight smile, her cheeks flushed. "I always wanted to, but your dad wanted me home with the girls."

"Really?" I'm having trouble wrapping my head around the information.

"Yes, so please, trust me, we'll be fine. Besides, as an investor in Katie Bird's, I think the girls and I should see a nice return, don't you?" she continues, giggling in excitement. "I was thinking about it, and I figure we split the value from the sale of the car four ways—myself and you three girls get equal shares. I feel like your dad was telling me to do this."

"I can't..." My mouth is hanging pen, I'm shaking my head, steadying myself on the countertop.

"And why not?" She looks hurt.

"Because I can't," I insist.

"That doesn't sound like much of a reason to me."

"Fine, how about I'm not ready. Dad loved that car, and what if I fail?" I'm shaking.

Percy stands and walks up to me wrapping a tender arm around my back. "Sweetie, you have family, friends, and now investors. I'd say you're more than ready."

"I'm scared," I whisper.

"I know, isn't it great?"

I laugh; she's right. It's awful and exhilarating all at the same time. "I don't know."

"I do, and it's going to be amazing. I'm honored to help you. Your sisters are already talking about working there with you," Percy says.

"Seriously?"

"It will be just like when you were little—a family business."

"I don't know what to say,"

"Say you'll do it."

My heart is aching. I want to cry out 'no,' tell her I won't do it—can't fail everyone. But the adrenaline is pumping, drowning out the doubt just enough to get me to say, "Okay, let's do it."

Percy releases a high-pitched squeal, throwing her arms around my neck and squeezing firmly.

"Oh God," I moan.

"What?" Percy stops, staring at me with nervous eyes.

"Now we have an entire menu to plan."

"Oh my God! We're actually doing this."

"I guess we are," I confirm with wide eyes.

THIRTY

PULLING from my trunk the handmade basket I picked up at one of the farmer's markets while on tour, I turn and walk in the direction of the market place. One of the things I used to love doing with Travis and Katie was visiting a local historic fixture in the city called Findlay Market.

As one of Ohio's oldest public markets, it's the place to go to find locally sourced goods. It's only blocks from downtown and the space we found for the restaurant. For weeks I've been building relationships with the local farmers and butchers who sell out of the location.

When Travis and I first started coming to the market it was struggling—an area of the city that had been neglected and forgotten by time. I wish he could see it now. Since the gentrification efforts, it has become a gathering place for friends and families. Sometimes I like to come and just sit on a bench and people watch. I can forget how diverse and amazing this city is in the hustle and bustle of my day-to-day life. Who would have ever thought my life that used to be filled with tubs of ice cream and reality television would be this full again.

Today, however, I'm on a mission; there is no time to sit and take in my surroundings. We were lucky enough to find a space for Katie Bird's that already had the majority of the equipment we needed for our kitchen. Besides a major facelift on the place, there would be very little large equipment to invest in. Things have been moving so rapidly. It's hard to believe it's already time to bring in tasters.

I've prepared menu choices that are about double what we will actually offer once the doors open. Monica handled the invitations. Over one hundred people will stream in and out of Katie Bird's tomorrow, tasting our food and completing a survey on what they like and don't like. This will help us fine-tune the menu to what the majority of our customers want.

My first panic attack was when I found out we wouldn't even have our tables in before the event. It's very much still a white box—and simply another instance of why I'm so thankful for Monica and my stepmom. Percy stepped up immediately and started making phone calls. She rented tables with linens for a buffet-style set up, along with some cocktail tables for people to set their plates and taste while standing.

I would have served everyone sitting down at tables. With Percy's genius thinking, standing will encourage them to taste and move on quickly so we can fit the next wave of people in the door. The more feedback cards I receive the better informed I will be, helping me to make the best choices for opening night.

As the fall has descended on us, the outdoor booths at the market have retreated into the indoor space. Taking a deep breath, I pull open the heavy metal door and stand at the end of the long aisle, drinking in the various options in front of me. As a chef it's like a utopia. The shop menu will change based on the season and local foods that are available.

In front of me are a number of various shops, from butchers to those serving confectionary delights. A smile makes its way across my face. It's hard for me to believe sometimes, but I am actually doing this. I wake up every day with a purpose. Katie Bird's has become a part of me. There are a million things to consider and some days I only manage to fit in a few hours of sleep, but I love it. I love everything about it.

In the next case I find bread pudding, pecan tarts, buckeyes, chocolate chip cookies, and ... macaroons. When my eyes catch the colorful version of the treat I freeze. I can't move. Dean's voice is replaying in my head, the way he whispers my nickname. The way he kisses me. The way my skin feels under his touch.

Every fiber of my being wants to call Dean—just like it has almost every day for the past six months. I want to hear his voice. I want to tell him about the restaurant. I want to share every detail with him from the menu choices to the decorating Percy has been working on. Sometimes it feels like none of this is real because I'm not sharing it with him. And, in a way, that infuriates me.

It's not Dean's fault, and I know that. It's something broken inside me. I've had a lot of time to reflect. I've realized that the way I used to be wasn't healthy. The person I was with defined me. If I didn't have someone to call mine, then I was nothing. This is why, when I lost Travis, I became nothing. A complete waste to those around me. I never want to be that type of person again. I want to be strong. I want to be independent. You are strong. You are independent. You're opening your own restaurant.

Dean is beautiful and sweet and perfect in so many

ways. Even his life scars make him seem more appealing. And that is the exact reason I can't pick up the phone. I can't call him. I can't share all of this with him. I'm not strong enough to lose the little bit of self I've found inside of him.

I force myself to continue moving, continue my job, continue this journey, all on my own. This is the only way. I look at the list in my hand. It's time to get started.

THIRTY-ONE

I LOOK AROUND, ensuring that all of the linens are pulled into their proper place, the chairs are under the tables, the flatware is in the perfect position. Taking a deep breath, I take a step back and drink it all in.

My eyes lock on the freshly applied logo on the door of the small restaurant; it's very similar to the bird tattoo on my arm. The tattoo Dean took me to get.

Damn it, I'm doing it again. Come on! It's been seven months; you need to get him out of your head.

I thought the night of the soft opening would be the most stressed out I had ever been. After all, all of the food critics and press from the city were there to critique my work. They were all eagerly waiting to tell the world how I'd failed and to stay away from this restaurant at all costs. I haven't actually seen any of the stories yet, but I've convinced myself this is what they must all think. But somehow, tonight, the grand opening of Katie Bird's, is stressing me out even more. This will be the truth. Tonight will be the regular people—the customers who will either love me and help us succeed, or hate the experience and sink us in an instant.

Keys jingle in the front door; I look up to see Monica entering. She slips inside, her purse and a paper tucked under one arm. She locks the door behind her and crosses the long and narrow dining room. I smile.

"You're freaking out, aren't you?" She grins.

"What? Why on earth would I be freaking out?" I ask, my heart racing.

"Oh, please, I know you too well," she answers, dropping her purse and paper on the bar.

"Okay, maybe I'm freaking out a little," I confirm.

"Is someone here?" Percy calls, emerging from the kitchen. "Monica!" They greet each other with a hug. In the past seven months, the support of Katie Bird's has somehow created this super weird friendship between my stepmother and best friend. I've found it easier to try and ignore it.

"Percy, this place looks amazing," Monica nearly squeals. "I still can't get over the fact you found all these farm chairs at a flea market—they're amazing."

"Aw, shucks, thanks." My stepmother waves a hand playfully in the air as she speaks in her best Southern accent.

"Do you know how lucky you are, Mac? I mean really, this woman, she's pure heaven, am I right?" Monica asks, slugging me gently in the arm.

I lift my eyebrows and quietly agree with my friend.

"You girls are too sweet," Percy begins, stepping forward and giving us both a quick embrace. Then she teases, "Okay, we all know how much Mac loves mushy moments, but I actually came out here for a reason. The prep work's all done, so I told the staff to grab a bite to eat before the official opening."

"Thanks." I smile, scanning the room again for anything out of place.

"Has she been obsessing like this all day?" Monica inquires.

"Yes," Percy confirms.

"I'm not obsessing!"

"Whatever you say." Monica laughs. "Oh! I almost forgot. Guess what I got?"

"What?" Percy asks, nearly scaling my side in excitement.

"Will you get off me?" I huff.

"Sorry," she giggles.

Monica moves over to the bar and retrieves the paper. She turns to face us, waving it back and forth as if it were a trophy. "Hank Crumplemeyer's review of Katie Bird's."

"What?" I gasp, grabbing onto the bar stool closest to me. Hank is the harshest and most admired food critic in all of Cincinnati. A bad review from him is considered a death sentence in this city.

"Read it!" Percy exclaims, taking two steps closer to Monica.

"No, don't," I interject. They both look at me.

"What?" Percy gasps, "Why not?"

"Have you read it, Mon?" I inquire.

"Not yet ... I wanted to do it with you two."

"Well, what if he hates it? We have an opening tonight, and I don't want to throw us off our game," I answer. But honestly, I'm more worried if she reads it, I might vomit.

"Oh, that's just silly." Percy sighs, then instructs Monica, "Read it, now."

I pull out the stool and shift up onto the edge, holding the countertop with a white-knuckle death grip. Monica is staring at me for permission. I expel a huge breath of air and nod.

Katie Bird's name left me a bit stumped when I first heard it. What kind of food could I expect at such a place with a name like this? Upon further investigation, I was intrigued to find out this was a new farm-to-table establishment. You get the distinct feeling as soon as you enter the Gateway District restaurant that they truly adhere to this in every form.

The tables are adorned with vintage mason jars that are overflowing with hydrangea pom-poms, and the decor is a mix of wood, metal, and reclaimed materials of yesteryears. While the restaurant deserves points for decor, what really matters to everyone is the food. The menu boasts the names of local farms that their foods' ingredients originate from. I was eager to see if the trouble to locally source the menu was a complete waste.

On this particular evening, there was a special of a rib-eye from a grass-fed cow, raised without antibiotics. The steak was darker and had beautiful marbilization throughout the cut. It was as if a hush fell over the room when I slipped the piece of meat into my mouth. The flavors exploded, and the tenderness was as though it were melting against my tongue.

MacKenzie Phillips, a local born and raised chef who was brought up in a family restaurant, leads the kitchen, and it's clear she learned a few things as a kid. It's not just the wonderfully pure ingredients she offers, but also the creative menu offerings. One of my favorites was the pork belly mac-and-cheese. The pork is crispy, there is a hint of truffle oil on the pasta, and a delightful three-cheese blend that makes you moan with every bite—the ultimate comfort food.

This chef doesn't, however, shy away from the classics. Mussels in a butter and garlic sauce, baby back ribs with a dry-rub that I am still trying to figure out, and a homemade barbecue sauce on the side. My companion chose a half-chicken that had been sautéed in a white wine sauce and served on a bed of rice, which she was quite happy with as well.

One word to summarize Katie Bird's: unexpected. The drinks had a great pour, and the bartenders are clearly experienced. The atmosphere is warm, welcoming, and yet maintains a tasteful elegance. It's clear that the owners and staff have a passion for what they do.

If I have one complaint, it would be that I only had room for one of the delicious desserts, and the coffee was lukewarm at best. I recommend reservations; I think this place is going to be a shining star in our city.

Monica sets the paper down and is peering up at me. She has a grin on her face, but I'm still trying to process the information I just heard. All right, lukewarm coffee ... that we can fix. Percy screams and hugs me tightly, pushing me into the counter. I close my eyes tightly, and suddenly Monica makes this a group hug. I hear my sisters running in from the kitchen.

"What's going on?" one of them asks.

"Katie Bird's just got an amazing review by Hank Crumplemeyer," Percy shouts, and, in an instant, my sisters are squealing and joining in on the group hug.

"Okay, okay, everyone, calm down," I say, bursting from the huddle of gleeful women. I try to keep a straight face.

"We have an opening to worry about tonight. Doors open in less than an hour."

Everyone begins to clear the room, heading back into the kitchen. My hands are sweating, my heart is racing, a smile is creeping in, but I'm fighting it as fiercely as I can. Suddenly, I feel a hand on my shoulder. I turn my head, and my eyes lock with Percy. What is she doing?

She pulls me against her body, squeezing her arms tightly around me. Releasing me, she grips my upper arms and pushes me back a step, locking her eyes onto mine. "You did good, and it's okay to be excited about that. And tonight is going to be even better. We're all proud of you, but I know your mom, dad, and especially Travis and sweet Katie are very proud of you."

I feel my heart drop. Her words are the last thing I want to hear, and at the same time they're the sweetest. The tears are threatening to spill out. I grit my teeth; I can't allow myself to come unraveled in this moment. There is too much riding on it.

Percy releases me, but just before she walks away I grab her arms and mouth the words 'thank you.' She nods and joins everyone else in the kitchen.

I swallow hard. This is it. My entire world is about to be turned on its head. Again.

THIRTY-TWO

PERCY TOOK care purchasing the flowers for all of the tables. They're beautiful, and for a moment I actually started to think things were going to go smooth for my big day. Then the thing that everyone warns you about began to happen—everything started to go wrong.

My hostess called in to tell me she was quitting before we even opened ... with no notice. The pork chop order was short by half. The vodka that came in was the cheap brand and not the top shelf I'd requested. However, even with all of the complications, our hard opening to the public is starting to come together, and I'm doing my best to swallow my fear and bury it deep inside.

Monica stepped up and has been playing hostess for the evening—a job she is surprisingly good at. We've made do with the other incidents, and the night I was wondering how I would ever get through is close to coming to an end. I know I couldn't have pulled this together without my amazing partners, but I can't help feeling a huge sense of accomplishment. I'm a twenty-five year old culinary school dropout, and I did this.

"Madge, you can go ahead and take off. I think the rest of us can handle the last hour," I instruct the sous chef. While we've counted carefully every penny that has gone into Katie Bird's, I still find myself worrying constantly about having enough in operating expenses to keep us going while we get our name out there. I know the full house you have opening week can disappear just as quickly as it came. Hiring talented help is expensive but key, and I plan to watch their hours closely to ensure I can keep them around.

"Yes ma'am, and congratulations on a great grand opening," Madge offers.

Madge is at least fifteen years my senior and has worked in some of the greatest restaurants in the city. When she applied for the position, I was surprised she was even interested. Apparently she'd heard a story about a young widow who was opening a restaurant in honor of her daughter she had lost. She has three children of her own, but in the interview I learned she used to have four. One of her daughters died after a diagnosis of leukemia years ago. Instantly we had a bond. I never imagined death could bring people together, but I could tell she wanted to see Katie Bird's succeed as much as I.

"Thanks." I smile and nod, pouring the sauce over the roasted chicken plate. "I couldn't have done it without you."

"Oh Mac," Monica taunts as she steps back into the kitchen. "There's someone out front asking to meet the chef."

"Okay, let me finish up these platings." People asking to meet me feels so odd. It's kind of amazing how many times it has happened considering it's opening night. I wonder if this will change as time goes on and the newness of our little restaurant wears off.

"Oh, you do not want to keep this one waiting," Monica says.

"Why?" I furrow my brow. "Another food critic?"

"Not exactly." She grins.

I huff, placing two more plates onto the serving counter. "Seriously? What's the deal?"

"Umm … let's just say, he's fine as hell, and he asked for you by name." The kitchen goes quiet when they hear Monica's statement.

"Let me see!" Percy exclaims, moving to the kitchen door and peeking into the dining room.

"By the window," Monica instructs.

"You two should be ashamed of yourselves. I'm sure he just read the article in the paper and that's how he knows my name," I dismiss, plating up the last order on the ticket.

"Well, I don't care how he knows your name. He's fine, that's all I care about." Monica laughs, while Percy scans the dining room.

"Is it clearing out in there?" I ask, ignoring her drooling.

"Yeah, the reservations have all been seated so it's just a few late night walk-ins at this point," Monica replies.

"Oh my God!" Percy gasps, turning around and rushing over to me. She grips my arm, digging her fingers in.

"What's wrong with you?" I snarl, pulling my arm from her grasp.

"It's him!" she exclaims.

"What are you talking about?" I question, a knot twisting in my stomach. "Him who?"

"That guy from Head Case." Her words make my chest ache and my throat tighten.

Rushing over to the door, I peek through the crack to confirm. It only takes me a second and I see him; he's sitting at the table by the window, his gaze scanning every detail of the restaurant. His hair is shorter, and he's sporting a five o'clock shadow that defines his strong jawline.

I gasp, and turn to face the kitchen, greeting all the prying eyes of my friends and family. "It's Dean," I state at last.

"Wait, Dean? Like Dean Dean, the one you slept with?" Monica attempts to clarify.

"You slept with him?" Percy blurts out in disbelief.

"Thanks, Mon, that's really something I want my sisters to know about." My cheeks are hot, and I avoid looking at anyone's faces.

My oldest sister rushes the door immediately, peeking out, then ducks her head back inside. "Oh my God, seriously?"

Percy nods.

"He's gorgeous," she adds.

"What the hell is he doing here?" I whisper, more to myself than to anyone else.

"How about you go find out?" Monica suggests.

I look down at my food-splattered apron. Slipping it over my head, I shove it on the counter, straighten out my clothes, and tuck a few fallen strands of hair behind my ears.

Swallowing hard, I ask, "How do I look?"

Monica licks her thumb and wipes away an invisible smudge on my cheek. "Better."

I roll my eyes and suck in a gasp of air, wipe away her spit, then mutter, "Thanks."

Approaching the kitchen door, I pause and close my eyes for a moment. Why is he here? What does he want? You can do this. You're strong. Reaching out my hands, I push open the kitchen door and begin to walk. The dining room is still half-full, and one of our waitresses is delivering the food I just plated. There are smiles all around. I look down at my robin egg blue chef's coat, jeans, and comfortable shoes. Confidence. You opened a restaurant for Christ's sake.

With one foot in front of the other, I move in the direction of Dean. He still doesn't notice me; it looks like he's inspecting the centerpiece on the table. I'm six steps away ... five ... his smell hits me. It has changed a little, but it's still him.

His head turns, and our eyes lock onto one another. He doesn't smile; he's just staring at me. He stands, and now he's less than a foot away from me. Neither of us speak. Is he as unsure what to say as I am? But he's the one who came here, so there must be a reason.

I watch him lick his lips, then open his arms, hesitating, waiting for permission to embrace me. Don't touch me. I can be strong as long as you don't touch me. I'm waving the white flag. I surrender, please, just don't—

He's holding me, touching me. I give up; I give in to the touch of your skin. I can't resist the warmth of your touch.

"Macaroon," he begins, and my heart aches in a way that I thought I'd escaped. I left so I wouldn't have to feel that. Why are you here? Why are you making me feel again?

"You look ... beautiful," he whispers against the flesh of my neck, and though I try to resist, I'm crumpling against him. My heart is racing. You can't go back to that place. Let go of him. Take your hands off.

I muster everything inside of me, grip his arms, and push myself back from his body. "Hi Dean," I offer with a soft smile.

He looks around and lifts his hands in the direction of

the back of the restaurant. "This place ... it's amazing. You're amazing."

I shake my head. I know I can't give him encouragement. I need to get through this as quickly as possible. "What are you doing here?"

His throat vibrates with a deep swallow. "Storm told me about the opening." I suddenly regret telling her, though I know somewhere in the back of my mind I was hoping she would do just what she did, even if I don't want to admit it.

"So you're here to eat?" I ask with a narrowed gaze.

He throws his head back and laughs. "Yeah, I guess I am."

"Great, I'll send the waitress over." I grin and take a step backward.

"You're just as stubborn as ever, aren't you?" he huffs, a smile breaking through his frustration.

"Dean, I'm the chef. I really can't be away from the kitchen long," I lie.

He shakes his head. "Of course, how rude of me. Before you go, could you at least recommend something?"

I bite my lip, I know better than to say it, but I do it anyway. "The mac-and-cheese is a favorite."

He moves in closer. "You put our dish on the menu." I say nothing, trying to fight the blush that is warming my cheeks. "That sounds perfect," he adds.

"Great, I'll go get your meal ready," I say, breaking free.

"We need to talk," he calls after me.

I nod and keep walking. I thought I was strong enough. I know now I'll never be strong enough to resist Dean.

I GRAB the rag and begin scrubbing the counter. I scrub it harder than I have ever scrubbed anything in my life. I'm scrubbing away all of the urges welling up inside me, the desire to have him hold me again, the yearning to have his lips touch mine the way they once had.

"I think he ate all of it," Monica announces from the door of the kitchen.

"Will you get away from that door and let the poor man eat in peace?" I demand, moving over to the stack of dirty dishes.

"So tell me exactly what he said," Percy instructs, moving next to me.

"Oh dear Lord, not you too." I sigh.

"What? We're just curious. You looked like you were really enjoying that hug." Percy isn't wrong.

"Tell me again why you can't be with him?" Monica questions.

"Shouldn't you be hostessing?" I suggest, scrubbing a pot. Percy takes it from my hand, dipping it in the rinse water for me. My sisters have left. Everyone except a waitress, bartender, and the three of us have gone, but he is still here.

"And who should I be hostessing? He's the only one left, and we're closed," Monica argues.

I turn and glare at her. "Then maybe you should go tell him we're closing."

"So let me get this straight ... you two were actually a couple?" Percy inquires, taking the next dish from my hands.

I shake my head and continue scrubbing. "For a short time. A very short time."

"And why can't you be together?" Percy asks again.

"Is he leaving?" I ask over my shoulder.

Monica presses gently on the door, peeking out from the crack. "Oh no, I don't think he's going anywhere."

"There's not much left to clean, sweetie. I think you're going to have to talk to him," Percy suggests. I know she's right. I know Dean, and he won't go anywhere until I talk to him.

"I know," I relent, scrubbing the last few items in the sink and pulling the drain plug.

"You don't have to talk about him to me if you don't want to," Percy adds, reaching over with a wet hand and squeezing my arm.

"I guess it doesn't matter," I start, drying my hands off and unbuttoning my chef's coat. "There really isn't much to tell. Everyone makes a bigger deal out of this than it is. I started falling hard for Dean, and I knew that he was becoming the center of my world. I had to leave him to learn how to be alone. Christ, does that even make sense?"

"You were alone for three years," Monica interjects.

I smile a tight-lipped grin, shaking my head. I lay my coat on the prep counter, and continue, "No, I wasn't. When Travis and Katie died, I did too. I quit living. I've never really lived, truly lived, life alone."

"Until now." Percy smiles, placing a hand on the small of my back.

"What?" I huff.

"You've lived more in the last seven months than I think I've ever seen. You're devouring the world around you, my dear," Percy explains.

"I live with you," I argue.

"Semantics, and you know it. You might be under my roof, but you are a strong and independent woman."

I stand silent, absorbing her words.

"She's right," Monica begins. "You don't have to be

scared of having nothing if you lose someone, because you have yourself now. Mac, you're an inspiration."

I laugh. "Okay, everyone shut up before I have to punch you ... or something."

"Even if you don't want to hear it, it doesn't make it any less true," Monica adds, walking over and guiding me to the kitchen door. "Go talk to him, and we'll lock up."

"But..." I have nothing. Monica pushes me out the door with a thundering clatter. I stumble forward into the dining area.

Dean is sitting, watching, waiting, his foot propped up on one of the wooden chairs.

"There you are. I thought you were going to hide out in that kitchen all night," he teases in a loud voice.

I swallow, take a breath, and cross the room confidently. "I do a have a restaurant to run."

"Fair enough." He smiles, standing and moving directly in front of the main door. "Any chance you'll be done soon?"

"I just finished, why?"

A huge smile beams across his face, splitting his head in half. "I was hoping you would go for a walk with me."

I glance at my watch. "It's midnight."

"Don't worry, I'll keep you safe," he says, opening the door. I agree, even though apprehension is coursing through my veins. You're not safe with him. Don't get comfortable.

THIRTY-THREE

THE SOUNDS of the city change at night. This is something I noticed after all the late evenings getting the restaurant ready. During the day there is the bustling of hipsters and young families visiting the trendy shops and eateries, eager to spend their money. But it's at night that the city reclaims the little strip of gentrified bliss. Horns sound to the left of us, and up ahead I hear an argument in an alleyway. The lonely souls who have had too much to drink have not yet wandered out into the streets. They are still tucked away in the few remaining untouched bars, but soon they will filter into the night. The broken come out in the dark. This is why I feel at home here, in the blackness. Scared, but at home.

"I wanted to write," Dean says at last.

"Why didn't you?" I ask the question that I've been wondering.

He presses his lips together, and a clicking noise sounds as they part. "I didn't think you'd reply. I'm not sure I could have handled that."

We can't go back. Don't let him dwell on what you were together. "How's your mom?"

"Good. We talked to her lawyer, and she's up for a parole hearing later this year. We have high hopes."

"Really?" I can see he is trying to restrain his excitement. Perhaps he fears he will be disappointed if it doesn't go the way they hope. "Dean, that's amazing."

"We'll see," he says with a half smile, avoiding looking directly at me. "We've got a long way to go."

"What will she do if she gets out?"

"We're not sure yet. She wants to live wherever I settle, so she'd have to apply for relocation and a parole officer in the area."

"What do you mean where you settle?" I turn to the right in the direction of Washington Park and the parking garage; he stays close to my side.

"Have you talked to anyone from the band since you left?" he asks.

"No, I mean maybe Christian a couple times, and I keep up with Storm; she gives me updates about Pete."

"Did she tell you what we decided?"

"Who decided? About what?" My impatience is growing.

Dean pulls one of his hands from his back pocket and places it on my lower back. There's a chill in the evening air, and I have to resist the urge to push my entire body into his for warmth. Perhaps more than warmth. I know what I really seek is intimate contact with another human being. An urge he awakened in me all those months ago.

"Pete decided he didn't want to be in the band anymore. He's going to ask Storm to marry him."

"What?" I exclaim in disbelief.

"She doesn't know the last part, so keep that between us."

I nod.

"The crash changed something in him. I wouldn't have believed it myself had I not seen it with my own eyes."

I smile from ear to ear and softly answer, "I'm happy for them." Then I realize there's more he hasn't told me. "Does that mean you replaced him in the band?"

"We talked about it, but ultimately decided it was time to call it quits."

We stand at the corner, waiting for a walk signal. He doesn't seem upset or disappointed with the information he has relayed to me. I'm not sure how to react or how he wants me to react. The light changes, and we cross silently, walking through the park and toward the stairs to the underground parking area.

"Are you okay with that?" I ask at last, realizing he isn't going to tell me without prompting.

"Can we sit?"

"What?"

"I want to talk, but do you mind if we sit down on a bench?"

"It's kind of cold..." Don't give in. If you sit, you will keep talking to him. If you keep talking to him, you'll be weak. Don't be weak. Weakness will swallow you—everything you've become.

"I'll keep you warm." He grins.

"Dean..." I shake my head, taking a step back from him.

"I need to talk to you," he presses, his serious tone making my heart race. Something's wrong, I can feel it. I take a deep breath and tell myself, you can do this. Though I'm terrified I can't.

I nod and we walk to the closest bench. At first I sit at

the opposite end, but when he laughs at my actions I give in and scoot closer, accepting his warmth.

"So what do we need to talk about?" I ask, praying it's not about us.

"I'm so happy for you," he says peering out at the park.

I laugh briefly. "What?"

"You were pretty damn spectacular when I met you, but what you've done lately, it's amazing."

"You've said that a few times now. I opened a restaurant ... it's not that big a deal," I dismiss, but I know I'm lying, and he knows I'm lying. It is amazing, and spectacular, and I'm proud, and I feel like I'm more in control of my life than I have been in a very long time. I'm in charge—not my pain, not my feelings for someone else.

He's smiling; I've missed that smile. I'll never let him know that. I think of the way we used to laugh all of the time. I miss laughing. Losing yourself in someone only leads to pain.

"I miss you," his voice is deep and smooth. His tongue slips out to moisten his lips in the bitter air, and I close my eyes for a moment, remembering the texture of it.

"I can't do this, Dean. I told you when I left."

"Well, I can't do this either," he answers firmly.

I try to hide my shock, but can't be sure I'm successful. "Good, then we agree."

"No, I didn't say that," he corrects me, closing the distance between us until it all but disappears. "What I can't do is fight this need to be near you anymore."

"Dean—"

"Let me say this," he continues "I haven't been able to get you out of my mind since you left. Food and smells, and even colors remind me of you. I've been working on starting my own production company, and it's growing."

"That's fantastic," I exclaim.

"It would be, but working a million hours only keeps the thoughts of you at bay for so long."

I understand this in more ways than he could ever imagine. Katie Bird's has been that for me. Something to immerse myself in so I'm not constantly thinking about him. But still, he manages to find his way into my thoughts more than I would like.

"Can I talk now?" I ask.

He nods.

I sigh, knowing these words make me vulnerable in a way I never want to be with another person, but until he understands, I know he won't stop. "I was used up and sad. I needed someone to tell me I was worth something, and that was my problem. I don't want to be someone who is worthless without another person. People mourn and miss the ones they love, but they continue to live. I didn't."

I stop. My eyes are wet, and the cold stings them. I close them for a second and feel his hand on my knee, but I don't brush it away. It anchors me to this place. With a deep breath I continue, "I was doing more than mourning. I realize now I didn't exist without them. It took me a long time to find out who I am, and I can never go back to that."

"Babe, don't you see ... you are someone, even without another person. You freaking opened a restaurant that, from what I saw, is pretty damn incredible."

"It is incredible," I admit with a laugh, my cheeks stinging from the surge of warm blood in the cold.

"So why shut me out? I don't want to take away what you've become, but I want to share in it," he offers.

I'm trembling. You're not strong enough. You'll lose yourself in him. It's just who you are. Then when you lose him, like you've lost everyone else, it will end you.

I shake my head. "It's been too long. You can't just show up and think we can pick up where we left off."

"Why not?"

"It doesn't work that way," I insist.

"Who says? I say love is patient. My heart feels the same about you now as it did back then. I can't turn off loving you."

"Because I left for a reason. Nothing about that has changed."

He clears his throat and delivers me a half smile that is so sexy I have to remind myself not to come unraveled. "I was never quite clear on what that reason was."

I shake my head slightly, panic washing over me. He's beautiful, why did I leave him? Why can't I quit thinking about kissing him? He'll die, remember? I remind myself. Everyone you care about leaves you eventually. He's looking at me ... he wants an answer. "I have no desire to deal with a long distance relationship."

He smiles again. Dear God, I wish he would stop doing that. I'm now literally sitting on my hands so I don't wrap my arms around him. I shift awkwardly and move his hand. It had blended with my own warmth, and now that it is gone, it's like some part of me is missing. "What if you don't have to?"

"I don't want to play this game. Was there something real you wanted to talk about?"

"Damn, there it is again. I was right; you're still just as stubborn, aren't you?"

I start to stand; I've had enough of this conversation. His hand grabs my wrist, and my flesh burns where he's touching me. A burn that I want to feel on my cheek, my neck, my hips, my legs, everywhere. Take my body, my heart, every piece of me wants to crash into you ... and that's why I can't be with you.

"Let go," I instruct firmly.

He doesn't listen, but instead, he pulls me back down next to him with a jerk. I'm staring into his eyes. In the night they appear completely gray, the blue disappearing. Look away from his eyes. His warm hand slides up to my cheek. Run, damn it. Don't you see it? He has you; your control is spinning away from you.

No matter how hard I try I can't move. I am glued to this bench, to his hand, as if there were a thousand feet of chain wrapped around me. I'm a prisoner of my desire for his touch.

Though it's cold and bitter all around us, we seem to be in a bubble of warmth. My limbs are tingling as it surges through them. I know what's coming, I know once it happens I will be powerless.

"Stop," I whisper faintly and turn my head slightly to the side. He doesn't release me. His hand is still cradling my cheek as his thumb strokes my chin. His eyes are wide, a longing in them that mirrors my own.

"I don't think you really want me to stop," he says. I know if I tell him again, he will do as I ask, but I'm silent.

He leans in, and his lips touch mine, soft at first, then it grows into an intensely feverish lustful union that has my head swaying. My chin is trembling as my lips part, wild tremors shoot out through every end of my body. I'm kissing him back ... there's no stopping it at this point.

Excitement and fear swallow me, and I like it. I want more of it. I drink in the panic, the softness of his touch. I feel like at any moment life could explode from my fingertips like massive branches sprouting leaves and flowers in the middle of the winter's canvas of death.

My heart sinks when he pulls away from me. Opening my eyes, I can see the smile in his pupils; it's the way they glisten in the moonlight. What have I done?

"I like your little corner of the world here, Macaroon. I want to move my production company here."

"What?" My head is still swimming from the kiss. I can't think straight.

He stands and takes my arm into his hands. "Let's get you to your car. We can talk more about it later. But I want you to know—I'm not looking to be your world. I'm looking to be part of it."

THIRTY-FOUR

IF I LET MYSELF LOVE, isn't that the gateway to despair, to hopelessness, to nothing? Last night, Dean gave me a choice. He wants me to change this life I've made to include him. Afterward, I stood in the darkness of my room. Percy came home soon after, but I didn't respond to her knock. I knew she would have questions to which I did not have answers. I lay in my bed, staring at the ceiling, but the answers never came.

It's raining out, and today is the first time we will include lunch service at Katie Bird's. I hoped it would prove as a distraction, but all I can think about are the words that Dean left me with last night. I'm not looking to be your world. I'm looking to be part of it.

No matter how much I continue to tell myself I'm incapable of retaining a piece of myself in a relationship, the idea keeps rolling around in my head. Loss is supposed to be painful, but what I felt when I lost Travis and Katie was so much more than the word 'pain' can describe. I don't want to be that vulnerable again in my life. And no matter how many times I reason with myself and tell myself I am incapable of not getting lost in another human, the thought keeps coming back to me. What if I can? What if I'm stronger now? What if this is my chance at joy?

I think about my mother ... it hurt me when she was gone. I was devastated. I used to look at my father and wonder, How can he go on? How could he have ever loved her if he could love someone else so easily? Sometimes I'd see glimpses of his pain, the loneliness of her not being near him, even though he had Percy. That person you once loved missing from your life never really goes away.

I'm lying on the cool tile in the office of the restaurant. Curled up on my side, it is the only way I fit in such an awkward place. I don't feel like moving or thinking, let alone cooking for a lunch crowd, but I don't have a choice. No matter what thoughts creep in, I have duties now. Duties that keep me functioning in the real world. I like that. I like that I can't get lost in my misery anymore ... it's simply not an option.

There's a knock at the door. I shift, sit upright, and slide my body under the desk. The door cracks, and Percy sticks her head inside. It contorts with confusion as she sees me in my hiding place.

"MacKenzie, are you okay?"

I shrug my shoulders. I don't have the energy to lie to her. She slides inside and closes the door behind her, taking a seat in the roller chair next to me.

"You want to talk about it?" she asks, and I can tell she's concerned.

I shake my head, remaining silent.

Her head tilts. "Is this about that musician?"

I nod and look up at her. I've given her no information, yet somehow I am hoping she relays some sort of amazing wisdom to me.

"I know I'm not your favorite person," she begins.

"That's not true," I insist.

"Please, I know you've hated me since you were a kid. I get it; I'm not your mom. But I still love you. I still care about you. If I can help you at all, please, let me."

I look at her face, and I see a different kind of pain—one I've inflicted on her for many years. In that moment, so many mistakes become clear to me. I made my own world of pain, and I forced others to live in it. I built those walls. I'm not who I am because of what I've done; I'm who and what I am because of the people around me. When I lost Travis, I may have shut people out, but they continued to love me, and care for me, and they waited for me. Percy waited for me. My dad was waiting for me. Jesus, how did I not see what I'd become?

"I don't feel that way anymore," I offer, sliding out from under the table and sitting on top of the desk so our eyes meet more naturally. "I was a foolish kid. I've been a complete witch to you for most of my life. After Dad died you could have shut me out. You didn't have to deal with me anymore. Instead, you helped me open this restaurant, you gave me a place to live. I'm so sorry."

A tear escapes from one of Percy's eyes, rolling down her cheek. She bites her bottom lip, her face suddenly red and splotchy. She shakes her head at me, speechless.

I reach out and take her in my arms. I risk the pain of caring for someone and losing them because I'm better with her, I'm better with my sisters, I'm better with Monica, than on my own. If I lose one, it would hurt like hell, but I like who I am with them.

"I think I love him," I whisper in Percy's ear. It's a confession I need to make.

She pulls back, laughs, and wipes away a tear with the back of her hand. "Then tell him."

My head is spinning. I'm still terrified. I nod, a slight smile on my face. "I will, but first, we have a restaurant to run."

We both laugh. Percy opens the door and exits the office. I pull out my phone, scroll through my contacts, and find Dean's name.

Me: Can you talk tonight?

I hit SEND. That's it. I'm doing this. My phone dings almost immediately.

Dean: I can talk now.

Me: I can't.

Dean: I can be there in five. Are you at Katie Bird's?

Me: I have to work.

Dean: I'm looking at a space for my company later today. I want you to see it.

Me: After close?

Dean: Whatever works for you.

Me: After closing.

Dean: See you tonight, Macaroon.

I slip the phone into my pocket. My face is burning, and my cheeks ache from smiling. If I can hold it together for an entire day, it will be a shock. If I can keep myself from chickening out, it will be an absolute miracle.

THIRTY-FIVE

I'D TAKEN MY TIME, making sure each and every dish was washed, countertops and floors polished, and I even restocked all of the toiletries. Dean came in an hour before closing, ordered our mac-and-cheese dish, and has been patiently waiting for me at the small table by the front door of the restaurant ever since.

I glance in the mirror, lick my fingertips, and wipe away the black mascara rings that have formed under my eyes. I press my lips together, attempting to move around the last bit of balm left on my pink lips. With a deep breath, I place my chef's coat on a hook near the kitchen door, straighten out my shirt, slip on my coat, and take my first step in his direction.

The moment I walk through the kitchen door Dean notices me headed toward him. My heart's racing, my mouth is suddenly dry, and all I can think about is the fact that he's looking at me. More than looking, he's staring, studying me. It's the strangest sensation. I love having his eyes on me, on my face, my body, but at the same time I feel the urge to lower my head, hide from his probing gaze. I'm so confused, so all I can do is smile and say, "Ready?"

He's smiling at me, still probing with those beautiful eyes. "I am if you are."

"Why are you looking at me like that?" I immediately regret asking.

He shakes his head. "You're beautiful. I can't help myself."

"What?" I gasp and realize I'm grinning from ear to ear.

"You're different." I can't hide the surprise on my face from his statement. "Wait—I don't mean that in a bad way. You're amazing."

This seems like the perfect opportunity to have a little fun with him. "Oh, I see. So back when we first met, you didn't think I was amazing. Well ... I take that back ... amazing enough to sleep with."

"Ouch," Dean hisses.

I burst out laughing and his posture relaxes. "You should see your face."

"Are you teasing me on purpose? You have changed."

I shove him in the arm. "And apparently you've lost your sense of humor."

My breath catches in my throat as his hand grips my wrist. I'm no longer laughing. I'm not breathing. I'm just watching and waiting. He leans in closer to me. "I'm sorry, what I meant before was how much you've done with your life since you left the tour. You always were incredible, that hasn't changed."

"All right, you have to shut up now."

"What?" He laughs at me. I look away; I can feel that my cheeks are hot. "Okay, I'll stop. I wouldn't want to embarrass you."

"Oh, please, you love embarrassing me," I correct him.

He grins, "Who, me?"

"Don't we have somewhere to be?" I can't quit smiling.

"Oh right," Dean exclaims, rushing over to the main door, waiting for me to exit.

He's so close to me now, just behind me, over my shoulder. My hair flutters as his warm breath tickles the back of my neck. An electric surge runs down my spine. I'm hesitating. Move, damn it! Open the door. You look insane.

"Let me get that," he offers, his voice is deep and smooth.

He reaches over me and pushes the door open. I step outside, the cool air washing over me and snapping me back to reality. He follows me out, and I turn, slipping my key into the bolt and locking the door behind us.

As I turn, I feel his hand slip down to my lower back, and it arches. He lifts a single hand and points north. "It's this way."

I move forward quickly, trying to increase the distance between Dean's touch and myself. "Where?"

"A place called Neons," he replies.

"Oh yeah, I know that place. They've got a great outdoor patio area right in the middle of it." I attempt to continue the conversation, focusing on the passing traffic and sidewalk instead of his eyes.

"Yeah, the owner seems really cool. She said she would leave the keys at the bar so we could check the place out whenever," he answers.

"That's nice. I think her name's Molly," I say hesitantly.

"You know her?"

"She's involved in a lot of places around here. She has a book out about cocktails as well. Kind of looks like an old fashioned pin-up girl, right?"

"Yeah, that's her."

I smile and coyly peer up at him for a moment. "I'm a bit envious of her ink."

"What? You have beautiful tattoos."

"But she really went for it, you know? Double sleeves and everything."

"Nothing says you can't do that," he starts, "but I think you're pretty perfect."

Damn it! There's that heart flutter he keeps causing.

"Can I make a confession?"

"Juicier the better," Dean adds without missing a beat.

My cheeks are hot before I even say the words, "I kind of have a girl crush on her. She's so beautiful." He's quiet. I feel panic rush over me. I laugh nervously. "Okay, have I totally freaked you out?"

I glance up at him, and he glares down at me mischievously. "No, I'm just trying to think of horribly depressing things so I don't get a raging hard-on."

My mouth drops open as we come to a stop directly in front of the bar. "You wait here," he directs. "I'll run in and get the keys."

The words 'raging hard-on' keep repeating in my mind. I turn and lean against the exterior brick wall, watching the people around, trying to think of anything besides the image Dean just placed in my thoughts. A local taco food truck is parked directly out in front of the bar, and a long line of staggering patrons are waiting patiently with their mouths hanging open. My thoughts shift to what geniuses the owners of that food truck must be. I have a monstrous monthly overhead for the restaurant, and they park right where there is peak demand and then park in their driveway when they're done. Pure genius.

"Hungry?" Dean's voice startles me.

"Huh?" I gasp, then giggle. "Oh, no, I was just thinking what a smart business model food trucks are."

"Expanding already?" he asks, walking to a door on my right and slipping a key into the hole.

"Oh God, no, my hands are full as it is."

"This way, my dear," Dean announces, waving toward the entrance.

I climb the wooden stairs. They're creaking, and there is a smell of saw dust in the air. The music from the bar is loud. Climbing up beyond the top stair, I turn and make my way into the space. Somewhere behind me Dean flicks on the light. In a flash, the space becomes clear. It is a large, open, and narrow room. The floors are a rough finish that show the age of the building, the walls brick with flaking white paint. At the front of the room there are four massive windows that I can only imagine would allow in a ton of natural light. The space is big, and I can picture it being spectacular with a little work.

"So what do you think?" he asks.

I pull my lips tight. "Good, I guess."

"You guess? Is there something wrong with it?"

"I'm just not the person to ask about a recording studio. I would think the bar would be a bad thing since it's so loud."

"Nah, by the time they get going my clients would be done," he explains. "Do you like it?"

I begin to pace the room from one side to the other, looking out the window and watching the taco line slowly move. "It's a pretty awesome part of town, and it does have a lot of character. Jesus, how high are these ceilings?"

"I know, right? This place has some kick ass acoustics," he adds.

"But—" I stop myself.

He crosses to stand next to me. "But what?"

"Nothing." I shake my head. "Never mind."

"Mac, please. I asked you here because I wanted your opinion," he pleads.

I swallow hard and hope what I am about to say doesn't offend him. "Is this really your dream?"

"What? Owning a studio?"

"Yeah, when we met you were touring and seemed to be pretty successful with your band. You looked so happy on stage."

"We had our run," he answers.

"And you just want to give that up?" I press.

He sighs deeply. "I don't know. I guess I don't feel like I'm giving up anything. I like working with music, so I think as long as it's in my life I'm happy. Besides, life on the road can get exhausting."

"You sound like an old man or something."

"I'm serious. Sometimes all I want is to put down some roots, you know?"

I shrug. I had roots, and I know that doesn't always stick. "Why here? Why not be close to your mom?"

"Too many ghosts in Atlanta."

"Yeah, I know how hard that can be."

"Oh God, Mac ... I'm sorry. I didn't mean—"

Shaking my head, I stop him, "I know you didn't. I'm fine. But just a warning, ghosts tend to follow you. And I still think it will be too hard to be this far from your mom."

"I can visit until she gets paroled, and if I live here, it will be easier for her to petition to move residency when she's released."

"You've really thought this out, haven't you?"

Dean moves closer to me, and I feel the urge to step

back, create more distance between us, but I don't. "Wanting to get away from my past wasn't the reason I chose Cincinnati."

My face goes hot, and I lick my lips. "Oh yeah?"

He's even closer to me now. He reaches out and takes my hand into his. My hands are dry from the cleaning products at the restaurant, and I can't help wonder if he notices. "I think I made it pretty clear why I'm here."

"I know, but—"

"But what? Have you met someone else?"

"No, but I'm focused on the restaurant and making it a success. I don't know if I have time for anything else." I want to tell him I've been a fool. That I want to share this exciting journey with him, but I'm still too scared to say the words. Old fears keep creeping in.

"I stayed away because you said that was what you wanted. Mac, I was miserable. In my entire life, you have been the only woman to actually understand me."

I can't let him go on. "I'm still broken, Dean. I'm not good for you."

"It's because you're broken that you're perfect for me. It's the reason we connect, and I know that now." His words make my chest ache. I've missed him, his smile, his laugh, his sense of humor, those eyes, and oh God, the touch of his skin.

"Mac? Say something," he pleads.

"What do you want me to say?" He lets go of my hand, and a loneliness washes over me immediately.

"Tell me you want me here," he replies, staring at my face.

I shake my head. He's asking too much of me. "I can't tell you to stay."

"Why not?" His bluntness shocks me.

I maneuver around him, walking to the top of the stairwell, but he matches me stride for stride. I'm trapped; I can either turn and face him or go running down the stairs and out to the street like a mad woman. I turn, look at him, and decide to tell him the truth, "Because, I can never be what you want me to be."

"And what do I want you to be?" He's grinning, and it infuriates me. Why is he smiling? "I never asked you to be anything but yourself." There's a laugh at the end of his words.

"What's so funny?" I demand defensively.

"It's ... just ... don't you see? I stayed away because I thought I couldn't be what you needed. You're trying to avoid even giving this a shot because you think you can't be what I need. We can't get out of our own damn ways to make this work."

"You want me to be available in ways I'm not ready for."

"I'll wait."

"I may never be available."

"Damn it, Mac! There comes a point when you have to let go," Dean says in a tone I haven't heard since our fight that night in the bus station. My defenses immediately go up as my spine stiffens.

"Screw you! I don't have to do anything."

"I'm sorry, I didn't mean it that way."

"How else could you have meant it? You commit your life to someone, then when they are ripped away from you I want to know how easy it is for you to just let go." My voice is trembling.

"Think about it ... what's so terrible about letting someone love you again? Wouldn't Travis want you to be happy?"

"He's not here to tell me that, is he?"

"Wouldn't you want him to be happy if the situation were reversed?"

"No!" I'm shouting. I don't shout. But right now I am. "I'd want to be here with him, with our daughter."

"It's not fair what happened to you, but you can't change it. I wanted to grow up with my mother in my life, but that's not the hand I was dealt."

"I can't do this," I huff.

I try to take off, retreat down the steps and into the safety of the night. Anywhere but here. I'm not moving. I can feel his hand gripping my wrist. "I'm not letting you run away."

"Let go of me."

"Not until you talk to me."

"I have nothing to say," I snap.

"Then maybe I should go." His words sting. I wish the battle between my head and my heart would end. I know I'm better with him in my life, so why can't I say the words to him? Why is a piece of me still holding onto this fear? Let go, damn it!

"Maybe you should," I reply, standing firm. You don't mean that.

He releases me, lowering his eyes. There is despair and sadness on his face. I wish I hadn't been the one to inflict the pain. His voice is quiet as he asks, "Is that what you really want? You want me to go away?"

I hesitate; if I tell him to leave, I know he will. At last I answer, "I don't want anything."

He's practically on top of me. If I take one step back, I will topple down the stairs. I can feel his breath on me. He is so close I am forced to look into his eyes, and in a flash I'm locked in his gaze. The silence sits between us for a moment and the anticipation grows. What will happen next? Do I speak? Will he say something?

"You don't want anything?" His voice is a rugged whisper now.

I shake my head.

"So you don't want me to kiss you right now? Because that's what I want more than anything in the world."

"Dean," I squeak out in protest.

"Help me understand. Is it guilt? Is that why you can't let yourself be happy?"

"Not anymore," I answer honestly.

"Is it me? Don't you think I could make you happy?"

"For a time." My words seem to wound him, and he staggers back slightly. I probably should use the opportunity to escape, but instead I foolishly move forward, reaching out and touching his arm in an attempt to soften the blow of my previous statement.

"So you think I'll hurt you?"

"Of course, it's inevitable. Everyone leaves and that hurts." I know he understands this from what he experienced in his own childhood.

"I used to think the same thing—my dad, my mom, and then Grams died a few years ago. It took me a long time to realize none of it was my fault."

"Is that what you think? That somehow I think I'm to blame for everyone in my life who has died? People die, it's no one's fault. I get that."

"But—"

"No, you don't get it. I can't lose anyone else. I can't lose you ... it would kill me."

"But I'm right here."

"Until you die, too. Everyone dies, Dean, and that's just how it is. It hurts too much. That night when Pete was in the motorcycle accident, and I thought it was you, it felt like Travis all over again. That's when I decided I'd rather be alone than feel that pain again."

He's quiet, and I can tell he's thinking about what I've said. Then he plainly says, "I'm going to die, you're right; but we all are, and if I have ten minutes left on Earth, the only way I would want to spend them is with you."

His words are like a sucker punch to the gut, knocking all the air out of me. "Shut up," I gasp.

"I mean it. The best day of my life was when you came into it. And I think you feel the same way."

"Don't say that."

"Why not? Too close to the truth? You might be risking pain, Mac, but you will be gaining so much happiness for the risk."

"You don't know that."

"I know how you make me feel, and I also know I would do anything in my power to make you feel the same."

There is a buzzing in my head, and my knees are weak. I turn to walk away. I need to get away from him. His hands easily ensnare me, pulling me in against his body, his heat consuming me.

"What are you—" Dean doesn't wait for me to finish asking the question. He presses his lips to mine, and without any consideration, I don't resist. His tongue parts my lips, and the deep and passionate kiss causes the rest of my body to go limp. He's there, though, his strong arms waiting to catch me.

The kiss blurs all other thoughts—thoughts of what I've lost, thoughts of running, thoughts of resisting. I'm here and, in this moment, I am his. When his lips pull away, I speak the first words that pop into my mind.

"I'm scared," I whisper, his arms wrapping around me.

"Good. Scared means you're feeling something, that you're alive." And he is right. I'm so alive.

THIRTY-SIX

I GLANCE AROUND, taking stock of the meal I've prepared. Behind me I hear my phone ding with a text message alert. I don't rush over to look at it, as I am pretty confident I know who sent it.

"Mac," Monica gasps, looking at me as if I must be in some other world. "Your phone."

"I heard it," I confirm, continuing to take stock of the containers.

Shoving the remainder of the apple slice she had been munching on into her mouth, she moves swiftly. She retrieves my phone and begins flipping through the screens. A huff escapes her lips.

"Is there a problem?" I pause, turning and receiving her disapproving glare.

"Clingy much?"

"What are you talking about?" I snap.

"How long have you and Dean been dating?"

I furrow my brow in an attempt to let her know I don't like where this conversation is headed. Based on her face, though, I can see she doesn't care. "I think dating is kind of a strong word."

She drops my phone on the counter, the clash of it against the metal causing her to wince. Grinning, she whispers, "Sorry." She then seamlessly continues with her interrogation. "The two of you eat almost every meal together, and last weekend you went antiquing. If that's not dating, I don't know what is."

"We were not antiquing," I quickly defend, then grin at the humor of her statement. "We were looking for vintage music equipment."

"Yeah, like I said, dating."

"We've decided we're not labeling it."

"Please." She laughs at my statement. "That's only because he knows how terrified you are of relationships, and he doesn't want to scare you off. You're a couple."

I smile, and though I won't admit it to her, I know she's right, and it feels amazing. "I don't know, whatever we're doing together, it's been a few weeks, why?"

"You don't think these kind of text messages from him are a little clingy?"

I don't have to look at our message history. I know exactly what is in there, and confidently I answer, "Not at all."

Monica raises her hands in the air as if she is calling an imaginary truce with someone. "Fine. All I'm saying is he moves here because of you, and now he texts you every time he gets somewhere. I mean, look at these." Retrieving the phone, she flips back through them, but before she can read them out loud I stop her.

"I know what they say, and I don't think he's clingy," I inform her.

"Mac! I'm really happy you are getting back in the

saddle and all, but you have to be smart about things." She reads a message anyway. "'At the studio' and then there's 'Back at my place, goodnight.' Now today we get another one, 'Made it to the studio.' Christ, how do you keep yourself from replying 'Why would I give a crap?'"

"Because," I answer in a flat tone. I can feel my cheeks growing hot. "Aren't you here to pick up an order for your office? It's waiting for you on the counter over there."

"Oh, come on, don't be like this. I'm trying to be a friend. Normal guys don't do that stuff. He's giving me the stalker vibe."

I press my teeth firmly against one another and tightly ball my fists. She doesn't understand, but I still can't help but get angry with her. "Just drop it. He's not a stalker," I warn her.

She stands up and turns toward the door, "Why don't we call Percy back here and ask her what she thinks."

"No!" My body recoils as I realize I'm shouting. I take a deep breath. "I'm the one who isn't normal."

"Huh?" She moves back toward me, taking her seat once again on the stool. She reaches out and briefly touches my hand. "What are you talking 'bout, sweetie? Did he tell you that?"

I shake my head. I know she is trying to protect me, but if she could only understand how damaged I am and how Dean is the only one who gets it. "The texts are for me," I answer, but I know it's not enough.

"Of course they're for you ... it's your phone."

"No, it's not him who wants the texts. He does it for me," I attempt to clarify, but her puzzled stare signals otherwise. "When he came here, I told him I couldn't see him. He kept pushing me to try and figure out why, and he thought it was because of some sort of guilt about Travis and Katie."

"And it wasn't?" There is a sound of surprise in my friend's voice.

I shake my head again. "No, it was because I was scared. I still am."

"Of what?"

"The pain of losing him. I never realized how much I loved Travis and Katie until they were gone. Don't get me wrong—I knew they were my life, but after the accident, it was like there was this gaping hole in the center of me. It's a constant ache that nothing can fill. I don't ever want to feel that again, so I don't want to let anyone in."

"So what does that have to do with the texts?"

"Don't you see?" I smile and take my phone from her hands, pulling it close to my chest and wrapping my hand tightly around it. "He doesn't want me to worry, or be afraid. There's no guarantees in life, and it terrifies me, but Dean texts me so that when we're apart I don't worry."

"Oh hell," Monica groans.

"What's wrong?"

I see her eyes grow moist. "That's the sweetest thing I've ever heard. I might have to go puke."

"It kind of is, isn't it?"

"I was wrong; he's perfect for you. God, I need to meet a man." Monica's voice quivers before she forces a laugh.

I laugh, too, reaching out and embracing her firmly. "Thank you."

"For what?"

"For being there over the past few years while I was falling apart," I explain.

"I'm proud of you." Her words surprise me.

"What?"

She shakes her head and looks around the kitchen. "I've got to admit, I wasn't sure a year ago if you were going to pull yourself out of this downward spiral, but look at you now."

"Gee, thanks," I grumble.

"No, I'm serious. You've really done something amazing with your grief ... by putting it into this place. It's amazing—you're amazing."

"Thank you."

"You really like him, don't you?" I can feel her eyes penetrating me, and I wonder how deep into my soul they can see.

Shrugging my shoulders, I swallow hard and reply, "I think I love him."

"Have you 'done it' again?"

"What are we, back in high school?"

"Oh, come on, I thought I was supposed to be your best friend," she whines.

I lean across the table and shove her firmly in the arm. "You are, and no, we haven't 'done it.' We're taking it slow."

"Now I know he's too good to be true. Hot as hell and a gentleman; they don't exist. Take your picnic basket of goodies to Dean before he sends you another dozen text messages, and I'm forced to eat all of the food you made my office to drown my boyfriend sorrows," she teases.

I laugh, leaning over and dropping the last of the containers into a basket. "I love you, Mon."

"I know." She smiles. "I love you, too."

She follows me out to the main area, retrieving her bag of meals as she exits. Pressing open the door, I lock it behind me. I turn to the right, wave to my best friend, and begin walking.

Dean's new studio is only a few minutes' walk from me.

There's something comforting in knowing he is so close to me all the time. It's hard not to want to spend every second with him. It's an instinct I've had to fight, a struggle to find a balance. I begin to coach myself. You're going to retain your identity. You're going to be a sane and non-clingy girlfriend. Oh Lord, you just said girlfriend; you are dating.

I look up, and I'm here. Only a flight of stairs separates Dean and me. I realize I'm not breathing when my phone begins to vibrate in my back pocket. Then I hear the window above me slide open.

"There you are," Dean's voice calls out.

I glance up; the sun is creating a halo effect around his head, blinding me from seeing his full features. "Hi."

"I was just calling you to see if you wanted me to come over for lunch," he quickly adds. My heart is still racing ... why is my heart racing? Dean and I have been around each other every night for weeks, and I've never gotten like this. Damn it! Why did Monica have to say anything?

"Too late, I brought lunch," I reply, motioning toward the basket.

"Oh wow, I'll be right down."

And before I can calm my rapidly beating heart, he's standing in front of me, scooping the basket from my hands and delivering me a huge grin that makes my stomach flip. The only thing to do now is follow him up the stairs.

Climbing the narrow stairwell to the studio loft, all I can see directly in front of me are Dean's jeans hugging his perfectly shaped backside. One corner of a back pocket is torn and frayed, and I fight the urge to reach out and run the threads through my fingertips.

He moves quickly, the stale air shifting around him, carrying his scent to me. I close my eyes for just a moment, drinking it in, a mingling of mint and soap. When we reach the top of the stairs I glance to my right, where a window overlooks the bar below.

"This place is really coming together." I attempt to make small talk, but really I'm just trying to distract myself from the way his arms look as he shifts things around on the nearby table, making room for our lunch.

"Thanks. Once I get the booth done I'm going to actually have some design elements put into the space." He motions to the partially framed wall in the corner.

"What kind of design elements?"

"Oh," he begins, clearly excited. "I was talking to Molly from the bar downstairs, and she said she knows a mural artist who can paint the huge brick wall for me. He's working on some design ideas right now."

I pause. Instantly I am uncomfortable when I hear Molly's name. Don't be that girl. You've never been the jealous type ... don't start with him. He likes you, I remind myself. "That sounds amazing," I say, then force a smile.

I scan the oversized room one last time then turn to see Dean hesitating over the basket, unsure where to begin. "Here, let me do that."

I rush over, welcoming something to focus my attention on other than his broad shoulders. I've managed to hold it together for weeks now around him, and one comment about sex from Monica, and I can't carry a cohesive thought in my head. I'm going to kill her.

Staring intensely at the basket, I first pull out a Tupperware container with a special treat I made specifically with Dean in mind. He'd made a comment the other night that he saw no fault with adding bacon to every dish conceivable.

"What's that?" he quickly asks, moving in close.

I smile, pleased he notices so quickly. "Candied bacon."

"Oh no, you're not teasing me, are you?"

"I swear, I candied it in a mixture of honey and maple syrup," I insist, pulling a piece from the container. "Here, try it."

Cupping my hand with his, he doesn't take the bacon from me; instead, he uses me as a utensil and eats directly from my fingertips. I feel my knees buckle slightly, and I attempt to steady myself. He pulls the bite into his mouth, and his eyes roll back in his head, but he doesn't release my hand, still holding it with both of his. He lets out a groan that signals he has found a level of ecstasy.

"Like it?" I giggle.

"Like it? Oh please tell me you're putting this on the menu." Just as he says the words, I watch his eyes shift down to our hands, still joined together around the bacon. He goes in for another bite, but instead, the corner of his mouth shifts it aside, and he takes my sticky fingertip into his mouth for just a moment.

He lets his lips linger before pulling away and, with a wicked grin, he adds, "Delicious."

I set the half-eaten bacon strip on the nearby lid of the plastic container, and without thinking I lick the last of the sticky residue from my fingertips. I realize my fingers are still wet from his mouth, and it's all I can think about. His mouth, those lips, anywhere and everywhere on my body.

The one time we had sex before, I couldn't quit thinking about Travis. I want Dean so badly, but I also don't want to put myself through that again. I try to think of anything except Dean's lips. My fear of losing self-control and being at the mercy of his mouth fades away when I feel his arms wrap around me. My heart is racing, and I can't think straight, but there's a sweet relief of being here in his arms. An overwhelming feeling that I'm not alone. An intoxicating idea I haven't experienced in a very long time, and one I've missed desperately.

His arms pull in tighter, pressing my back against his chest. I release my muscles into him, allowing the lines between us to blur. His warm breath is on my shoulder, and I wish I could see the deep blues and grays of his eyes, but I dare not move for fear of this moment disappearing.

"What are you thinking about?" His words are soft and deep.

Swallowing hard, I push down the scattered thoughts of doubt that are creeping in and force a smile. Words said with a smile are, after all, always more convincing. "Just enjoying the moment."

He breathes out again, his exhale syncing perfectly with mine. He runs the back of his fingertips down the bare skin of my arm, causing my entire body to convulse in delight. I continue to shiver as his hand traces the outline of my hip before traveling back up my side, my arm, and then my shoulder.

"Are you all right?" he whispers in my ear. I can feel the delight in his words, the pure joy it brings him to put me in such a state.

"I'm just worried about the food getting cold," I answer, feeling my control slipping away.

Reaching around me, he uses my hips to turn my body until we are facing one another. My eyes avoid his as my tongue slips out and moistens my lips. I'm trying my best to cling to my sanity with every passing moment, but with each inch that closes between us I'm more and more frightened because I feel the last pieces of restraint slipping away. My lips part, a breath escaping as my gaze meets his.

He pulls me closer, a smile in his eyes. He breathes a small laugh. "I'm not really hungry right now—well, at least not for food." And with those words, it's as if a thread snaps, and I'm lost in him.

"Oh yeah?" I grin, surprising myself by the playfulness in my question.

"MacKenzie Phillips! Are you flirting with me?" Dean asks. My stomach twists as I hear my last name, a connection to my past, a connection to Travis.

I hold my breath, staring at him. Travis is gone; he'll only haunt you if you let him, I tell myself. Dean is perfectly broken. He thinks he is just like me, but I know I've reached that point beyond broken. That place where a person is completely shattered, and no amount of the king's men will ever be able to put me back together again.

"What just happened?" Dean asks, moving in close to my side. He must have seen the reaction on my face when he said my last name.

Shaking my head, I insist, "Nothing, I ... we ... I just don't want the food to get cold. Besides, I'm starving."

"Bullshit," he curses. This unsettles me. I cross the room and hover near a couch, then begin to pace. "What the hell just happened?" He raises his voice slightly.

"Maybe I should just go," I suggest, biting my nails and purposely avoiding eye contact. One passing thought of Travis has managed to derail the entire meal.

He crosses the room, stopping me in my tracks. "No, I felt you shift back there. What's going on? We've been getting so close lately, I don't want us to move backward."

He's right. I don't want to move backward either. I like the way I feel when I'm with him.

He reaches out and takes hold of my shoulder, forcing my eyes to connect with his. "I've been waiting my entire life for someone like you. You're my person. I'm not going anywhere, so you might as well tell me what's going on with you."

"I ... You'll think I'm crazy."

"I already do, so no worries there," he laughs, and suddenly I am too.

"Shut up," I huff with a grin.

He sits on the couch and pulls me down next to him by my waist. "Take a deep breath, close your eyes if you have to, and just tell me what's going on inside that beautiful head."

I follow his directions. After a few deep breaths the truth isn't ready to come out. So I close my eyes, the blackness sinking in and enveloping me. My breathing shallows and with one final swallow, I speak to the darkness, "It was my name. You said 'Phillips.' All I could think about was Travis when you said it."

"You're allowed to think about him," he reassures me.

"I don't want to think about him anymore. I want you."

"You have no idea how happy that makes me. But I want you to know, I don't expect you to give up your memories of Travis. He was part of your life. He helped make you into who you are," Dean explains.

His hand is on my cheek, and his thumb wipes away a tear that has escaped. His fingertips lift my chin. I'm shaking, and I jump when I feel Dean's lips press against mine. Just as quickly, they're gone.

I open my stinging eyes, but I see Dean staring at me, a smile on his face. "Why are you happy? I'm so messed up."

"You love me." His words stun me.

"What?"

"Yup, I know you well enough by now," he boasts smugly. "You're freaked out because you love me."

"Oh, is that right?" He looks so proud and confident in

his conclusion that I can't help but smile. "Then what's to be done?"

"Well," he begins, scooting closer, narrowing the gap between us. "Luckily, I love you too. So there really is only one thing to be done."

I furrow my brow. "I see. Care to enlighten me?"

"We're going to have to have mad, passionate sex until all you can think about is me," Dean informs me in a low growl.

My heart's pounding, and I'm smiling so much my face is starting to hurt. I don't pull away when he moves in closer; instead, I lift my head so my lips meet his, and with our mouths pressed together, he moans as his tongue slips past my teeth. I can taste the mint I had smelled earlier. Placing my hand on his thigh, I shift my body weight toward him. I can't get much closer than I already am, but I still try. His stiffness grazes my wrist. I don't pull my hand away, and through the denim, I feel it grow harder.

Though I don't want to break the seal between us, he needs to know how I feel. Pulling my mouth away from his for just a moment, I sigh and whisper, for fear the words might make me cry, "I want you."

Wasting no time, Dean lifts a hand to my hair and, with a fistful, he moans, "I love you, Mac." This time I do not think of Travis. I think of Dean's lips, on all the various parts of my body.

I allow the terrifying words to slip past my lips, "I love you, too." I say the words and the world does not come to a crashing halt. Before another breath can escape me, his mouth is on mine again. My eyes widen, and I willingly release all control, allowing the moment to lead us wherever it may.

I hear Dean's shoes hit the floor behind me and, without

hesitation, I kick mine off as well—not an easy task in my current position. When my second shoe hits the ground Dean presses against me and continues to do so until he has me standing in an upright position. He leans back on the couch and stares at me, starting at my head and following the length of my body all the way to my toes.

His gaze settles back onto my face, and he is lost somewhere between a smile and a predator's glare. I know what he wants, and I can't wait to give it to him. I bring down the zipper of my jeans, slowly, so as to tease him. Pulling one flap down, I expose flesh and just the hint of black sheer underwear. I'm suddenly very thankful I took the time to make a recent run to Victoria's Secret and trade up what Monica would call my oversized granny panties.

Dean lets out a whistle, and instantly my face flushes red. Leaning forward, he rips away his T-shirt. It happens so quickly. His lean and hardened chest distracts me, and I forget I'm in the middle of a strip tease.

"More," he pleads.

Shaking off the entrancing hardness of his body, I turn my backside toward him and slip my pants to the floor, bending over as I do so. I hope my actions are driving him crazy. I'm quite sure my pale skin must be startling for anyone, but he seems to be enjoying everything I have to share with him. Kicking off the last leg, I turn to face him so he can watch as I unbutton my shirt, one button at a time. I'm smiling, and he's staring eagerly.

He reaches to unzip his own pants, but I stop him with a well-placed foot. He looks at me, puzzled. "I'll get to that," I assure him.

His eyes widen, and a thrill rushes over me at the idea that I've shocked him. With the last button, I pull open the shirt and allow it to drop to the floor. Standing there in my bra and panties, I feel sexy in his gaze—sexy in an entirely new way.

I lower myself to my knees, leaning in and kissing his side, his hip. Releasing the top snap of his jeans, I pull them open slowly, pressing my lips against the flesh that had been hidden by the denim. He moans as he exhales, and I feel a shiver run through my body. He lifts his pelvis toward my face to pull his jeans from under his bottom. Once they are free, I take it the rest of the way, pulling them from his legs. He leans forward, slipping off his socks, and I can't help but giggle at his eagerness.

Licking my lips, my eyes shift to his erection, then with a grin, I look back into his eyes. There's an intense longing in them that excites me. He shifts and moves toward me, reaching around, and with ease, he unhooks my bra, pulling it from my shoulders and allowing it to fall to the floor. Lifting me by my upper arms, he places me on the couch next to him.

Gladly, I relinquish the reins to him. He lowers himself on top of me, our skin pressed against one another's, the only barrier at this point the underwear we each wear. His lips caress my neck, my shoulder, and as I take in a sharp breath I feel him take my nipple into his mouth. There's a comfort between us; I'm his and he's mine.

I rock my hips as I moan and then thrust eagerly upward again.

"Oh God, Dean, please, I..." My words trail off into a deep breath.

He lifts his head from my breasts. "You what?" he asks with a smile.

"I need you."

One of his hands shifts down and slips inside my panties, and he begins moving two fingers. My body convulses, as he once again takes my nipple in his mouth. My face is hot, and I feel like I'm floating above the scene and only he is keeping me from drifting off into space. A pulsating sensation that excites me begins to build inside.

He doesn't relent with my moans.

"I want you to take me," I beg, not recognizing the sound of my voice. His hand slips away for a moment, and he wiggles on top of me. I realize he's removing his underwear, so I move, tugging at the waistband of my own. Propping up onto his knees at the foot of the couch, now completely naked, he lunges forward to assist me. I lift my bottom, and he slides off the black lace in a flash. My stomach is no longer fluttering, but instead it's aching with desire.

Leaning forward, I take his length into my hands and guide his path. He's over me now, staring into my eyes. He doesn't move any farther. He's simply looking in my eyes, and I wonder what he's waiting for. Does he want me to beg for it, because at this point I will.

I give a nod and realize that is exactly what he is waiting for. An indication that I am ready and that he is welcome. My thoughts scatter as I feel him thrust deep inside of me. The tightness of me around him renders me in a state of complete bliss.

A glimpse of Travis flashes in my mind, but I don't panic this time. I close my eyes and bite my lip and pull Dean flat against me. My chin is pressed over his shoulder. I whisper both to Dean and to my Travis, "I'm okay. It's all going to be okay."

As the words leave my lips, I can feel Dean collapse deeper into me. I dig my fingernails into his back and squeak, "Oh god!" Warmth floods me as my abdomen begins to pulse. Feeling my release, Dean pauses and pulls away, our eyes meeting as he allows the pleasure to deliver him into ecstasy as well. The look in his eyes is one of the most satisfying I have ever seen.

I can't look away from him. After he collapses to the side of me, the first instance of sadness occurs when I feel him pull out of me. It's an emptiness I don't want to feel again, but I take comfort in knowing I will, many times.

"Wow," he laughs, sweat beading on his forehead.

"Yeah," I giggle in agreement.

Our bodies press up against each other, side by side on the couch. He's staring at me. "What?" I groan, covering my face for a moment. He pulls my hand away, still looking at me.

"You're beautiful." When he says it I believe it.

"You're not so bad yourself," I joke, before leaning in and giving him a quick kiss.

Propping himself up on one arm, he hovers over my face and asks me, "Are you happy?"

I smile, pleased to share the answer, "More than I ever thought I could be."

Licking his lips, he continues, "Until this moment I never felt like it, but now I can see, I really am the luckiest man alive." His fingers trace the outline of my cheek.

Taking in a deep breath, I slowly press all the air out from my lungs. I used to hate when people talked about luck, but from Dean, a man who knows what it means to be stuck between hope and doubt, it is one of the most beautiful words I've ever heard.

EPILOGUE

THREE YEARS LATER...

The initial sign is staring at me, but I wait impatiently for the second test result to materialize. I can't say anything to Dean until I'm certain. What do I say to him if it's positive?

"Baby, you're all I want, your love is all I need, and when I'm with you, I feel like I'm in my personal heaven." He spoke those words to me two weeks ago, and I'd never felt so thankful Dean had come in and turned my life upside down. "Mac, will you do me the honor of becoming my wife?" He had asked in front of our restaurant full of patrons. After, he joked that it was his clever way of forcing me to say yes.

I can already see the plus sign begin to materialize.

My heart rattles in my chest as there's a knock at the door. I stand and open it. Dean is staring back at me.

"Oh baby, what's wrong?" he asks. I'm puzzled by his question at first. But then I realize tears are streaming down my cheeks.

I open my mouth and try to speak, but no words come out. I look back at the sink, and his eyes follow mine. He sees the pregnancy test, and it suddenly becomes clear. I brace myself for his reaction.

"Are you?" he begins, his voice full of excitement. "Jesus, really? Are you sure?"

I nod, still sobbing.

"That's amazing! We're going to be parents."

My crying becomes heavier; Dean wraps an arm around me and guides me to our bedroom, helping me to the bed. He sits next to me, and I wonder if he thinks I've finally lost my mind.

"Why are you crying, sweetie?"

I can only manage one word, and I hope it's enough for him to understand, "Katie."

He pulls me in tight against his body, smoothing my hair, and I hope I haven't upset him. I can't imagine what it must be like to experience life events in the way he has had to endure. As soon as he escapes from Travis's shadow, now our child must deal with that same weight of Katie's memory.

I feel his lips press against the top of my head before he pulls away from me.

"This is a good thing, I promise."

"But what about Katie?" I ask, knowing full well I don't make sense.

"What about her?"

"I don't want her to think I forgot her," I say, pinching my nose for a moment in an attempt to stop the snot flow.

"Macaroon, that will never happen. Our babies will know all about Katie, and we'll make sure they know that one day, after they have lived their full lives and have great-grand-babies of their own, it will be time to go and meet their big sister in heaven." Dean's words make my chest ache. I look at him and, in my gaze, I know he can see how much he means to me.

"Well, you do have this nifty tattoo to make sure she knows you're always thinking about her." His fingertips run over the lines. "But, I think the only thing we can do is make sure Katie is everywhere around you all the time."

"And how do we do that?" I ask in a nasally tone, my eyes stinging.

"Come on," he says, standing up and pulling me up by my hands. "This calls for some fresh ink."

"What?" I gasp.

"Well, not you silly, you're pregnant. No tattoos for you for nine months." He smiles, pausing and turning to face me. Pressing my hair behind my ears, he delivers me a gentle kiss. "I'm going to get a tattoo for Katie, so that whenever our baby sees it or you see it, you will know she was a part of you then, and will therefore always be a part of us."

"Seriously?" I chime in disbelief.

"Yeah! What? You don't like it?"

"Dean Johnson, I do believe I am the luckiest woman alive."

"Absolutely." He smiles. "I'm quite sure you're right about that. I mean, I'm a catch."

Even though he's joking, I know it's the truth. I really am the luckiest.

READ ANNABELLE'S STORY NOW

DO ANYTHING

Are you ready for another story about Stubborn hearts and second chances? Try the first book in The Wandering Hearts Series, Do Anything.

A broken heart is only the beginning for her.

Bookworm Annabelle Hart thinks she's found the love of her life. But when her fiancé's philandering ways shatter their happy future, she decides she's through playing the victim. Now, rather than read about life, she wants to live it —starting with a sabbatical from her editing job in Chicago to travel the world. But the past refuses to let her go so easily.

He thinks he has his life figured out.

After watching the woman he thought he loved walk away from him, Holden Blackburn is still picking up the pieces. Content with his life as the owner of an English Inn, just outside the sleepy town of Alton, he's living his new and peaceful normal. That is, at least, until Annabelle stumbles into his life, and he's overwhelmed by a desire to learn all he can about her. Now if only he can get her to stay in one place long enough.

Will they risk their hearts on a new chance at love?

When her past returns in a way she can't ignore, Anna panics, running from any possible future with Holden. She's determined to keep her life from falling apart again, but she soon discovers the only place she feels safe is in Holden's arms.

But some things even he can't protect her from.

PREVIEW OF DO ANYTHING

As the rain falls on the metal roof, I stare, my head cocked back sharply in the chair I am slouching in, and watch as the droplets gather together in the ridges of the skylights, veining outward across the glass. I'm not sure how long I've been sitting here; it seems time has lost meaning in recent days. I run my fingers over the tan line on my finger. I don't need to look at it because the place where the ring had been has become an obsession. I've tried everything to lighten it. I scrubbed it with soap, and I even tried bleaching the area in hopes it would fade, even slightly. All it did was give me a headache and leave my skin dry and irritated.

I hear Kenzie running around my apartment frantically, rambling on about something or other, but I tuned her out at least twenty minutes ago. Don't get me wrong—I'm not sure where I'd be without her. She is the one person who has been there for me through all of the drama; it's just that sometimes she can go over the top with the pep talks. A girl can only hear 'you need to get back up on that horse,' or 'there are plenty more fish in the sea,' so many times before she wants to physically remove her ears from her head.

On the other hand, when I told my parents what happened, they expressed what a shame it was and how much they liked Jack. Leave it to them to point out the strong qualities of a man who pulled my heart out of my chest cavity before stomping it into a thousand pieces.

I know they had undeniably truthful arguments, but even though there were a lot of amazing qualities about Jack, there were some things that couldn't ever be undone. I met him during college; I was a freshman and he was a senior. He had the greatest smile I'd ever seen. You know, one of those where the teeth are so perfect and white that you can't imagine they're natural, but then there was a slight lift on one corner of his mouth that made it all come together perfectly. He came from a prominent political family, and I couldn't believe out of all the girls on campus, he noticed me. It really is such a cliché when you think about it.

He was smart and funny; he always knew what to say in a crowd of people. I'd preferred the characters in my books to the real thing. People made me nervous—they always had. But not Jack, and I never had to worry about other people, because I always had him.

When we met, I wasn't looking for a boyfriend, but that didn't matter to him. He had been so suave about it, too. I didn't even know his name, but one day, while reading at the campus cafe, he came over and asked, "Should we meet there, or do you prefer I pick you up?"

"Excuse me?" I'd asked.

"This Friday, at six ... oh, I mean, I assumed you would be going."

I had peered at him, quite puzzled, but he didn't miss a beat. "You must have me confused with someone else," I assured him.

He looked around the cafe, then pressed his finger against the book I'd been holding. "Nope, you're the only girl around here I see reading a Jonathan Franzen novel."

"What?" I remember my voice had cracked slightly when I spoke.

"He'll be signing at the campus library this weekend, and I assumed you were a fan given what you're reading. But hey, if you don't want to go, I guess I can go by myself."

"Are you serious?"

"About Franzen or the date?" That was the first time I saw that sly and captivating smile from him, that lip that curled at the edges. I wanted to climb into the tiny ridges around his lips and stay nestled there for an eternity.

I squeeze my eyes shut tightly, wishing I could erase the memory from my mind somehow. Jack wasn't someone you could just forget, though. I didn't even want a boyfriend, yet after only three dates I was certain I was going to marry him one day. He popped the question at my graduation last year. Life had seemed so perfect in that moment. Jack could be very romantic, but he was also the practical type. I liked that about him. He wanted to finish law school before we took the leap, and now with his bar exam right around the corner, the wedding plans had moved full steam ahead.

While I love romance novels, I wasn't the little girl who had always dreamed of her wedding day and what it would be like. In fact, the details of the actual day concerned me very little. I just wanted to get through the event and move on with our lives together. I didn't have any family here in Chicago, so Kenzie took care of a lot of the planning. My mother, who lived in Ohio, didn't seem to mind either. This was not surprising, considering we had never been what you would call close.

Had Kenzie not been planning the wedding for me, I'm

not sure I would have ever discovered Jack's dirty little secret. Would I have been at our apartment when he didn't expect me to be, had she not sent me home from the office in the middle of a workday to pick up the measurements for the bridesmaid dresses? I'd forgotten the paper on the counter that morning, and despite several attempts at calling Jack to request he bring them to me, I found myself begrudgingly making the trek home. To think, had I not, I may have never known about Jack's study sessions. He was supposed to be cramming for the bar, but instead I discovered him in our bed, cramming himself into our across-the-hall neighbor, a blonde bombshell who looked like a Swedish super model. I can still hear the sounds of them going at it.

The only thing I have in common with the woman is our long hair. Hers was a pale yellow in color with a silken texture, while mine is wavy and coarse with deep chestnut tones. Her skin was tanned while mine is pale; her eyes blue, mine brown; her features slight all the way down to her slender nose, while a round ball sat at the tip of mine. I'm not ugly, and I've never thought of myself that way. Well, not until I saw this naked goddess in my bed. That moment had definitely been a solid blow to my self-esteem.

I think I handled it well. Okay, no, I didn't handle it well at all. When I first walked into the condo I heard them. Initially I thought an intruder was lurking around our place, and my heart had begun to race. Quickly, I realized exactly what type of noises I was hearing, so I then thought I had walked into the wrong apartment. Somehow, in that moment, it was making sense in my mind ... that my key had fit into someone else's lock and worked. I never said I was thinking rationally. Then I saw a picture on a side table—

the one of Kenzie and me during our vacation to Mexico senior year.

It was confirmed that this was my apartment, these were my things, and whoever was making those noises was in my bedroom. *What would Jack do when he found out someone was using our apartment to have random stranger sex?* When I walked into the room I wasn't exactly quiet, but neither were they, so I went unnoticed. I just stood there, watching. Honestly, I still have no idea why I watched. It was a horrific display, like two wild animals pawing at each other, but I was helpless, a captive prisoner, forced to stare at the sweaty primal union.

The next part is where I like to gloss over the details when I tell people about what happened. I'm pretty sure most people would have started shouting and screaming at their cheating partner, or perhaps just turn and leave. *Oh God, why didn't I just leave?* I walked up to the edge of our bed, the entire time thinking about completely pointless details, like how that bed was the first thing we had purchased together in our relationship. I suppose I was hoping one of them would notice me and stop the appalling display. And luckily, Jack did see me, eventually. He rolled off Elsa, or whatever the hell her name was, and started screaming at me.

I'm not sure what he was saying, but knowing Jack, he was probably making excuses. I couldn't hear him because I was busy regurgitating the burrito I'd had for lunch on the way over to the apartment. Not only did I vomit, but I managed to spray it all over the bed, thoroughly dousing Jack and his Swedish Barbie. It was at that point I turned and ran out of the apartment, not looking back. I can still remember their faces; it's one of the few things that gives me satisfaction when I think back on the horrific memory. As embarrassing as it is to vomit on someone, I can't imagine it being nearly as traumatizing as being the recipient of the discharge.

What happened after I ran out is a blur. Somehow I'd managed to give the low down to Kenzie over the phone, who in turn came and found me at a local Mexican joint somewhere between greasy taco number four and five. I stayed with her that night, which was terrible considering she recently had to move back in with her parents due to her shopping addiction and lack of money management skills. The entire night her mother brought me baked goods and kept asking me if I was all right. Every time I would try to answer her, it came out as a whimper, which would just send her running back into the kitchen to bake more. I have no clue how Kenzie is so slender after growing up with that woman and her incessant need to cure sadness with brownies.

The next day Kenzie had gone with me to deliver the official break up speech. I'm not sure if I could have resisted his charms in my current state of mind; for that, I will always be grateful to her. Jack pulled out all of the typical statements one would expect in a situation like that. 'It was just that one time,' which of course I didn't believe, and 'I still love you,' which again, I didn't believe and was now quite confident the slime-ball had never loved me. The condo was in my name since I was the one with an actual job while he was in law school, so I told him to get his crap and be out by the time I got back. For dramatic effect, I also threw the engagement ring at him. I remember the sound as it bounced across the wooden floors. I half expected it to be waiting for me on the counter when I returned, but it and Jack were gone.

Jack wasn't one to take things lying down. The next

morning he was back, begging for another chance, asking to come home. I still shudder when I think about the display that happened on our front stoop. It was worthy of the Jerry Springer show. I stood quietly while Kenzie berated Jack for being a piece of scum. He tried attacking Kenzie, telling her to mind her own business, but that only made my conviction in what I was doing all the stronger. The last thing I had said to him was, "Please, just go. I don't love you anymore." I think he knew I was lying, but he left. Maybe he thought time and space would cause me to change my mind.

Looking back, it didn't feel like I was actually in my body. I couldn't imagine myself saying or doing any of that when it came to Jack. But I did, and these past four weeks Kenzie has been my rock. Even when I hatched my crazy scheme of finding myself, she was there, backing up my decision with nothing but support.

I have—*had*—a job I loved. I was an editor for a publishing house. I loved books, so it was like a dream job for me. When I told Kenzie my plan to quit my job and travel the world, I'll admit she flipped out at first, but once I explained she could live in the condo for half the mortgage payment, she was sold. I think she would have done anything to get out from under her parents' roof. I like to think she also believed in the idea, but I'm not even sure I think it's that great of an idea, so I didn't push the subject.

You probably shouldn't make major life decisions right after your heart is broken. In fact, that's probably written in many self-help books. But that's exactly what I did. Two weeks ago I decided Chicago, and all the things in it, were merely painful reminders of Jack and our history together. I wanted to go somewhere I could get back in touch with the real me. It made sense two weeks ago, but now I'd realized something—something that was even scarier than a life without Jack. I have no clue who I am, and I'm not sure if I ever did. I met Jack so young, and he became part of my identity while it was still forming.

How do you find yourself again if you're not sure who the hell you ever were? I began selling my possessions, at least as many as I could in two weeks. While I'm away, Kenzie can sell more for me. This money will help pay the other half of the mortgage and bills she needs help with while I'm gone. I also have some savings; after all, Jack always told me I needed to be responsible for the sake of our future.

I also decided to take the money Jack's parents had given us for the wedding and use it to fund my travels. Now, I hadn't actually gotten permission for this last part, but honestly, after what went down between us, I doubted anyone was going to say anything. I even had the funds in my personal account for the honeymoon. If I live frugally, it should be enough to keep me going for quite a while.

"Are you even listening to me?" Kenzie demands, her wavy red hair bouncing up and down as she speaks.

"Huh? I mean, yeah, of course I am."

"You're such a terrible liar. You have your passport, right?"

"Yes, I have my passport, for the tenth time," I huff, sitting up in the chair, noticing a noise outside my window.

"Then we better get moving. The cabbie has been honking for so long I think his head might explode if we keep him waiting any longer," she informs me, glancing out the bay window and waving at the impatient driver through the rain.

I smile. I can't believe this is actually it. I'm saying

goodbye to my home, to my friend, to the only life I've ever known as an adult, and setting off for the unknown.

"Thank you," I whisper, standing and looking at her. Kenzie's eyes look wet. She's always very emotional, so we are a great balance to one another.

"Oh, shut up already, this is what friends do." She waves me off, her voice cracking slightly.

"Especially when they get cheap rent on an apartment in exchange," I jest, trying to smile, though my heart isn't in it.

"Well, there is that." Kenzie laughs, tossing my backpack over her shoulder and grabbing an umbrella from the stand next to the door. "Come on, let's not start with goodbyes. It's just going to piss me off or make me cry. I don't know which, but one of the two."

I follow Kenzie down the stairs, glancing at the door across the hall. I wonder if Elsa the Barbie would report back to Jack I was leaving on a trip. I don't want to wonder anything about him ... or her for that matter. *Damn him.*

"So I never asked you, why England?" Kenzie inquires as she hands my bag to the impatient cab driver.

"Why not? Seemed like as good a place as any," I reply, staring at her, wishing I could take her with me. "Plus I thought it was a good idea to start with a place where I could speak the language."

"Excellent reasoning my dear." Kenzie giggles, shifting the umbrella to her other hand. "Call me as soon as you get there, promise?"

"Of course." As I hug her, it feels like I might never see her again. I know this isn't true, but everything has begun to feel so uncertain in my life. I'm ready for an adventure—ready to become the heroine in the books I love to read. Now if I can manage to make it to England without having an all-out panic attack, everything will be perfect. At this point, I'd do anything to forget what has happened, and I'm confident the answers I seek lie over the ocean.

https://wendyowensbooks.com/books/

ACKNOWLEDGMENTS

As always, I wouldn't be here if it weren't for my readers, so from the bottom of my heart, thank you. You all have shared my books with other readers, purchased my books, and left reviews. I couldn't do any of this without you; I'm still in awe every day.

Thanks goes out to my editor, Madison Seidler, fantastic job as usual. I'm a royal pain in the butt who never meets her deadlines and has about a million panic attacks yet you still keep on supporting and pushing me.

Thanks as well to Rare Bird Editing for polishing up the final product. You have been an awesome addition to the team and I look forward to working with you on future projects as well.

I can't forget my community of Indie Authors who supports me daily. There are far too many of you to list, but you all know who you are and how important you are to me.

To my husband, Joshua, I love that you love all the broken pieces of me. You're my rock and without you I couldn't do any of this. To my three amazing children, mommy is so proud of you. And thankful you understand why we always have a messy house and a back up of laundry around deadline time. I love you to the moon and back.

———

ABOUT THE AUTHOR

Wendy Owens was raised in the small college town of Oxford, Ohio. After attending Miami University, Wendy went on to a career in the visual arts. After several years of creating and selling her own artwork, she gave her first love, writing, a try.

Wendy now happily spends her days writing. When she's not writing, she can be found spending time with her tech geek husband and their three amazing kids.

For more information:
www.wendyowensbooks.com
me@wendyowensbooks.com

ALSO BY WENDY OWENS...

**Find links to all of Wendy's Books at
wendyowensbooks.com/books/**

PSYCHOLOGICAL THRILLER

My Husband's Fiancée (book 1)
My Wife's Secrets (book 2)

The Day We Died

An Influential Murder

Secrets At Meadow Lake

COZY MYSTERIES
Jack Be Nimble, Jack Be Dead
O Deadly Night
Roses Are Red, Violet is Dead

YA ROMANCE
Wash Me Away

CONTEMPORARY ROMANCE (adult)
Stubborn Love
Only In Dreams
The Luckiest
Do Anything
It Matters to Me

YA PARANORMAL (clean)
Sacred Bloodlines
Unhallowed Curse
The Shield Prophecy
The Lost Years
The Guardians Crown

Made in the USA
Monee, IL
23 November 2023

470894 59R10167